DARING SUMMER

A Novel

Elyse Douglas

COPYRIGHT

ISBN: 9781093138429

Who has a daring eye, tell downright truths and downright lies.

—Johann Kaspar Lavater

A single feat of daring can alter the whole conception of what is possible.

—Graham Greene

… The wild, mad love when it overtakes you… the world can go to pieces. If love hits you that way, you're lucky… and you're lucky if you survive it.

—Joseph Campbell

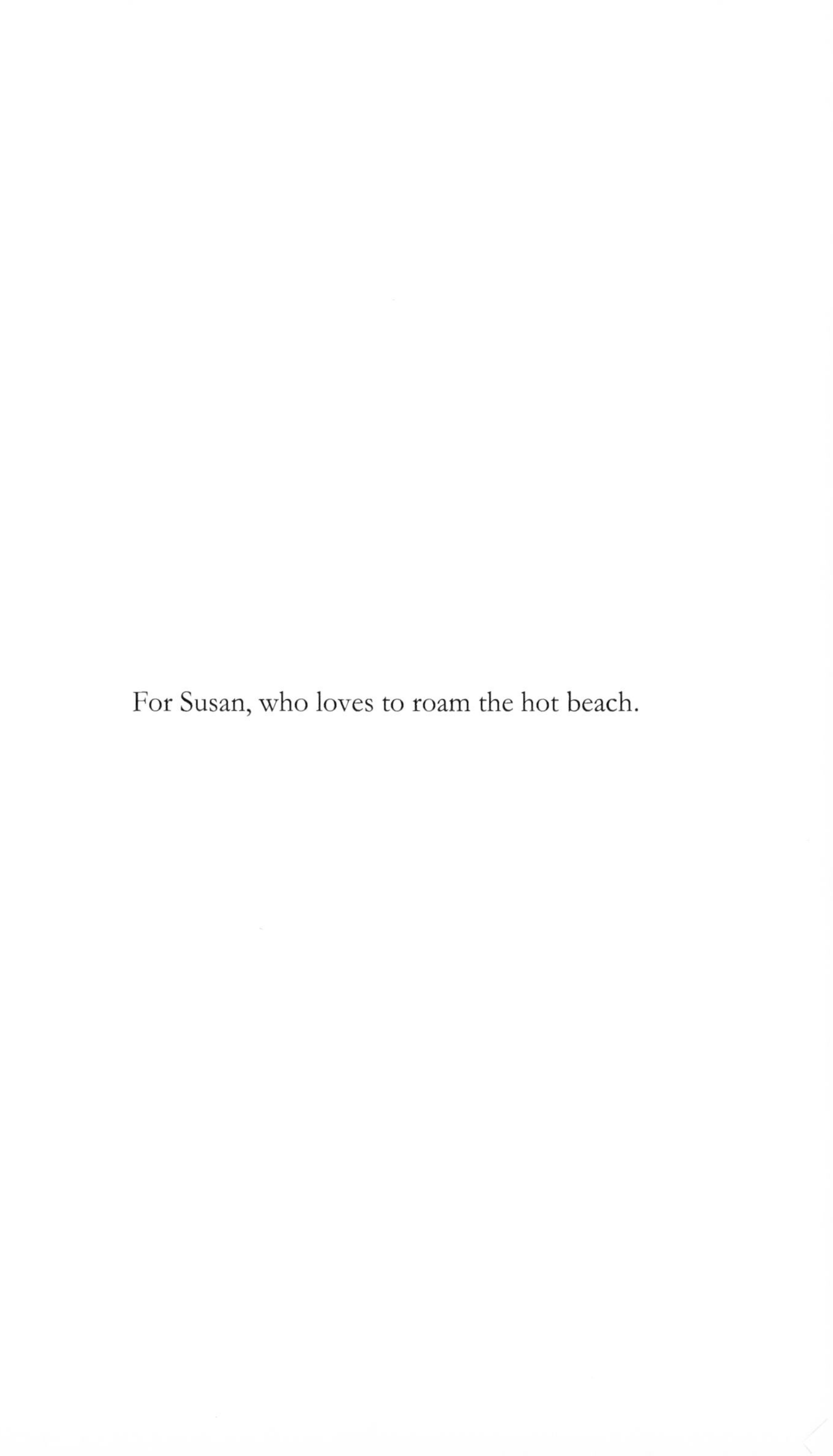

For Susan, who loves to roam the hot beach.

DARING SUMMER

PROLOGUE

The metallic gray Mercedes raced across the two-lane road through clouds of rolling fog. It bounced and ramped, bending around curves, tires squealing, wipers slapping away splotches of charging rain. Kim Ryan's hands gripped the passenger seat, her knuckles white, her face pinched with stress, her anxious eyes throwing darting glances toward her husband, Ben Maxwell, who ignored her. His expression was hard and resolute. His hands were jerking the steering wheel about as if the car were an amusement park thrill ride, and he was searching for something to slam into.

"Slow down, Ben," Kim pleaded, raking a loose strand of blonde hair from her face. "Please."

Ben's jaw tightened. His grave, pallid face was fixed in a frown.

"You're going to kill us both," Kim said. "Stop this!"

Ben stomped the accelerator, a menacing delight flickering in his brown eyes. The tires sought traction across the rain-washed asphalt road, while Kim watched the ghostly autumn trees rush by. She was close to panicking. Her neck stiffened, her throat tightened, and her heart kicked at her chest.

"Ben. Please stop the car. Just stop it!"

Ben laughed, harshly. "Look ahead, Kim. See the fog? Watch how it vanishes for a few seconds and then returns. Just like our marriage. Mostly foggy, with a few brief patches of love and honesty."

The road leveled out, and through the blowing patches of fog, a deer leapt across the road and vanished into the trees. The car shot past it, back tires slinging water.

"Oh, for God's sake, Ben, I've told you. Nothing happened. Carl and I are just old friends. You know that."

"Old? Well, I don't think so. I mean, let's get real here, Kim, you're 29 and he's 31. How *old* can the friendship be?"

"You know what I mean, Ben," Kim said, her frightened eyes blinking fast. They burst into another heavy gray blanket of boiling fog, and she was barely able to see a few feet ahead.

"All my friends told me I was a fool to marry you. They said, 'Ben, she'll get bored with the money, the trinkets and the old man. Especially, the old man.'"

Angry now, Kim turned to face him. "You're *not* an old man, Ben. You're only 58. I'm sick of your jealousy, but I'm not bored with you."

"Not now, my sweet. Not now, when we're traveling the speed of light down a curvy, bumpy Long Island country road. But you will be tomorrow when you wake up in the morning and have to look at a 58-year-old man who's losing his hair and his mind. That's when you'll get bored. That's when you'll go looking for Carl Lancer again."

"How many times do I have to tell you? I am *not* in love with Carl Lancer! Why do you do this to us, Ben? Why? Why are you trying to kill our relationship? I love you. We used to have so much fun together until you started this shit. Now stop it!"

"You married me for my money. Admit it."

"For the thousandth time, I don't give a damn about your money."

"Good, because I'll make sure you don't get a cent of it. Nothing."

Kim looked away. "Fine. Good. Now stop the car!"

"Just stop lying to me, Kim! Don't you think I have friends who tell me what's going on?"

Kim snapped him an angry glance. "Who are you talking about? Your restaurant investors? Your accountant? Are they really your friends, Ben? What are they after? What do they want? Why do you believe them, but you don't believe me?"

"Because they don't lie to me! Okay? Oh, to hell with it. To hell with the whole thing."

His eyes were moving from fury to hurt to contempt. "We could have lived so well, Kim. But then, who cares about living, anyway? I mean, if I lose you, the only real thing I ever loved in this swindle of a life, then who cares about living? You're the only thing that ever made me happy, if you can call agony happy."

"You're not losing me, Ben. Stop saying that."

The windshield wipers were a blur, the world a blur, Kim's mind a blur.

A car burst out of the fog heading straight for them, its headlights glaring. Kim screamed.

"Look out, Ben!"

Ben whipped the Mercedes right, horn blaring. It was a near miss as the car skidded along the narrow shoulder of the road. Ben righted the car and continued on, beads of sweat pimpling his broad forehead. He pushed a hand through his thinning gray hair.

Kim struggled to recover, her pulse high and racing, her face hot with a new panic.

"This is stupid, Ben. Stupid! Stop the car. Now!"

Ben hit the brakes, throwing her forward. Her hands braced against the dashboard as the car skidded and finally came to rest on the narrow shoulder of the road.

Ben sat breathing hard, his haunted face pale. "Get out," he said, his voice low with defeat. "Just get out of my life, so I can finally have some peace."

Kim drew in a breath of defiance. "No. I'm not going to let you kill our relationship over some silly jealousy."

"What do you care?"

"Stop being a pain in the ass, Ben. Stop acting like some high school kid! Anyway, I'm not getting out. It's pouring rain, and I'd get soaked."

Rain drummed on the roof and washed the windows. Ben's weary eyes looked at her, carefully. Kim noticed a change of mood. She turned and stared at him as a slow pleasant smile crept across his face. Could she trust it? She studied him closely. He often had sudden mood swings, especially when he'd been drinking. But he hadn't been drinking today. In fact, he hadn't had a drink in months, ever since his doctor and college friend, Lawrence Eaton, had urged him to stop.

"What is it, Ben?" Kim asked, watching him curiously. She reached for his hand as she'd done many times during similar fights. He pulled away, a dazed look on his face.

"Hey, kid... remember that wonderful day two years ago? Remember how you got lost on the path going down to the beach and I had to come find you?"

"Of course I remember. It was the day you asked me to marry you."

"I was outside talking on the phone, and I heard you

call to me."

"A heavy mist blew in and I got disoriented. I could hear the ocean but I couldn't find the path. Everything seemed to be spinning around. It was so odd, and I got frightened, so I called for you. I kept calling your name."

"I heard you, and I got off the phone and went running down to find you."

"I was so relieved you'd come."

"And after I found you, I led you back to the house…"

"… and you said you wouldn't make any more business calls the rest of the day. You opened a bottle of wine and pulled me toward the Jacuzzi. We stripped, got in and played around like high school kids. We listened to Frank Sinatra and drank wine all afternoon. And then you popped the question and another bottle of champagne. Of course I remember! How could I forget? It was such a happy day."

Ben stared at her, wistfully. "I wish I could believe you, Kim, but I haven't had much luck with my women. My first two wives screwed around on me too."

"I have not screwed around on you, Ben!"

He shook his head. "I wanted this one to work. I really did. I needed it to work. You were my first love, Kim, just like in all those goddamn romantic movies."

Kim touched his cheek. She stroked it.

"Okay, Mr. Romantic, then let me be your love and stop all this crazy jealousy. Stop listening to your stupid friends! They're just jealous of you and our relationship, and they're driving you and me crazy."

His smile vanished into a frowning memory, and he looked down and away, picking at his fingernails. "We had something special until you killed it, Kim."

"I did not kill it!"

He gave her a sad, tragic look, and his voice dropped an octave. "I have pictures, Kim. Pictures of you and Carl holding hands, going into the Plaza hotel in Manhattan."

Kim drew back, stunned. "What!? You had someone follow me and take pictures!?"

Ben stared out the front windshield, seeing nothing, resigned to this final moment. "Goddammit, Kim, stop denying it! Just stop. It makes everything so much worse."

Kim gave him a feverish, burning stare. She shook her head, unable to find any words. She grabbed her purse, shoved the door open and got out, slamming it hard. A hard steel rain pelted her as she stormed off into the opposite direction, drenched in seconds, her long blonde hair hanging in strings about her face.

With an intense agony and with lowered eyelids, Ben watched her tall, willowy body disappear into the rain and fog. He smiled ruefully.

"Goodbye, kid. Goodbye, Kim, my love."

He shifted the car into gear and shot away, tires screeching.

Kim walked aggressively, lost in anger and hurt. How could he do that? Hire some private detective to spy on her? It was revolting! Sick! Why did he distrust her so much? He hated every male friend she had, especially Carl, even though she'd explained a dozen times that she and Carl were just friends. They'd been lovers a few years back, but she broke off with him. Was he still in love with her? Maybe, but so what? She wasn't in love with him. She was in love with Ben. She married Ben.

Kim slowed her pace, chilled and shaking, her wet clothes sticking to her.

She and Carl had run into each other the last time she

was shopping in Manhattan. They'd gone to the Plaza to have a quick lunch because it was close by and they both loved the burgers there. That was it. Nothing else happened. He'd taken her hand, briefly, but just because they were playing, like they always did. There was nothing to it. She purposely didn't tell Ben because he would have suspected the worse. He wouldn't have believed her.

Ben's jealousy was clearly out of control. He was suspicious of every man who looked at her, who even smiled at her. He'd even slapped her around a few months ago, before he'd stopped drinking.

"You're just too damned sexy!" he'd shouted. He slapped her across the face and flung her down on the bed, ripping off her blouse. He fought to kiss her. She fought him off, kicking, punching. She slid out from under him, snatched her coat and ran for her car. She drove around for hours, finally going back to their apartment in the City. Before that happened, she'd felt so safe with him, so loved. His jealousy had seemed a harmless part of that love, something she thought he'd outgrow with time, as he realized what a good, faithful wife she was.

In the beginning, their relationship had seemed like a fairy tale come true. They'd met at one of his Upper East Side restaurants. She was teaching jazz dance at a midtown dance studio, after a long run with a Broadway show that had closed a few weeks before.

She remembered every detail of the night. She and a few friends were celebrating a friend's birthday. She'd worn 3" heels and a tight, knock-out strapless dress that accentuated her large breasts and hugged her dancer's figure. Her shoulder-length honey-blonde hair looked particularly lush that night. Every man in the place was staring lustily at her.

But it was Kim who had fallen in love first. She fell in

love with Ben after he drifted over with a warm smile to ask if she liked French Burgundy.

"Well, I don't really know," she'd said, not knowing much about wine. "I don't know what that is."

He smiled, charmingly, and then gave her a courtly bow. "Then do you mind if I send you over a bottle of 2005 Damoy Chambertin? It's one of my favorites."

She looked up into his very dark, very warm eyes and smiled flirtatiously. He'd seemed so familiar, as if she'd known him before. She'd even felt a little shiver of recognition when he'd smiled and bowed. "No, sir, I wouldn't mind. I'd be honored," she said.

He frowned. "Please don't call me sir. It makes me sound more mature than I want to be."

"Then what should I call you?"

"Why not Ben? Ben Maxwell."

She stared at him. He was a new idea. A gentleman. A very distinguished man, with salt and pepper hair combed back from a broad forehead and a square face. This was a man—a real man—and not one of the silly young actors she'd been dating. Yes, Ben was utterly appealing and charming.

And so the relationship had begun, and they were married six months later.

Kim was jerked from her memories by the sound of thunder, or what she thought was thunder. But she quickly realized it wasn't thunder. The thunder and lightning had stopped minutes ago, as the violent part of the storm went roaring off to the east.

She stopped, pivoted and peered down the highway that disappeared into woolly fog. She froze, every sense awake, feeling the cold beating rain on her head and face. She brushed the hair from her eyes, caught in a sudden nightmare. A swift ringing alarm went off in her head.

She shouted out. "Ben! Ben!" and she kicked off her heels and broke into a sprint. As she tore off down the road, the wind threw gushes of rain into her face. She ran frantically, calling Ben's name, tears forming.

Minutes later, breaking through stringy fog, she saw it. Something ahead—something that shouldn't be there. A car off the road, down in a ravine. It was pitched forward, looming out of the gray curtain of rain, wedged into a row of trees, appearing and disappearing in a filmy haze. The tail lights were blinking, as if shouting out disaster.

Kim hurled herself down the slope, across low shrubs and rocks, slipping on wet stones, falling branches slashing her face and feet. She got up, stumbled, reaching for him, fell and reached for him again, pushed to her feet, reaching for him, calling to him.

In the relentless downpour, she finally tumbled against the car, chest heaving, head throbbing. She didn't notice the broken, scattered glass—didn't notice or feel shards piercing her bleeding feet. Peering in from the passenger window, she saw Ben slumped over the wheel, the airbag only partially deployed. Blood splattered his white shirt—his faced was turned away from her.

Terror swelled her chest. "Oh God. Ben!"

She frantically pulled and yanked on the door handle, but it didn't budge. The car had slammed into an embankment of rock and mud, so it was impossible for her to approach from the driver's side.

She glanced about, her eyes wild, as sliding curtains of rain drenched her.

Nearly exhausted, she fumbled into her purse for her cell phone. Wiping her eyes, she dialed 911. She was cold and shivering, her hands shaking. Into the phone, she shouted out the location. She shouted for help. She shouted for an ambulance. She hung up, leaned into the jagged open window and called to Ben. He didn't stir. She wept, as the hard rain slanted into her, as the wind circled her.

It was only when she heard the loud, wobbling siren that a strange calm came over her. Her head cleared, and, despite the uncontrollable shivering and her chattering teeth, she didn't faint. She didn't waiver. She looked at Ben as they lowered the stretcher into the ambulance, and she told him that everything was going to be okay.

"Do you hear me, Ben? I'm calling for you. I'm here with you. I'm calling to you, Ben, just like I did when I was lost on the path. Remember? Do you hear me, Ben? You came to me, Ben. You came for me and you found me. Find me again, Ben. Ben, wake up. Wake up!"

CHAPTER 1

June—

Eight Months Later

Kim stood in front of the dining room windows, staring out at the distant, turgid sea. The morning mist was cool and refreshing as it washed across her face, tasting salty on her lips. She lifted her nose and inhaled a good breath, hoping it would help ease the agitation of her mind. Fog was clinging to the ocean, crawling along the dunes and faraway cliffs, obscuring the sprawling beach houses on the bluffs, creating a lonely, pensive seclusion.

She peered down. Scorpio Beach was mostly fogged in, but she could see a single dog-walker and his black Labrador emerge, disappear and reappear, as if they were shadowy players in some ghostly dream.

Kim narrowed her eyes, focusing. Even from the high beach house, as the dog-walker materialized from the smoky fog, she could tell he was tall and in good shape. He was barefoot, wearing khaki shorts and a blue T-shirt, his long black hair combed back smoothly from his forehead. He strolled along the edge of the tide, slinging a stick high in the air, up onto the beach. The playful Labrador sprinted for it, barking, leaping, snagging the stick between his teeth. The dog pivoted and brought the stick back to his master for another round of play.

Kim had seen this guy and his dog on the beach a couple of times during the past two weeks. Had he just moved to town? You noticed new people and new things when you're a prisoner. And that's what she felt like, a prisoner.

She reached for a cigarette, placed it between her lips and lit it, blowing a feather of smoke toward the open door. After Ben's accident, she'd started smoking again. She drank more too. Wine mostly, but she wouldn't have turned down a cold vodka martini—if offered—not that she had been offered one in the last six months. Since they'd returned to the beach house, they'd lived in almost total isolation. She rarely left the house, going out just to shop or take Ben to his doctors' visits. Only recently had she allowed herself to leave the house at night, to stroll the beach, get some air and clear her head. She had wanted to be there for Ben, just in case there was any kind of emergency.

Though friends had called, wanting to get together in Manhattan or in town, Ben would fly into a rage, accusing her of leaving him to meet one of her old boyfriends behind his paralyzed back. Kim told her protesting friends that Ben just needed more time. He was still emotionally fragile after the accident. He'd come around eventually, and she'd catch up with them then.

Maybe it was the fog that was bringing back the awful memories of that night. Maybe it was a hundred other things, but then again, it didn't take much to bring that nightmare back. It was always with her, wasn't it?—a living hell incarnate. A prison sentence. A gothic horror story right out of a bad Hollywood movie.

Maybe it was being alone for so long in the beach house, and Ben's refusal to let anyone see him—not his friends nor his family, and certainly not her friends. Mostly, though, it was her living with Ben's hate. Hate for life, hate for his dead legs and hate for her.

He never wanted her to forget his accident. Accident? No, it hadn't been an accident. She'd recycled through all the pointless, incendiary memories hundreds of times over the past eight months, blaming herself, forgiving herself, cursing herself and then cursing Ben. Therapy hadn't helped. Sleeping pills hadn't helped. Booze helped a little. Medication made her crazy.

Ben had tried to kill himself. It was as simple as that. He'd tried to kill himself to punish her for something she hadn't done, and since he'd survived, he wanted her to pay for the accident for as long as he lived. He wanted her to be marooned and alone, just like he was.

Ben was paralyzed from the waist down and there was no possibility of recovery. Part of his spine had been crushed. He sat in an electric wheelchair most days, pouring over real estate contracts and investments, staring out onto Scorpio Beach and the endless sea, brooding and moody. He'd sold his restaurants but continued to manage his stock investments and vast real estate holdings, like a miserly king, ordering everyone about, including her.

Why did she stay with him? Stubbornness. Guilt. Fear. And hope that Ben would finally overcome his bitterness and anger, move on with his life, and fall in love with her all over again. As crazy as it sounded to her friends, she still loved him and believed they would one day fall in love again.

In dark moments, when she was honest with herself,

she was aware that her pride had something to do with her holding on. She was too proud to fulfill Ben's prophecies that she would leave him someday.

Immediately after the accident, she'd heard enough of his conversations to know that his "friends" were still poisoning him against her. They blamed her and her infidelity for the accident. She'd heard herself referred to as a bitch, a whore, a silly dancer, and a low-class slut. Ben's upper crust friends couldn't imagine why he hadn't just set her up in an apartment instead of marrying her. That way, he could have ended it quickly and easily as soon as he was through with her. They told him, with sneering confidence, that she would walk out on him after the accident, because she was "just a pretty gold digger." The last time two of his friends visited them at Scorpio Beach, Kim had seen their meager smiles and disapproving eyes. She'd overheard their conversation.

"You'd be better off without her, Ben. She's terrible for you and she always has been," one said.

"She brings out the worst in you," the other added.

"She married you for your money and you know it. To be brutally honest, Ben, she's just not our class of people. Divorce her before she makes you do something else crazy."

Kim had overheard these comments as she stood outside Ben's bedroom door, holding a tray with a pot of green tea and a plate of cookies. She stood there, in that hurtful silence, waiting to hear if Ben would defend her. But he didn't defend her. He didn't say anything. When she finally entered the room, the friends lowered their eyes and put strained smiles on their faces, like royalty does when a servant enters the room.

Finally, she had stayed in the marriage because she felt a persistent guilt. After all, if Ben had never met her, he wouldn't be paralyzed. How could she leave him when he needed her most? What kind of wife would she be if she abandoned him when times got tough? Didn't she vow to love him in sickness and in health? Didn't her father abandon Kim's mother, Kim, and her younger brother, Scott, when times got tough? He left them and never returned. She still didn't know where he was, and now she didn't care. But she'd vowed to stick out her marriage to Ben, no matter how hard it got. Surely things would improve in time. Didn't time heal all wounds?

But now, they were both lost—he in anger, resentment and bitterness, and she in regret and depression. She knew from Martin Peterson, Ben's friend and lawyer, that Ben had completely written Kim out of his will after the accident. So be it. She didn't want Ben's money, anyway. If he died, she'd manage. She'd saved money and she could always go back to dancing, teaching or choreography. Her mother had taught her to manage—to survive no matter what.

"Kim!" Ben shouted from his office. "Kim! Get in here."

Kim turned from the window, staring into the extravagant living room with its shiny pool-blue tiles, deep white carpet, designer furniture and wrap-around patio with wicker chairs and blossoming plants. She crushed out her cigarette, turning to pass a final glance toward Scorpio Beach. The man was still there, strolling along the tide line, his dog prancing about, splashing in and out of the waves.

It looked like they were having such a good time. How she longed for a normal, peaceful life. She folded her arms tightly across her chest and watched in fascination as the man peeled off his T-shirt. He had wide shoulders and a muscular torso, but it was a working man's body, natural, not pumped up from lifting weights. She liked that. Kim knew about working men. Her father had worked construction and her brother, Scott, was a pipe-fitter still living in her hometown of Binghamton, New York.

Aching with loneliness, Kim imagined what it would be like to be with that man. She studied his movements, becoming gently aroused by his easy walk, and his strong but gentle play with the dog. She inched a little closer to the open door to watch the man slowly retreat into the distance of mist. And then they were gone, obscured by a thick scrim of fog. It was June third. It was Kim's birthday.

"Kim! Where are you?" Ben called, pulling her out of her fantasy.

Kim hurried into Ben's spacious, well-lit office, with its heavy oak desk, floor to ceiling bookshelves and floor plants. His stout, stern and stoic middle-aged nurse, Lois Carson, was sitting nearby, reading a paperback novel. She attended to Ben's necessaries, as he called them. Lois was a strong, no-nonsense woman, whom Ben had heard about from a friend. He seemed to trust her, and Ben did not trust easily. It puzzled Kim a bit, their relationship. Kim had asked him once where he'd found her. He just passed the question off with a flick of his hand.

"A friend."

Ben was at his desk, facing the beach and the sea, tirelessly pouring over a stack of papers, dressed in pajama bottoms and an old white polo shirt. He never dressed much now—he wasn't the stylish man he'd once been. Instead, he was full of his duty: acquiring property, calculating his stock investments, and barking orders.

"Where's my tea and toast? It's after 9 o'clock, for God's sake. What the hell were you doing out there?"

His anger still stunned her, but she'd given up trying to answer it. Instead, she built a wall around herself. Once she asked Ben's primary doctor if it might be one of his many medications that was fueling his frustration and anger, but Dr. Eaton denied the possibility. And when Kim tried to discuss it directly with Ben, he told her to shut up and leave the medication decisions to his doctor and to Nurse Carson.

Despite his indifference, she'd decided to dress up today. It was her thirtieth birthday, and she wasn't going to let her depression and his bitterness stop her from celebrating. And maybe, just maybe, today would be the day that Ben would see her for who she was and love her again. Maybe today they would rebuild that loving cocoon that used to surround them, and she would sit on his lap and he would hold her in his arms and hug her, like the grateful, fun lover he had once been.

She stood before him now, in tight designer jeans and the low-cut pink blouse he'd given her last year for her birthday. Her thick blonde hair was piled on her head, the way he liked it, "accenting her elegant dancer's neck," as he said. She dressed this way to let him know that she was ready for love if he was. If he couldn't make love to her in the traditional way, there were other and equally playful and satisfying ways she could pleasure him, and he could gratify her. They'd even discussed the possibilities with a therapist after the accident. But the first time she'd attempted to arouse him, it hadn't gone well. Since that fiasco, he hadn't allowed her to touch him. He seldom even looked at her. If he did, it was with cold contempt.

As she stood there, waiting, his eyes never left his papers. He sat hunched and frozen, like a solid piece of ice.

She retreated to get his breakfast. Of course he hadn't remembered it was her birthday. How much more rejection and isolation could she take? How much longer could she wait for him to come back to her? She had never felt so alone.

CHAPTER 2

Kim spent the day shopping and cooking her own birthday dinner. Preparing healthy gourmet meals had become her passion, a safe way to overcome loneliness and feel she was doing something for herself and Ben. Though he didn't always join her in the dining room, Ben insisted on eating at six o'clock every evening. Everything was different from pre-accident days, including meal time.

Ben barely touched the filet of sole, haricot verts with shallots, and scalloped potatoes she had so lovingly prepared. He was an erratic eater now and, as a result, he'd lost weight. When Kim expressed concern about it, he snapped back. "The thinner I am, the easier it is for me to hoist myself up on the bed, and the less there is for Lois to lift."

Though he wasn't eating much, he was drinking a lot of wine, so Kim made sure there was a supply of good quality wines in the wine cellar. As they were drinking the last of a French Pinot Noir, Kim quietly hummed *Happy Birthday*. Ben looked up scornfully, turned his wheelchair around and ended the evening by going back to his office.

Alone again, Kim sat at the table, fighting tears, knowing anger and depression would overwhelm her if she didn't get up and move. She found the CD of *Chicago* music and danced around the kitchen while she cleaned up, imagining she was in the show again, one of the sexy dancers in *Jail Block Tango.* She struggled to remember the choreography, kicking and whirling until she finally gave up, slumped into dejection.

"I'm in jail again," she thought, as she walked through the house to her bedroom. "Only this time it's not fun."

Her bedroom was white and wide and had a stunning view of the silky-sanded beach below. In the early dusk, she could see the rise and curve of the cliffs and the beach as they stretched away into the misty distance, and the faint silhouette of the Scorpio Beach lighthouse, which was no longer in use but remained a tourist attraction. She stepped onto her Juliet balcony and then ascended to a private upper deck that seemed so close to the sky you could touch it. During the day, she sunbathed, stretched, did yoga postures and practiced old dance routines here. This, and the occasional jog along the beach, was how she stayed in shape.

She stared out at the horizon, wondering how she had ended up here, alone, on her thirtieth birthday. She felt so lost—as though she were thousands of miles from civilization.

Their house sat on a high cliff overlooking the sea. It was a 5-bedroom, modern house with lots of windows, lofty interiors, wrap-around porches and a new heated pool. It was airy and sun-filled and there were water views from every room, where sunrises and sunsets dazzled. A serpentine private beach path led down to the sea and, although the beach was open to the public, most people preferred the public beaches closer to town, because there were life guards on duty.

Ben's master bedroom was large and comfortable with a fireplace and two flat-screen TVs, where he watched business news and sports, often at the same time. An adjoining bedroom served as Ben's private office. It was spacious, with spectacular lighting. Two additional flat-screen TVs were installed here after the accident. That's where he spent most of his time, seated behind his massive oak desk facing out to sea. Between the two rooms was a marble bathroom with a Jacuzzi in the tub.

About eight o'clock, Kim checked on Ben, since Lois had the night off. Ben was dozing on his bed, with both TVs on. The physical therapist had taught him to roll the chair to the side of the bed, push up, sit and roll, and he refused to let Lois or Kim help with this. He'd become quite good at it, although he snorted that he was no more than a trained monkey.

Kim slipped a sweatshirt over her shoulders and left the house, wandering down the winding dirt path that led to the beach. The big orange sun sat on the edge of the sea, just hanging there, as if waiting for a command to drop and finish the day. Purple and rusty clouds stained the late blue sky and two sailboats were far at sea, their white sails glowing.

Kim thought of her mother and her friends, who had all sent birthday cards and texts. Some had even sent gifts. Early that morning, she'd sent a group text to them all and lied, saying she was going to have a very special day. It was too hard to admit that her fairy tale marriage had gone so wrong. Nonetheless, one of her dancer friends, Denise, who was currently in a Broadway show, had called her in the afternoon. She recognized Kim's guarded answers as painful half-truths. Denise told her to get the hell out of there and come back to the City before she went crazy. She needed to be dancing.

"Have you been working out at least? Are you keeping in shape?"

Kim presented her face to the warm, humid breeze that blew in from the thundering sea. Yes, she was still in good shape, although she didn't have the flexibility she had when she was twenty-two. A Yoga class would help, and she intended to start taking one soon, despite what she expected Ben would say about her leaving him: "Who are you screwing this time in the Big City?"

She shook that thought away as she stepped onto the beach, unfastened her hairpin and shook out her hair. She took in the pastel sky and the charging, curling waves that came sliding in, pounding the beach. She took a deep breath, suddenly feeling the tension leave her body, as it always did when she was released from that multi-million-dollar prison of a house. She *would* have gone crazy if she hadn't had the beach to escape to.

She removed her sandals and rambled, feeling the sand give way to her toes, feeling the return of that haunting loneliness that was particularly acute when she was away from the house and on her own. But then, wasn't she always on her own?

Kim leaned her head back, gazed up into the wide dome of sky and drew in another deep breath. As she released it and turned her attention back to the beach, she saw him again. The same man she'd seen that morning. The same man and his dog, drifting toward her. She froze, feeling a warm stirring across her skin, feeling an unexpected tingle of excitement. He was about thirty feet away, shirtless, wearing only swimming trunks, his hair and chest wet from a recent swim. The last of the sun fell on him and he gleamed with oil and perspiration.

The black Lab snapped at his heels, willing his owner to throw the stick which he teasingly held aloft. The dog barked and jumped. The man flung the stick out into the rushing, churning sea, and the dog broke for it, splashing into the water, racing and diving into the charging waves. He was tossed and bounced but persisted, and with a lunge, he finally snatched the stick between his teeth, turned and paddled back to shore. He did the wet dog shake, and with a proud lift of his big head, he pranced forward, presenting the trophy stick to his waiting master.

On impulse, Kim applauded. The man snapped a glance toward her, as if questioning her right to invade his privacy. The sun was nearly lost behind the horizon and the last light of day bathed him in golden light. The man looked at her with suspicion and reluctance.

She became self-conscious. "Beautiful dog," she called, feeling the need to say something. The sea was loud and she wasn't sure he heard her.

"That's a beautiful dog!" she called again.

He nodded but was silent. They stood there, their eyes exploring. Kim swallowed a breath, caught by the unexpected pleasure of staring at his powerful body and tanned, handsome face. She was surprised by sudden desire.

His sharp jaw stiffened.

"Yeah…good dog," was all he said, barely audible over the restless sea.

Kim lowered her head and turned away. She felt his eyes on her. As he passed, he turned.

"Do you have a dog?"

"No… No, I don't."

"Maybe you should get one."

Kim smiled back at him. "Maybe."

He drifted away.

Kim went back into the quiet house and spent a mostly sleepless night drinking a bottle of Chardonnay, watching old movies and smoking half a pack of cigarettes. At four in the morning, she stepped outside into the humid night and started to cry. She wiped the tears with an angry, impatient hand. "Stop it!" she said. "Just stop it."

The sound of the sea seemed to call to her and she answered it, taking a beach towel and a flashlight to help guide her along the rutted path down to the beach. There was a half-moon hanging over the water, casting a shimmering path of golden light, and Kim took in the loveliness while she spread out her towel and sat down, pulling her knees up to her chest. She looked about numbly. She was the only person on the empty beach. The soft rasp of the sea and the distant stars made her feel like she was the only person left on Earth.

At some point, Kim nestled into the towel and fell into a deep sleep. She awoke with a start, the early morning sun warm on her face. As she sat up, rubbing her eyes, she heard a dog's barking and turned to see the Labrador galloping along the beach, splashing into the rushing surf. Through the misty haze of morning, the man emerged. Kim straightened her back and stared, hypnotized, holding her breath. A shiver ran through her body and she exhaled, a soft breath of desire.

She glanced down at her watch. It was almost 7 a.m.!

Ben would be calling for her. He was always awake by 6:30. He had a doctor's appointment at 9 a.m. Although Lois was there, Ben preferred that Kim accompany him. She suspected that he still wanted people to see him with his young wife, the sexy blonde.

Kim shot up, gathered the towel and finger-placed her hair as she walked briskly toward the path that led to the house. Out of the corner of her eyes, she saw the man wave to her. She stopped, staring at him, and then waved back. She dropped her head and pushed on, but at the first curve of the rising path, she twisted around to view him again.

He was closer, standing near the lower entrance of the path, watching her, waiting, his dark, steady eyes taking her in. The sun was hot on her face and neck. He waved again. Kim lifted a tentative hand and waved back, feeling heat rush to her chest, as rowdy emotions awakened a sense of swift desire. She was much too vulnerable and confused to take this in. She pivoted and hurried up the path.

CHAPTER 3

Derek Gray was driving his red Nissan Titan truck down Ocean Beach Road. He had to check on his landscaping crew. They were working on the property of a hedge fund manager, who owned a massive modern beach house with three acres of lawn, shrubs, gardens and trees. The house sat high on the cliffs and had a superior view of the beach and sea. The rich guy and his friends were new to the area, and they were potentially very lucrative accounts.

Derek had low-balled the guy to get the account. In fact, he'd low-balled all the jobs he'd landed since he'd arrived at Scorpio Beach five months before. He'd pissed off some of the local guys who'd had the local accounts for years, but Derek didn't really care. He didn't care if they threw him dirty looks in town or slashed his tires, or left threatening notes on his windshield, telling him to get out of town. They would just have to get used to a little competition.

On Scorpio Beach, most of the landscaping jobs and construction jobs were kept in the family, passed down from father to son. But Scorpio Beach had recently become the new hot spot on Long Island, where new rich blood came from Wall Street, from the new tech millionaires, and from the ever-expanding real estate market, and Derek wanted in on the ground floor of this new market. Nothing or no one was going to shake him off.

He was able to get a foothold in town only because of an old Army Ranger buddy, Bill Parker, who had grown up nearby and had married a real estate broker. She was new in town, too, and new at the market, but she was pretty, savvy and smart. Whenever she closed a sale, she called Derek with names and numbers.

Derek traveled along the two-lane road that curved and rose above the shining beach. He gazed out at the scintillating sea, seeing kites trembling in the wind, distant fishing boats drifting in the bright sun, and lazy white clouds hugging the horizon. He smiled with pleasure as he always did whenever he took this road. The beach was crowded, with bright umbrellas, beach chairs, candy-colored beach towels and kids.

This is where Derek wanted to be, and where he wanted to settle down. Scorpio Beach would be his permanent home. After three tours of duty in Afghanistan, and a stint in the hospital recovering from shrapnel wounds on the left side of his body, thanks to a mortar shell, he wanted stability and a home. And not just any home. He wanted his own beach house, and not just any ordinary beach house. He wanted one with a stupendous view of sky and sea. He wanted fireplaces, lots of windows and a broad, wrap-around deck. He'd been dreaming about it since he was a kid, working two jobs, one as a stock boy in a supermarket and the second one as a construction and landscaping worker.

Now he was going to get it and nothing was going to get in his way, and that included a woman. He wanted no part of them—at least no permanent part of them. He'd seen what they'd done to his Army Ranger buddies. The good and patriotic soldiers had gone off to war, only to return to find their girlfriends or wives had left them or had had affairs. Many guys got divorced. One buddy, Juan Gonzales, shot his cheating wife and then shot himself.

If Derek needed a woman—after all, he was only thirty-two years old and not a saint—he could find one, no problem. He'd never had a problem. One or two nights was all he needed, and then he wanted to get the hell away from them. He didn't trust them. He'd never known one to be faithful or supportive, and that included his own mother. She divorced his dad—a former Marine and a Brooklyn cop—and she'd married some loser from Chicago. Guess what? That marriage didn't last either. Big surprise. His dad started drinking and died drinking. He died a lonely alcoholic.

Derek entered the town of Scorpio Beach, passing the village green with its quaint gazebo, driving by the tackle shop, designer shops, restaurants and bars. There was only one stoplight in town and just a few chain stores, another reason Derek loved the place. In many ways, it was a new town, just perfect for the ambitious who wanted to make a new start.

His eyes were suddenly drawn to Mac's Market. There she was. The same blonde he'd seen on the beach that morning. He watched as she exited the market, a bag of groceries swinging from her arm.

Derek slowed down, taking her in with new pleasure. His weren't the only male eyes appraising her tight designer jeans and perfectly sculpted body. As she strolled, her pony tail swished back and forth in a sexy rhythm and Derek suddenly saw himself gripping that pony tail, tugging her head back and licking her perfect, long, elegant neck, and then kissing those petulant red lips. Her tight blue top revealed firm breasts, which seemed larger and rounder than when he'd seen her on the beach.

Derek swallowed again, feeling desire flame, just as it had on the beach that morning, when he'd gotten a little too close to her, watching her climb the path up to that magnificent beach house.

What is it about this woman? he thought.

With an effort, he pulled his eyes from her and drove on, passing her one last glance through his rearview mirror. Whoever she was, he wanted no part of her. She was probably the wife of some rich-as-hell Wall Street guy and that was the last thing Derek needed. This was a small town, where people loved to talk and gossip, because people in all small towns loved to talk and gossip and stab you in the back if you were from the outside. Derek's competitors would love for him to screw up.

He drove on, absorbed by her, keenly aware that he was still absorbed by her. On the beach that morning, she'd looked back at him with an expression of confusion and longing. Her hair had been wonderfully tousled by the wind, her sleepy face so beautiful and sad. Had she slept on the beach all night?

She seemed both vulnerable and strong. Frightened and bold. She was one hell of a contradiction and he knew it was going to take all his will power not to walk toward her beach house, hoping to find her.

Five minutes later, he arrived at the hedge fund owner's extravagant house and found his four guys hard at work, mowing the lawn, scattering fertilizer and trimming hedges. Two guys were still in college, only working for the summer, and two were Mexicans, hardworking men in their 30s, with families and ambition. Derek paid them well—better than the local guys—and thank God they'd stayed on, despite the threats and insults.

Derek checked their work, chatted under a baking hot sun, and then walked back to his truck. He took a long swallow of bottled water while surveying the area. Every house he saw was massive, unique and worth millions. How did people make that kind of money?

Derek felt sweat trickle down his head, chest and neck. He pulled out a handkerchief and mopped his face. He hooked a thumb beneath his belt and leaned back against his truck. His mind cautiously strayed back to the blonde. Who was she? Where was she from? When he thought of her gently swaying hips, long legs and bright red mouth, he cursed.

He grabbed the bottled water and shook the thoughts away, angry at himself. No woman was going to bore into his head and spoil everything he was building. Especially that blonde, who was undoubtedly married to a rich man, who was undoubtedly connected to all the power brokers in town.

But he'd seen the want in her eyes. Derek knew that look of wanting, and he knew it well. It was a hungry animal look. A starved and fearful look that pretended confidence and strength but was really just a smoke screen for a woman who'd eat you alive, and then destroy you one way or the other.

He knew he was good-looking, and he was comfortable with his looks. He also knew he was often attracted to women who had big problems, or women who despised their husbands but stayed for security; or they wanted revenge for their husband's infidelities or lack of interest, or they stayed in the marriage just for the hell of it. It always seemed to go that way, and usually Derek didn't mind helping them out.

But soon there were problems: they wanted to own him. They wanted to tell their husbands about him, so they could enjoy the jealous flaring in their once beloved's eyes. Some wanted a divorce so they could marry him and live happily ever after. Some didn't know what they wanted, and they were the worst.

That's what had happened more than once—Florida was the last time. South Carolina before that. Derek had to get out of town both times before the angry, powerful husbands had him beaten up, or worse. Derek didn't mind a good fight now and then, but he didn't want to have to defend himself against a man whose woman he didn't love or really want.

Derek climbed into his truck and started off for the next job, another big, arrogant beach house owned by the board of directors of a tech company. Why didn't he go into computers? Why couldn't he get that sexy blonde out of his head?

CHAPTER 4

The next day was cool and rainy, and Kim stayed away from the beach. On the following day, a Wednesday, the sun came up hot and burning. There was a shimmering blanket of haze moving across the sea and the beach. A little after noon, Kim paced her room, trying to decide whether she should go down to the beach or not. She did not want to see the man—the Hot Man, she called him. That morning, she'd awakened sharply, the image of him staring at her with dark brooding eyes, exciting her body, a body that had been sexually asleep for months. Why this man? She'd seen other handsome men in the last few months—Hollywood handsome doctors, lawyers, even a bartender or two, and she'd always had a thing for good-looking bartenders. So why this guy?

Because he seemed to have a fire in him, a fire she recognized in herself, a fire she wanted to feel next to her. Because his chest was wide, his hands were big and his face was a little hard and terribly masculine. Because she'd noticed the signs of a scar on his left side, and she wanted to touch it.

Kim lit a cigarette and smoked pensively, even as she heard the echo of Ben's loud angry voice, coming from his bedroom. Ben's primary accountant, Howard Walker, was getting blasted. Howard was a diminutive man, who looked like a stereotypical accountant: pale complexion, short hair and black-rimmed glasses. He always wore dark suits, a white shirt and a gray or black tie. Kim didn't know how he stood it, or why he always came back for more. But then, why did she stay?

"You're losing me money, Howard!" Ben raged. "I pay you to look after my interests and you just don't give a good damn! So I lose money and you still make money. You're all incompetent assholes!"

Kim heard Howard Walker's small, contrite voice, but it was so low she couldn't understand his response.

And so it went. After she'd removed Ben's and Howard's lunch trays, and the teapot still half-filled with green tea, she cleaned the kitchen and pruned some plants. She grew edgy and restless. She sunned on the upper deck on a chaise, sipped a glass of white wine and tried to read a book. It didn't hold her. Her agitated thoughts kept wandering dangerously back to that Man who roamed Scorpio Beach.

It was about two o'clock when Kim finally told Lois she was going out. She slipped into a coral-colored bikini, applied sunscreen, and tied up her hair. She threw a towel, some lip gloss, and some bottled water into her beach bag, and then she left via the back terrace, shouldering her bag and glancing back toward the house as she started for the beach path. Ben would be at it for hours and he wouldn't miss her. She slipped on her sunglasses and started off.

There were few people on the beach. She fluttered the towel onto the sand and stretched out on her stomach, reaching her arms over her head, letting the sand sift through her fingers. She remembered the last time she and Ben had come to the beach together, less than a year ago. It was nearly sunset. He'd brought some wine and a wind blocker they could hide behind. After a few glasses, they started giggling and making out like teenagers. Ben got so excited he pulled her on top of him and pressed her hips against his groin, moving them roughly back and forth until he came, whispering dirty words in her ear. She recalled how firmly he'd held her, even when she tried to pull away. She hadn't fought him, but she felt used, as if she were just an actor in one of his sexual fantasies. It had come as a shock to her, how rough and almost angry he'd become.

Kim shot up off the towel and walked to the water, wading in and out of the tide, struggling to make sense of her life and how she'd wound up in such a crazy predicament. She'd been a professional dancer, and she'd loved it. She'd made fortunate connections and consistently danced in Broadway shows, taught jazz dance at a prestigious New York dance studio, and took occasional Bus and Truck tours to Chicago, Dallas and L.A. There was even talk of her throwing in with a gay dancer friend and opening their own dance studio in New York, near the theater district. That had really excited her. She loved teaching dance. She loved being with dancers and choreographers, watching them create, work and improve. The lifestyle was natural and stimulating.

So how did she get here, alone, a bit out-of-shape and terribly confused? How had it happened? She'd fallen in love with Ben, and even though she planned to keep working after the marriage, and in fact she did so for a few months, Ben's jealous rages had grown worse every time she left him for an audition or a class. Ben's stupid jealousy, and then the accident, had ruined everything.

It was almost seven o'clock when Kim gathered up her

towel and packed her beach bag. When she heard a barking dog, she turned sharply toward the sound, seeing the Labrador galloping through the water, kicking up spray, lunging and seizing the stick between his teeth. He whirled and raced off toward his owner, who was slowly working his way across the sand toward her.

She stiffened, staring at him somberly, the late sun on his broad naked shoulders, his hair wet and raked back from his forehead. Afraid he might pick up her vibes, she got up and swung the strap of her beach bag over her shoulder. Tucking her head, she started across the sand toward the path, feeling his eyes on her back. And then she heard him call to her.

"Leaving so soon?"

She stopped and turned, nervous now, pulling a loose strand of hair from her eyes, her mouth twitching as he approached. A late evening breeze stirred across them and then fell back to stillness. Her pulse quickened.

He stopped within ten feet of her. "Did you get that dog yet?"

She shook her head, pretending casualness, taken by his chiseled jaw and day-old shadow of beard. Taken by his tanned handsomeness. "No…"

His dog rushed over to him, tongue swinging, dark eyes focused lustily on the stick the man was holding. The dog nudged the man's hand with his nose.

Kim looked at the dog and then at the man. "What's your dog's name?"

"Colin."

"Colin. That's an unusual name for a dog."

"He was named after a buddy of mine in Afghanistan. Colin Bates. He was a Royal Marine from just outside London. He was killed."

Kim stared, seeing sorrow, seeing speculative appraisal. The impact of him was astonishing. He stood a good six inches taller than Kim, who was 5'9" in bare feet. She noticed the scar again, and he followed her eyes.

"I'm sorry," she said. "You were there? Afghanistan?"

Derek shrugged. "Yeah. Three tours."

Kim let that settle in. She turned her attention back to the dog. "Are you going to throw the stick?" she asked.

The man smiled, cocked his arm and flung the stick far toward the sea.

Their eyes met, his curious and cautious. Hers probing but nervous.

"Do you have time for a walk?" he asked.

"No, I don't."

"Meeting someone?" he asked.

"No."

"Something else to do?"

"No."

"Don't like dogs?"

"No…"

"Don't like me?"

Kim glanced away, forcing a laugh. "No."

"Do you ever say 'Yes'?"

The tension left her face. She smiled. "Yes."

"Can I take that 'yes' to mean you'll go for a walk with me? An innocent walk, with a man and his dog? Yes?"

Kim felt a little weak in the knees. The guy had a raw sexuality that was unsettling and thrilling. He seemed to pulse with it. Her cheeks flushed. Did he notice?

"Okay… a short walk," Kim said.

She dropped her beach bag and towel to the sand and they started off, silent for a time, each besieged with palpable attraction.

"I'm Derek."

"Kim."

Derek was entranced by the sound of her smoky alto voice. It had a breathless intimacy to it as if she were about to reveal some racy secret.

Derek indicated toward her beach house. "That yours?"

"I live there. It's my husband's."

He looked at her. "So it's not yours? Not yours and his?"

Her face told him nothing, and Kim didn't offer more.

Derek was disappointed. He was hoping she wasn't married. A single woman was a lot less complicated, and there was obviously something going on between her and her husband that was very complicated.

"Are you new around here?" Kim asked, kicking along the warm sand.

"Yeah, not long. I live in a little cottage on the beach, about a mile away."

"Just here for the summer?" Kim asked.

"I hope not. I came to Scorpio Beach to stay."

Kim lifted her eyes. "Really?"

He looked at her, surprised again by her taut stomach, tanned body and thin, gorgeous neck. She was even sexier close up than from a distance. How many women could he say that about?

Kim watched the orange sun color the water; watched seagulls sail and heard their piercing cries. She felt a little high, as if she'd drunk a glass of wine. It was a feeling she hadn't had for a very long time: a rising sexual high. But there was something about him that set off warning bells, and she sensed danger—danger burning in her gut. She'd been feeling angry and trapped, and just being with this man brought it all to the surface. She'd made a vow never to be trapped. Her mother had been trapped, lonely and unhappy.

Kim allowed her impulsive mind to wander, estimating things, like what would happen if she picked up this guy and had sex with him? They'd just met, so it wouldn't mean anything. It would just be a sexual release, an escape—but she could definitely use a release and an escape. But then what? Would it change anything? Would it solve any of her problems?

"What does your husband do?" Derek asked.

"He's into real estate, the stock market and other things. Investments… things like that. What do you do?" Kim asked.

"I have a landscaping business. Just started really. I've only been in town about five months."

"I guess that's why I haven't seen you."

Kim was just making conversation now. She could feel the sense of danger melting into forbidden longing, an impulse to rebel against her life's restraints and disappointments, against her loneliness and Ben's rejection of her. Yes, she knew they were nothing but convenient excuses to allow her to give way to the swelling of desire.

She imagined the weight of this guy on top of her—imagined him kissing her. She wanted to feel wanted again, needed again—even if it was just a sexual want, a sexual adventure. She wanted the thrill of sex and the delightful relaxation of coming back down to earth when it was over, feeling warm and satisfied. God, how she needed some kind of release.

"How's your business going?" Kim asked.

"Not bad. And what do you do?"

Kim turned away. "I used to dance."

"Dance? What kind of dance?"

"I danced in shows… shows on Broadway, and other places."

Derek stopped, looking at her brightly. "Broadway. That sounds like fun. Do you still dance?"

Kim looked back toward the house, anxiously.

"No."

"Why not?"

"It's a long story."

"I've got time."

Kim shook her head. "I don't."

Just looking at Ben's house frightened and depressed her. It snuffed out the candle of her desire. Of course she wasn't going to sneak off and have sex with this guy.

She stopped short. "I need to go," she said, abruptly.

"So soon?"

"Yes."

"Can we meet again?" Derek asked.

Kim swallowed away the knot in her throat. She wanted to meet him again, but it would be dangerous. She was feeling very vulnerable and very angry. And she was feeling agonizingly sexy.

"No," Kim said, swiftly. "I don't think that would be a good idea."

"There's that 'no' again."

Kim gave him a meaningless grin. "Yes, that is a 'No.' A firm no."

Derek watched her leave and move across the sand, a lovely, breath-taking beauty, with tall legs and broad fragile shoulders, and he felt a riot of heat burn his body. Keeping his eyes on her, he inhaled a deep breath and let it out slowly.

She disturbed him… really disturbed him. He ran a hand over his raspy beard, thinking.

He watched her climb the path to the house, hoping she'd turn back to give him a final wave. He willed her to wave. His lips moved as he called out at a whisper for her to turn and wave.

Then, just before she drifted out of sight, she paused, glanced over her shoulder and waved.

Derek sighed with pleasure. He eased down into the warm sand and sat, his body coiled and throbbing. Colin came up with a sloppy tongue and a wagging tail.

"Colin, old boy, that is one mysterious and sexy woman."

CHAPTER 5

Kim avoided the beach for the next two days. She took Ben for physical therapy, for cardiac tests and for various meetings with real estate agents, where he discussed his interest in purchasing another beach house that he could rent for inflated amounts during the summers.

By the weekend, Kim had regained control of herself, and she was able to push away her thoughts about Derek to some remote corner of her mind.

On Sunday night, a heat wave moved in and stalled, bringing calmer seas and high humidity. Ben had fallen asleep early, at 9 o'clock. Kim took her cigarettes and a bottle of Sauvignon Blanc to the upper patio and sat, intending to get drunk enough to sleep. She hadn't slept well in over a week.

She lit a cigarette and poured a glass of wine. In the stilted breeze, she caught the scent of burning wood, and lifted her torso to see a distant beach fire, with shadowy figures around it.

How lovely, she thought. How nice it would be to sit by a fire, roast marshmallows and hot dogs, drink beer and laugh. How she longed to laugh.

After a second glass of wine, she stood up, pondered,

and then descended the stairs to the lower brick patio. The house was quiet and the sea rumbling. The evening heat kept mounting. She walked gingerly down the beach path, the snappy, humid wind playing in her hair.

On the beach, she stood at a distance, staring at the fire and the four people seated around it. She heard their muffled voices against the low hiss of the waves. Feeling a little high from the wine, and desperately lonely, she ventured across the sand toward the fire. When she heard his voice, she abruptly stopped.

"Kim…?"

It was Derek.

"Is that you, Kim?" Derek asked, squinting a look, rising to his feet.

Kim was nervously pleased. "Yes. Derek?"

"Yeah. Hey, what a surprise. Come on over… join us."

She hesitated for a moment. "I don't want to spoil your party."

"No way. The more the better. Come on," he said, waving her over.

As she approached the crackling fire, she saw a young Latino woman stand. She'd been sitting next to Derek. She was a bit heavy, but very buxom and sexy in her low top and tight shorts.

The other two guests were boys in their early twenties, one with long blond hair and a toothy grin, the other completely bald and somber, with lavish tattoos on his arms and neck.

Derek took Kim's arm and led her. "Okay, listen up, gang. This is Kim. She lives in that very impressive beach house right up there. Kim, this is Anita, Kurt and Rick."

Kim said hello and waved awkwardly. In the glow of

the fire light, she could see that Anita's sweet smile was genuine, and her warm dark eyes added attraction. Kim could see why Derek might be attracted to her and, at the same time, she felt the rise of unwanted jealousy. The boys stared at her with curious interest, their eyes quickly sliding over to Derek to gauge his reaction. They lowered their eyes when they saw him gazing at her with bright interest. They put two and two together and sat down on a long, broad log.

Derek, Anita and Kim sat on a brown blanket, and Derek reached behind, yanked a beer from a cooler, twisted off the cap and handed it to Kim. Holding it from the neck, Kim tipped back her head, drank and swallowed. Derek focused on her neck, gleaming in the firelight. He suddenly felt like a vampire. He wanted to sink his teeth into that beautiful neck.

Derek took a sip of his own beer to help cool his sudden rush of desire.

"So Kim, Anita, Kurt and Rick work with me. There are more workers, of course, but some couldn't come, and the others have already left. It's Sunday night after all, and we have to be on the job at six tomorrow morning."

"We're the hardcore drinkers and partiers," the blond Kurt said, lifting his beer to toast Kim. And then they all toasted her, clinking their bottles against hers.

Rick pulled a pint bottle of whiskey from his backpack. "Hey, Kim, want some? It's Wild Turkey."

Kim *did* want some. She wanted to escape her stifling life for a while and feel free, wild and sexy. The wine had already made her high and feeling easy.

She reached for the whiskey bottle and Rick's stern face lit up with happy surprise. "Yo! I like this woman. Yeah."

He did a victory hand slap with Kim.

Kim unscrewed the cap. Derek handed her a paper cup, and she poured a healthy shot.

With great pleasure, Derek took her in. "Is there anything sexier than a woman drinking straight whiskey from a paper cup?" Derek asked.

Kim's eyes lingered on him, and he saw the warm invitation in them.

The others thrust their empty cups forward, expectantly. Kim poured the whiskey, watching it shine and glimmer in the firelight.

"To life and love," Derek said, lifting his cup high.

They toasted and took the whiskey down in a swallow.

When Kim coughed at the sharp burn in her throat, they all laughed. She laughed too as she grabbed her beer and took a swallow. It was the first time she'd laughed in weeks.

They sat in happiness, sharing stories about work, school, families and food. Kim munched on a hotdog, sipping her beer and enjoying it all, the delightful talk, the food and the pulsing sexual excitement of sitting close to Derek.

She watched him laugh, watched his big hands cut images in the air as he told a story. She studied his thick neck, muscled arms and wide shoulders. She imagined him in battle. Surely, he was a formidable opponent—a man who seemed crafted from hard steel. Surely, he'd be a good lover, she thought, allowing the booze buzz to light up her imagination. As they talked and laughed, as stories tumbled out, Kim stole glances at Derek, speculating and imagining.

Derek poked at the fire, and Kim watched the sparks flicker and rise toward the night sky, into the mass of blinking stars. The whiskey heated her chest, making her feel alternately cautious, sexy and daring.

Derek talked business with the guys, while Kim learned that Anita was from Mexico City, was married and had two sons. Anita told Kim she rode power mowers, trimmed hedges and did equipment inventory. She was also taking a course in bookkeeping, which Derek had paid for. "Derek pays us all well and treats us with respect," she said, smiling at her boss.

Kim's eyes wandered to Derek's face, as the fire cast shadows across it. He glanced back at her, a knowing, provocative look, as if he were about to reach for her. She wanted him to reach for her.

"I want to do the cards," Anita abruptly said.

Derek turned sharply. "Oh no, not the cards, Anita."

"Yes," Anita said, with a firm nod of her chin. "I want to do the cards for Kim. I sense something in her."

Kim sat up, alert. "Sense something?" she asked. "What does that mean?"

Anita reached into her purse and drew out a black velvet cloth. She laid it on the sand, opened it, and reached for a deck of ornately illustrated Tarot cards.

Anita began to shuffle, while she fixed her bright, earnest eyes on Kim. "Do you have a question, Kim? A question you'd like to ask. Anything? Ask anything."

Derek scratched his head, looking on. "Be careful, Kim. She did my cards once, and she was right-on. We got two more lucrative accounts, and that pissed off the competition. Two guys tried to run me off the road."

Kim swept the faces around her. They were shining with interest. Kim stared uncertainly. "No… I don't have any questions."

Anita kept shuffling, her fingers quick and agile, her focus on the cards. Her expression softened, her gaze glassy and inward.

"I sense a dark cave, Kim. I sense darkness. Things hidden."

"Do you believe in this stuff, Kim?" Rick asked, sitting in a slouching posture, the booze having relaxed him.

"No, not really. I had my palm read once, and the woman told me I'd meet the man of my dreams when I was twenty-two and have two children. Needless to say, that didn't happen."

Anita ignored her. She was locked in concentration. Sitting by the blazing fire with the night surrounding them, and the roar of the sea in her ears, Kim felt as though they were isolated, marooned on some lost planet.

Kim took the whiskey bottle from Rick and poured herself another drink. She sipped it slowly as she watched Anita spread five cards onto the black cloth. Everyone hovered near and fell into a hush, waiting for Anita as she studied, considered, tilted her head and then nodded.

"So what do the cards say?" Derek asked.

Kim stared down at one particular card. She cleared her throat and tapped her cheek with a finger. "What does The Lovers card mean? And why is it upside-down?"

Anita's forehead lifted, as she raised her steady dark eyes to meet Kim's.

"By itself, it only tells part of the story. It's an excellent omen for your love life in coming days. However, the reversal slightly weakens the overall positive energies for love coming to you."

Kim nodded. "And what do the other cards say?"

Anita shut her eyes for a moment. When they opened, she looked at Derek pointedly, and then she swung a hard stare back to Kim. "The Ace of Wands reversed."

"Come on, Anita," Derek said, in a tart, skeptical voice. "Let's have the worst of it."

Anita crossed her arms. "I see the beginning of a new crisis—but it's not clear. I see the potential for an explosive situation that threatens all who get too close. There are strong and primitive forces at work."

There was a long silence.

Finally, Kurt got up. "Okay, kids, I'm mostly drunk and I've got to get home. I'm fried. See you all in the morning."

Rick climbed to his feet, grabbed the cooler, and followed on Kurt's heels.

Anita gathered up her cards, her purse and sweatshirt. Derek stood, and Anita kissed him on the cheek.

"See you bright and early, Boss," she said, jabbing a finger at his chest, with a lopsided grin. "And don't be late."

"Okay, Boss," he said, winking at her.

Derek pocketed his hands, his eyes on Kim.

Anita took Kim's hand, looking at her carefully. "I like you…the cards like you. But there are dark clouds. The cards are not so clear about that. Take care, Kim."

CHAPTER 6

Kim and Derek sat alone and silent as the fire smoldered. It was almost high tide, and the waves came crashing in, loud in their ears. With a stick, Derek stabbed at the dying flames. He glanced over at Kim, who sat in an elegant melancholy, her knees pulled up to her chest.

"You built the fire just below my house," Kim said.

"Yes. I hoped you'd come."

"Didn't the others ask why you didn't build one near your place?"

"No… but they knew when they saw you."

"Where's Colin?"

"I left him in his house… a shed I built for him. He has a better place than a lot of people."

"How long have you had him?"

"Three years. I got him after I left the service."

Kim nodded. "Did you like the military?"

"Like most things, some good, some bad. I didn't like being shot at, and I didn't like all the confusion over there. I did like the guys I fought with. We did good things sometimes. I hope we made a difference now and then."

Kim nodded, looking at him with admiration and

speculation. The wind swept in, scattering her hair. He reached over, brushing it gently from her face.

"Come back to my place," he said, softly, intimately.

Kim looked at him, her eyes lowered on his chest. Indecision flickered over her face. "No."

"Why do you always say no?"

Kim played with her hair, twisting it with her left hand. "You heard Anita. You saw the cards. Explosive situation."

"And primitive forces," Derek said, his grin widening. "Does primitive sound good to you?"

"I'm a little drunk," Kim said.

"Good, so am I."

Kim gazed into the dying fire. "The beginning of a new crisis…"

"I don't believe in that occult stuff. Anyway, I don't give a damn. I live with some kind of crisis all the time. I always have. Hell, it's the way life is."

Derek drew closer, his lips close to Kim's ear. She shivered a little, feeling her temperature rise, smelling his musky scent, feeling the animal in her awaken.

"Let's tempt fate," he said, in a low murmur. "Let's see what happens. Come back to my place."

Kim pulled away and climbed to her feet. She crossed her arms, giving him a sweet, sad smile. "No, I can't do that."

He looked up at her, a near silhouette. "What are you waiting for, Kim? You know we want each other. You know we're going to have each other. We both know it. Anyway, it's just a night. One night. We're just two people, together for one single night and then…?" He lifted a hand and let it drop. "And then, it's over and no one will ever know, and in the grand scheme of this crazy world, who will care?"

"Yes, just one night," she said, reflectively. And then she thought, *And then all the walls of my life will come crashing down on top of me and bury me.*

She pivoted and started for the path.

"Kim… don't go," Derek called.

Kim didn't stop. She marched on, heading for the path, her bare feet kicking up sand. As she crested the dunes near the house, she stopped, paused, then glanced back. The blanket was gone. The fire was out, its smoke rising, being shredded by the wind. Derek was already walking away, a shadow drifting along the edge of the tide, slowly retreating from her. She felt a catch in her throat. God, how she wanted him.

She turned her cold eyes on the house, a dark and foreboding prison cell. With her jaw set in defiant determination, she turned, aiming her eyes on Derek's dark, receding shadow.

Derek wasn't aware he was being followed until he'd nearly reached his cottage. Colin barked from his stylish doghouse shed.

Kim advanced slowly, having been to this part of the beach only once. It was unpretentious, far from the main road, in a low-slung neighborhood of quaint, private beach bungalows, with a good view of the dunes and ocean.

Derek twisted around and saw her coming toward him, a dark figure with blonde hair gleaming in the moonlight. He stood watching her, in an aching desire, as she slowly closed the distance between them.

Kim approached, her breathing coming fast, her body ripe, her mind turbulent, like the sea that thundered in. She was going to have him now. She was going to take him—own him for a few hours—and the world be damned.

They stood close, the moonlight drenching them. He leaned a little and kissed her full lips. It was electric. She shut her eyes, trembling. Derek nibbled her open lips, licked them, sucked them. She moved into him, pressing her breasts against the wall of his chest.

Their tongues met, probed and plunged. Derek took her shoulders and pulled her closer. There was heat and breath and the loud sea. Colin barked out a warning, a call to move inside.

Derek took her hand and led her up the wooden stairs, across the screened-in porch into the dark living room. He kicked the door shut and backed Kim against the wall, pressing himself against her.

His eyes fluttered over her, a statuesque beauty, who in the tender moonlight looked back at him with an eager restlessness. Just feeling his body against hers overwhelmed her with a crazy pleasure.

They angled into the bedroom, touching, kissing, breath loud and hot. They tugged and kicked away clothes, stumbling, turning in a circle, their lips burning, their bodies pulsing. Derek lowered her onto the double bed and sank down on top of her. Kim stared into his risky, piercing eyes, wide and wanting. She called to him, reached and yielded to his taut, hard body.

CHAPTER 7

Kim stood on Derek's screened-in porch, staring out into the night, listening to the soothing sound of the sea. The moon was nearly full, casting an eerie glow, making shadows into twisted shapes and sizes. Colin must have fallen asleep. The shed was quiet.

Kim was wearing only her pink lace panties. She was barefoot. Derek came up from behind and waited. He was naked, his body slim, muscled and beautiful. Kim turned away from him and he didn't touch her, although she wanted him to.

"Do you have a cigarette?" she asked.

"No… I don't smoke."

"A drink?"

"Bourbon. Some white wine."

"Wine," Kim said.

She crossed her arms and waited, her body still having little tremors from the climax.

Moments later, Derek handed her a cool glass of wine. He had poured himself a short glass of whiskey.

"What should we drink to?" he asked, raising his glass.

Kim kept her back to him. "To bad little girls and boys."

She twisted and chimed his glass, then moved away to the far end of the porch and sat in a padded chair.

Derek drifted over. Kim looked him up and down with half-hooded eyes, then she took a sip of wine.

"You have a beautiful body," she said.

"And you are sexy magic."

Kim studied him. "Bad magic, you mean."

"Was it so bad?" he said, looking at her, pointedly.

She had a strange, dazed look. "Bad? Oh yes, it was bad alright… there's no doubt about that."

A minute later, she shook her head, lowered her eyes, but didn't speak.

"Can you stay the night?" he asked.

She lifted her eyes on him. "No. Anyway, don't you have to be up bright and early?"

"Yes, but I can go on three or four hours' sleep. In the Army, I got by on an hour, sometimes for two or three days."

The silence lengthened. Derek left, returning a few minutes later, wearing a pair of khaki shorts. He sat down in the wooden chair beside her.

"What happened to your husband? I asked around. They said he was paralyzed in a car accident. They said you were with him."

Kim ignored his gaze. She took a long sip of the wine, set the glass down on the floor and stood up. "I have to go."

While Kim dressed, Derek left the porch, waiting for her outside, with his hands in his pockets. He was staring up at the moon when she emerged, her hair finger-combed, her luscious lips drawing his eyes.

"I wish you could stay. I wish you would stay."

She avoided his eyes. "Derek… I did this because I wanted to… I shouldn't have, but I wanted to."

Kim waited, inhaling a troubled breath. "I've got to get back to my life now, and this is not part of it, and it can't ever be part of it. So, let's just… move on."

"Why do you stay with him?"

"That's none of your business," Kim said sharply.

"Do you love him?"

In her anger, her breathing increased and Derek watched the fetching rise and fall of her breasts. He remembered how they tasted—how she tasted. How she felt.

Derek shrugged a left shoulder. "Okay… If you want to play the role of the sacrificial lamb, the martyr, the good and loving wife who doesn't think she deserves to be loved, so be it."

Kim bristled. "Don't judge me. It's so easy to judge when you don't know anything about anything. When you don't know anything about me or what really happened."

"So tell me what happened."

"No."

"There's that 'No' again. Did you ever think that maybe you deserve something better?"

"Oh, so you can offer me something better? *You* can offer me love? Look, what we had tonight was just sex, okay? Good sex? You bet. It was even great sex. But that's it and let's not pretend it was anything more than that. We've just met. I don't know you and you don't know me."

Derek saw the fire in her. "This isn't finished," he said, in a strong, steady voice. "I think you and I both know that. Maybe it's just lust. Okay, fine, I'll take lust. I'll take all of it. Maybe it'll burn itself out the next time, I don't know. But you and I both know, there will be a next time, because our bodies fit. They fit perfectly, so we both know it's going to happen again. So, wherever you go, think of me, because I'll be around, thinking of you, and I'll be coming for you."

Kim swallowed, her body heating up; her mind ablaze with emotion and desire.

She burned past him and started up the beach. It was difficult to do. To leave him. Something had happened to her back in Derek's bed. Derek had touched her in some indescribable way. He'd moved her, and her body and mind were struggling to digest it, to understand it. If it was just sexual, then sex had taken on an entirely new meaning. Was it love? How could it be? They had just met. So, as the song went "*It was just one of those things. One of those fabulous flings.*"

Kim walked briskly along the beach, pushing down fear and confusion. She prayed that Ben hadn't awakened and called for her. He didn't often awaken in the middle of the night, but there were nights when he did.

"Let tonight not be one of them," she said aloud.

She'd always been there for him. She'd always been reliable and responsible. She'd prided herself on that. She'd always been faithful. Her heart sank a little at the thought. Not anymore. She'd cheated on him and she'd have to adjust her mind, body and soul to that. She'd have to see herself in a different way, and she'd have to learn to live with it.

Of course she could rationalize it, couldn't she? Ben treated her badly. He was angry all the time. He was unable to satisfy her sexually or emotionally, and on and on. Her friends had told her this, but she had made a commitment to work through all that—to be patient and persistent and trust that, eventually, Ben would come around. He'd change and see that she loved him. And, despite it all, she did love him.

At that thought, Kim stopped walking. Or did she love what was already passed; what had already died and could never be resurrected? Maybe his love for her would never return. Maybe he was too far gone, and she was just deceiving herself. Maybe it *was* time to think about leaving him. She shook the thought away, walking again.

Would Ben see the guilt in her eyes? Would he notice a change in her? He was one of the most perceptive men she'd ever known. He had a phenomenal talent for accurately judging people and situations.

And what if he'd had a heart attack or something while she was out with Derek? His heart was weak. He wasn't taking care of himself. Didn't he have a death wish?

She increased her pace as she approached the beach path. She glanced up at the house, apprehensively, her nervous eyes focusing on the windows of Ben's room.

Damn! His light was on. She checked her phone again. It was 1:20 a.m. He hadn't texted or called.

Kim entered the house through the back patio door, hearing insects screech and scratch at the night. She crept across the tiled floor to the bathroom, straining her ears to listen for Ben's voice. Nothing. With urgency, she entered the bathroom and stripped. She stepped into the shower and turned on the warm stream of water. As she washed her hair, she shut her eyes and saw Derek's face. She saw his naked wet chest, and she felt his salty kisses and raspy beard against her face. Kim had not been a saint. She'd had affairs with men. After all, she'd been a dancer and there were men who had a thing for leggy blonde dancers with big tits. She'd dated millionaires, sports figures and older men, and she'd slept with some. But she'd never experienced anything like what she'd experienced with Derek. She'd never felt that silky, thrilling connection with any other man. She didn't even know it was possible.

After her shower, she turbaned her hair in a thick towel, pulled on a cotton robe and padded across her room to her door. She cracked it and breathed with anxiety when she saw Ben's bedroom light was still on, spilling out into the living room.

She gently shut her door.

Later, just before she fell into sleep, she smiled at the thought of what Derek had said. "I'll be around, thinking of you and watching you. I'll be coming for you."

Kim ran her hands gently along her upper thighs. She liked the idea of being watched by him.

CHAPTER 8

The first summer heat wave rolled in during the week of June 10. Scorpio Beach was alive with sunbathers, fluttering umbrellas, surfers and swimmers, all cooking in a pot of stalled steamy air. The hot muggy weather brought hipsters from Manhattan, with their artisan tattoos, designer sunglasses, skinny jeans and fedoras. They found the cafes with vegan muffins; they packed the yoga studio and designer shops, and crowded into Hogan's Beach Bar, where live rock music thumped until the wee hours. Many were sunburned after the first day on the beach, impatient for that golden tan, so they hid away in a beach bar with a good view of the ocean and sky, sucking down beer and cocktails while searching for sex mates.

From Long Island came the loud families with jittery kids, wearing critter-embroidered swim trunks. They charged the beach and swarmed the new shiny pizzeria and family style Italian restaurant, chattering, texting, complaining and having the time of their lives.

NO VACANCY signs confirmed that the motels were off to a superlative start. The boutique and T-shirt shops were bursting, the cafes were hiring extra summer help, and the restaurants were looking at record summer sales.

With Anita in the passenger seat, Derek drove his truck through the over-heated town and turned onto Navy Road, a narrow two-lane asphalt road leading down to the water, where surfers and laid-back locals hung out along the surf amidst a sea of umbrellas and canvas chairs.

It was just after 1 p.m., when Derek drove into The Dock Café gravel lot and parked near the front entrance. Temperatures hovered in the high 90s, and heat shimmered off the cars and asphalt. Derek and Anita climbed out, adjusted their sunglasses, and saw that the thatched outside patio was full.

"Just as well," Derek said. "It's too damned hot to sit outside, anyway."

Inside, the room was rustic, with dim lighting, heavy oak booths and wooden tables and chairs. The music blasting through outside speakers was old rock: The Doobie Brothers, Grand Funk Railroad and Cream. There was a long mahogany bar with a wide tarnished mirror behind shelves of lighted liquor bottles. The tall, red upholstered bar stools were occupied with a rowdy beach crowd, slinging back beers and shots. Ceiling fans whirled lazily, and the smell of fried fish, fresh clams and grilled steak hovered in the chilled, air-conditioned air.

Derek and Anita found the one empty booth in the back near the kitchen. It wasn't the best seat, since servers and bus boys whisked by, rattling dishes, shouting out commands and dropping things, but it would do.

Derek slid into the booth. Anita flopped down opposite him, mopping her forehead with a paper napkin. Natalie came over, carrying two mugs of beer, and she plopped them down.

"Damn, Natalie, you may have just saved our lives," Derek said, sighing into the cold mug.

Natalie wore khaki shorts and the signature sky blue T-shirt with The Dock Café stamped on it. She was a bit chubby, with a round, serious face and short, dyed red hair. Her smile was good and genuine, her manner brusque. Derek was a two-month regular and he and Natalie had hit if off from the start. Natalie's husband, Mike, had been in the Army and sometimes when he was in, he and Derek shared war stories at the bar.

"Hey, Derek. Hot enough for you?" she asked.

"And this is only June," Derek said.

"Hi, Anita. You better be drinkin' lots of water if you're out there on a mower."

"Always," Anita said.

"The town's a madhouse," Natalie said. "Traffic is the worst I've seen."

"I see the back deck is packed too," Anita said.

"Yeah, people have fled the cities. They say this heat wave isn't supposed to break for a couple days."

"Is the money good at least?" Derek asked.

"You know it."

"How's Mike?"

"Fishing."

"Good."

Anita ordered fish and chips and Derek the cod fish sandwich with coleslaw. Derek and Anita talked business while they waited, draining their beers in three or four swallows. Natalie promptly delivered two more.

As Derek held the second mug to his lips, he saw

her. Kim. She entered from the back outside patio and sashayed toward the Ladies Room. She passed the crowded bar but didn't see Derek. Derek's eyes locked on her and Anita followed his eyes.

The bathroom was occupied, so Kim stood waiting, glancing about. That's when she saw Derek and she stiffened in surprise.

Derek smiled and winked.

Kim lowered her eyes for a moment as if in thought. A moment later, while Derek was still watching, she turned her shining eyes on him and gave him a coy smile. She wore red Keds sneakers, deep red lipstick, tight shorts and a yellow clinging T-shirt. Her hair was neatly rolled up and pinned, revealing that perfect dancer's neck. Men at the bar turned and entertained lusty wishes.

After Kim disappeared into the Ladies Room, Natalie hurried by and deposited Anita's and Derek's lunches. Anita dove in, famished, while Derek sat silently waiting for Kim. She emerged from the bathroom a few minutes later and drifted over to Derek's table. She paused, ignoring Derek, her full focus on Anita.

"Hi, Anita. It's good to see you again."

"You too, Kim. I love that top," Anita said.

"Oh, thanks. I bought it in town."

Kim felt Derek's eyes moving up and down her body. She allowed her smoldering eyes to drift toward him.

"Hello, Derek."

He nodded. "Are you here with a friend?" Derek asked.

Kim's eyes lingered on his lips. "Not a friend… my husband. He seldom goes out, but he likes this place."

"He has good taste, doesn't he?"

"Obviously."

Derek stared at the shiny luster of her hair, and he fought an irrational impulse to reach for her hand and pull her down into his lap.

"Well, got to go," Kim said. "Good to see you both."

After she'd gone, Derek ate quietly. Anita studied him.

"You're distracted by her. I've never seen that. Of course, I've only known you for a few months."

Derek glanced up. "Let's talk about the new account. He's that guy who bought that big bunker of a beach house up on Sandy Beach Road."

"Yeah. I talked to his housekeeper. A guy."

"He called me," Derek said. "He wanted a better price than what you quoted. So I gave it to him."

Anita stopped eating. "When we take clients like that, we're making more enemies."

Derek shrugged. "He called *us*. Not my problem."

"We might need more people," Anita said.

"So we hire more people."

"Some are afraid."

"Let's find the ones who aren't afraid."

Derek gave her a look of concern. "Are you afraid?"

"I have two boys."

"Have you been threatened?"

"Once or twice."

"Such as?"

"A couple of dudes said they'd take me behind some bushes if I wasn't careful."

Derek frowned. "Make sure you're always with

Rick or Kurt."

She nodded. "I will. Count on it."

"What's your man, José, think about all this?" Derek asked.

Anita dipped the last piece of fish into her plastic cup of tartar sauce. "He said he may have to call you for help some day."

"You have a good husband. Tell him he can call me anytime."

Anita grinned. "You like to fight, don't you, Derek?"

"Like it? No. Can I? Yes. Will I? In a minute."

"You be careful, Derek. Some of these dudes around here are pretty tough bastards."

"I knew when I started this it wasn't going to be easy. I knew it would take a couple of years before things settled down. But it will settle down. Things always do once the local folks know you're going to stay. It will settle down."

Anita drained the last of her beer, her stern eyes narrowed on him. "Not if you mess around with Kim."

Derek looked long and steadily at her. "Who says I have, or will?"

"You have. You will. I've seen the cards."

Derek dismissed the comment with a flick of his hand. "Ah, to hell with the cards..." He leaned back, averting her eyes. "Okay... but it will pass. It always passes. That's the way it is with me."

"I think she's different," Anita said. "I think you don't know that yet."

"It will pass," Derek said firmly.

Anita wiped her lips with the napkin. "Her old man knows lots of big people. I've seen him a couple of times. He's a little scary—even in that wheelchair. Have you ever seen him?"

Derek twisted around to see the back patio, buzzing with life. He couldn't see Kim.

"No... I've never seen him."

Anita's eyes dropped and came up again. "He uses Tom Bayless Landscaping."

"I know," Derek said.

"You gonna call him with a business proposition? Are you gonna offer him a discount?" Anita said, with a humorous glint in her eyes.

"Funny lady, Anita. You are a very funny lady."

Anita slid out. "Let's get back to work, Boss."

"Yes, Boss," Derek said, saluting her.

Anita started for the door and Derek turned and drifted toward the back patio. He casually glanced about until he saw Kim and an older man sitting at a private table under a broad patio umbrella. Kim had her back to him. Derek got a good look at the man who was surely Ben Maxwell. He was stocky, with a strong hard face, crinkly gray hair, a thin, stingy mouth, and small solemn eyes. Despite being in a wheelchair, he had an air of determined vigor about him, like a victorious wrestler ready for the next opponent.

Derek turned away, seeing that Anita was staring at him from the front door. She waved him over. Derek paid the bill, slapped a $20 bill into Natalie's hand and left.

After Derek dropped Anita off at the work site, he drove over to Beach Hill to speak with a potential client. As he crested a hill that had a glorious view of the ocean and cliffs, he saw a car in his rearview mirror, approaching fast.

Derek's danger meter shot up. He was climbing up over the cliffs on Fairview Road, a narrow two-lane highway, with a drop-off down to the sea of about ninety to one-hundred feet.

The car kept coming, glinting in the sunlight.

CHAPTER 9

"You seem a little flushed," Ben said, after Kim returned from the ladies' room.

She sat down, wishing her back wasn't to the door. She might be able to steal a look or two at Derek. Kim lowered her head, reaching for her glass of chilled white wine.

"It's hot. So damn hot today."

Ben finished his fish and chips, staring at Kim in a strange way. "You've been different these past few days."

Kim averted her eyes as she took another sip of wine. "Oh? Different?"

"Preoccupied. Distracted. A little happier."

Kim had finished her lunch, a lobster roll with coleslaw and French fries. She pushed her plate aside as the overhead speakers spewed out The Rolling Stones' *Let's Spend the Night Together*.

Kim struggled for words. "Well, you seem happier, too, so I guess that makes me happy."

Ben gave her a lop-sided grin of suspicion and then reached for his melting vodka on ice. "You disappoint me, Kim. You're not often a bullshitter. It doesn't suit you, and you're not very good at it."

Kim's eyes flicked around, searching for answers. She decided on a diversion. "Ben, I've been thinking that I want to open a kind of spa."

"A kind of spa. What the hell is that, a kind of spa?"

"Well… I'm thinking of starting a yoga studio."

"There's already one in town."

"But it's not very good. Mine would be better. I'd add some Swedish massage rooms, maybe hire an acupuncturist. I could offer dance courses for adults and kids."

Ben twisted up his mouth in thought.

Kim saw that she'd successfully deflected his suspicions. Anything business always interested him.

"Okay, it might work."

"It would work, Ben. Something upscale. Have you noticed that this town is growing?"

"Of course I've noticed. Why the hell have I been buying up property? There's a big future here. This used to be a little back-water town with old hippies, surfers and losers. Of course I know it's growing."

"There's a lot of money moving in," Kim said, leaning forward. "There are Wall Street guys, tech guys and even some movie stars. They have wives and kids and they have money to spend. And they want to spend that money on anything that will make them look good, and anything that will keep the kids from driving them crazy."

He studied her carefully, scratching his nose.

She held his eyes boldly, her face calm, though inside she was shaking. He'd almost caught her, and Ben was right. She wasn't a good liar or a bullshitter. What you saw was what you got. She found it nearly impossible to hide what she was thinking or feeling.

"Okay, let me kick it around," Ben said. "I'll get my shit-for-brains accountant to crunch some numbers, and

I'll get him to find out the numbers for that yoga studio to see if they're making any money."

Kim smiled. It was something she'd been thinking about but hadn't given much thought to—at least not until after she'd been with Derek. That next morning, the idea of the yoga studio seemed to blow in with the wind, and flower like a new bud on a fresh stem. And the truth was, she was happier. Nervous and scared? Yes. Working overtime to hide her thoughts and desires? Yes. Afraid of what Ben would do if he found out? Yes. Afraid of destroying her life? Yes.

She'd spent hours recalling Derek's kisses, his strong pulsing body and her extravagant climax—the best of her life. The memory kept her edgy, pacing and wanting more. She'd wandered the beach looking for him; went shopping in town and searched for him; sat in The Dock Café and wondered if he'd come. And he did come. When she'd paused at his table, she'd wanted to whisper, "When? When will I see you? When can we meet?"

Was he still hunting her? Was it over? Could she bear it if it was just a one-night fling?

"Kim…?" Ben asked.

Kim snapped out of her daydream. "Yes… Yes, Ben."

"Did you hear me?"

"Yes… I mean… Well, the music's loud."

"Are you ready to go?"

"Go? Yes, of course. Let's go."

Back at the house, Kim was busy watering the living room plants when she heard the wobbling sound of sirens out on the main highway. Ben was already back in his room, making calls and pouring over his stock investments.

Kim looked up as the sirens raced by, their horns blaring as they struggled to break through the beach traffic. She felt a sickening nausea and wondered if the lobster had been fresh. Then she realized it was something else—something she couldn't quite put her finger on. It was a dark foreboding, as if she or someone she knew was in imminent danger.

She stepped out on the patio, carrying her green watering can, and felt the hot breath of afternoon. The sky was hazy and thick with humidity. She wiped the hair from her eyes and watered her snapdragons, petunias and violets.

The sirens had faded, but her bad feeling hadn't. Kim paused, wondering if she should call her mother. Maybe something had happened to her or her brother.

A sudden fragment of conversation struck. Kim stopped, trying to remember. It was something Derek had said as they sat around the beach fire.

"*We got two more lucrative accounts, and that pissed off the competition. Two guys tried to run me off the road.*"

Kim turned toward where she'd last heard the sirens, troubled. She swallowed, feeling urgency rise in her chest.

CHAPTER 10

Derek saw the battered old Chevy through his rear-view mirror. It was closing in on him. He grinned darkly, seeing two guys in the front seat. They were obviously in pursuit.

"Come on, guys," Derek said.

Derek slowed down, checking to see what they'd do. They kept coming fast, the car glinting in the sun. He glanced ahead to see a car approaching from the opposite direction. He waited until it had passed, and then he yanked his foot off the accelerator. On the steep hill, Derek's speed plummeted, as his truck lost its climb. The Chevy driver slammed on the screaming brakes to avoid crashing into the back of Derek's truck. The sudden jolt threw the driver and the passenger forward.

Derek floored the accelerator and roared away, burning rubber, fishtailing. He was cresting the hill when he saw the car was stubbornly giving chase.

"You want more? Okay. Come on, boys."

Derek eased off the gas again. This time the chasing car whipped into the left lane and charged ahead, trying to pass him. Derek grinned. He tapped his brake abruptly, bouncing. Stopped. He slammed into reverse and shot backwards as the chasing car zoomed past. Both bad guys' heads whipped around in surprise as they whizzed by, seeing Derek recede behind them. Derek saw they were young—probably early 20s.

Derek hit his brakes, stopped going backwards and rammed the gear into drive and gunned the engine. He surged ahead after the car, watching as the bad guys recklessly swung their car into the left lane. To their shock, a UPS truck was barreling toward them, and at the last moment, the truck swerved wide to miss the car. It skidded on the narrow shoulder, spewing dirt and gravel from its back tires.

As Derek sped by, he saw the driver was still fighting the wheel, his arms and shoulders in straining motion, his face packed with fear.

Through his rearview mirror Derek was grateful to see the UPS driver finally regain control of the truck and swing back onto the road.

"You dumb shits," Derek said, lowering his head, his hard jaw set, his angry eyes focused ahead.

Derek crested the hill and started down the other side, gaining speed. The car was only fifty feet away, and they were slowing down, playing Derek's game.

"Good, boys. Good. You do that."

As Derek came up behind them, he tugged his seatbelt tighter. When the Chevy dropped its speed in a dare, Derek nudged up close, punched his accelerator and slammed into the Chevy's rear bumper. Both men lurched forward. The passenger twisted around, his face in shock. Derek rammed them again, hard, and they pitched forward, trapped, searching for a way out.

When the passenger flipped Derek the finger, he stomped the accelerator and butted them again. The driver fought for control as the car veered right onto the shoulder, the tires skidding, seeking traction, two feet from the guard rail and an eighty-foot drop-off onto the rocky sea below.

Derek watched in grim satisfaction as the driver jerked the steering wheel the wrong way. The car careened off the yellow guard rail. It bounced and ramped, finally screeching back onto the road. Derek went after them.

The passenger turned, his eyes bulging with fear.

"Welcome to combat," Derek said, his cold eyes locked on the car, now an enemy to be destroyed.

Suddenly, Derek was back in Afghanistan, in Paktia Province, in the heart of what the American military dubbed the K-G Pass. It's a gap in the rugged mountains of eastern Afghanistan that facilitates travel between Khost Province and the Paktia capital, Gardez.

It's so close to the border that the Taliban easily sent in replacement fighters from refugees in nearby Pakistani cities and villages, making for a near endless supply of re-inforcements.

On the morning of July 10, they attacked the American outpost where Derek, five other Rangers and thirty-five Marines were held up.

Derek was closing in on the car—now in front of him. He saw the bright sun wink off its back windshield. He saw the passenger's head whip around, anxious with fear. Oddly, the car was slowing down again. Derek was sweating. He wiped his eyes.

Then he was back at the outpost in Afghanistan, hearing the whistle of an incoming mortar round. Then the sizzle of a rocket. More than 200 Taliban were out there, ready to attack. Derek heard the scream of another mortar round. He saw soldiers running for the bunkers spread around the compound. Nearly everyone sought cover except the artillerymen. They sprinted to their guns, anticipating the computer-quick information from the team that handled targeting.

A mortar whistled in. It detonated with a muffled thud. It blew Mike Nelson into the air. He was dead. Jamar Gomez was hit and writhing in agony. Derek ran over to help, then more rounds came in. He dived for cover. More men were hit.

Having had some combat medic training, Derek frantically went to work, carrying the wounded into the outpost's tiny field clinic. He tried to stabilize the injured men until a medevac chopper could arrive. But two Marines died in agony. One had his leg blown off. Still the mortars came whistling in and Derek—a sniper—felt useless.

"You sons of bitches!" Derek screamed. "You fucking sons of bitches!"

Derek was back on the road in Scorpio Beach. He was side by side with the once attacking car, glancing over at the terrified driver, who was stomping the accelerator, trying to escape from Derek's attack.

But something was wrong. The old car was losing power. It was not gaining speed. It couldn't break away. Escape.

Gritting his teeth, eyes afire, Derek whipped his truck right, slamming hard into the driver's side. The driver panicked and lost control, his hands fighting the chaotic steering wheel.

Derek watched the car shoot off the road, jump, lurch and plow head-on into a telephone pole in a cacophony of exploding glass and grinding metal.

Derek wrenched his truck back into the right lane, narrowly missing an on-coming Mustang. He glanced back over his shoulder, seeing steam rising from the crumpled hood.

He shook away the Afghanistan nightmare and pulled over to the shoulder of the road. He took a couple of deep breaths and wiped his sweaty forehead. He swallowed away a dry throat. Through his rearview mirror, he saw the Mustang skid to a stop on the opposite shoulder of the road. The driver burst out of his car and ran across the highway to the broken Chevy.

Calmly, Derek drew out his cell phone, considering calling 911. If he did, they'd have his number. No, he'd let the Mustang guy do it. Derek rammed the truck into gear and drove off down the hill to keep his date with the man who had just moved to town, and who had connections with the country club.

He didn't think about the two guys slumped in the Chevy. They had attacked him. They had been the enemy, so he had simply taken them out. That was his job. That's what he'd been trained to do. He was a warrior.

CHAPTER 11

Late that night, Kim was sitting at a glass top patio table on the second-floor balcony, staring into her laptop. She was re-reading the news story about the car crash out on Fairview Road. Both the driver and the passenger—two 21-year olds—were in critical condition. They were from Riverhead, a town about forty miles away, and they worked local odd jobs, in landscaping and construction. Witnesses said both men had been drinking at The Dock Café bar earlier that afternoon, and as they were leaving, they boasted that they were going out to have a little fun and "Get rid of a piece of shit."

Kim lit a cigarette and smoked thoughtfully. Were they talking about Derek? It all seemed to add up. The police were waiting to interview the boys as soon as they improved—if they improved. If they had been after Derek, what had happened?

Should she call Anita? Should she go to Derek? What a wonderful thought that was. But why hadn't he come for her, like he'd done when he built that fire just below the beach house? Should she wait for him to come or should she go to him?

She poured a glass of wine, swirled it and drank. What

a fool she'd been for staying with Ben all these months. He hated her. He simply hated her and, like Derek had said, she'd played the lame role of a loyal wife because she thought it was the right thing to do. How foolish she was to believe he'd change. She'd wasted time on a man who would never be the man he'd once been. He was sick—filled with greed, jealousy, bitterness and hate. Couldn't she see that?

Kim heard the siren of a mosquito and she swatted at it. The humidity was still high and the temperature—even after 11 p.m.—was 81 degrees. Restless, Kim stubbed out her cigarette and got up, a glass of wine in hand. She went to the wooden railing and leaned in against it. As she stared out into the dark, hearing the restless sea, her body easily recalled the pressure of Derek's touch, and the smooth and erratic rhythms of their love making. The memories were exciting and hypnotic.

She pushed from the railing, set her wine glass down on the table and started down the stairs to the path. Crickets whistled around her as she made her way down to the beach. Would he be there? She had the strange and anxious feeling that he was there, waiting for her. Hunting her. Ready for her.

There was a rustling sound. She stopped short, nearly on the beach. A deer? A rabbit? She glanced about, took a breath and moved on.

When he stepped out in front of her, Kim screamed and jumped. He grabbed her, spun her around and slapped his hand over her mouth, his other arm tight around her chest. He squeezed a breast.

Kim squealed out fear.

He whispered seductively into her ear. "It's me. I've been hunting you. I've caught you."

He released his grip, and she whirled to face him. "You scared the living shit out of me."

Derek grinned. "Good."

"Good?" she shouted, eyes flaring.

He seized her shoulders and kissed her, hard and deep. His tongue stroked past her lips and played. Kim sank a little, surrendering, fear morphing into an urgent desire. She kissed him back, moving into him, her body pressing into his.

There was a waning moon, casting dim shadows onto the empty, turgid beach. Derek led her down to a secluded spot at the base of the dunes. There was a blanket there, waiting.

"You knew I'd come?" Kim asked, staring at the blanket.

"I was coming for you," he said.

"You were?" she asked, pleased.

"I started up the path as you started down."

Kim smiled darkly. "You bastard," she said, in a low breathy voice. "Then you must have been reading my secret thoughts."

Derek leaned and kissed her neck as she presented her face into the ocean wind, feeling it whip her hair, feeling Derek's tongue tickling her, teasing her. Derek grasped her hair and gently arched her head back into moonlight. He saw the pulse fluttering in her throat.

In a trance, he stroked her twisting thighs as her moving fingers found the ridges and hard muscles of his back.

They were exposed to the world, the beach empty, the night warm and private. Their sharp passion made them oblivious and wildly eager.

"You drive me crazy," he said.

"So show me," she whispered.

Kim lowered to the blanket, keeping him in her eyes.

She reached for him, drawing him down on top of her. His dark shadow of beard made him look dangerous—made the night fearful and thrilling. Feeling his magnificent body, she said something low in her throat, but the sea swallowed her words. The scorching pleasure made them foolish and high; made them shed their clothes and make love in the liquid moonlight.

Later, they were lying on their backs, naked on the rumpled blanket, staring up into the hazy swarm of stars. The sea seemed close, their emotions heightened, their bodies spent.

"I wanted to stay away," Derek said. "I should have stayed away. I couldn't."

"Yes, you should have stayed away, but don't."

He stared at her in the dim, silvery moonlight. "What the hell am I going to do with you?"

Kim was surprised by her swift answer. "Love me."

Derek looked away.

"Then don't love me," Kim said, sharply, hurt by his silence.

Derek's eyes locked on hers. "Leave him."

Kim looked away, and a fragile silence lengthened, leaving each in their private thoughts.

A minute later, Kim rolled and propped on one elbow, looking at him. "Were you involved in the accident with the two boys?"

"Changing the subject?"

"Yes. Were you?"

"Maybe. Maybe they wanted to kill me."

"What happens if one or both of them die? Will the police come for you? Do they know what happened?"

"I don't think so. I've played it all back in my mind. I don't think so."

They fell into silence again.

"Will you keep hunting me?" she asked.

"Of course."

Kim drew a line in the sand, staring down at it, deep in thought. "I'm going to leave him, Derek. I'm going to leave Ben."

Derek nodded. "I know. Tonight… Well, tonight we both know you have to."

In his room, Ben Maxwell sat at his desk in the dark, staring out into the low tide and the white waning half-moon. It was after 1 a.m. He'd heard Kim quietly enter the patio back door about half an hour before. He'd heard the pipes when she turned on the shower. He'd heard her close the bedroom door. That slight little metallic click. He still had good ears. Always had.

Ben held a lighted cigar. In the darkness, orange light blinked on and off as he puffed, pondering and considering power—the uses of power—how to wield power, and how he was going to wield his own power to get his own sweet revenge.

He puffed and stared into curling smoky worlds while carefully and pleasantly planning his strategies. He was stubborn and instinctive, knowing exactly what Kim was up to. Of course. He'd had her watched.

This time he wasn't going to destroy himself. No. He'd been a fool to try to kill himself over that lying, cheating bitch. She wasn't worth it, and now he saw that she wasn't worth it, and never had been. He thought she'd been different from his first two wives, but now he knew the folly of his belief. Kim was just like all the others: she was a slut.

But this time, he'd use his power to destroy *her* and her great hunk of a lover. He'd make them both pay for ridiculing him. For passing him over like he was an incapacitated cripple. For thinking he was an old fool.

He grinned with dark pleasure as he studied his cigar—a good tasting cigar—and he laughed a little, a low hollow laugh. He felt good and vital. He had a brand-new challenge. He felt new life pulsing through his broken body. Now it was just a matter of waiting for the right time to put it all together, and it wouldn't take long. Maybe just a week or so. And, of course, he had all the money he needed to put his plan into action, and to see it through to its delicious, destructive end.

Ben chuckled. "How pretty it is…"

CHAPTER 12

A week later, on Sunday afternoon, a violent storm came slamming in, bringing high winds, black rolling clouds, thunder that sounded like battle and pounding rains.

Just as the full loud force of it struck, Kim startled awake, sitting bolt upright.

Not asleep, Derek lifted, reached and stroked her hair. "It's okay, just a storm."

Kim relaxed with a sigh, took Derek's hand and kissed it.

"Bad dream?" Derek asked.

"Bad… Yes. How long have I been asleep?"

"Just a few minutes."

They laid back, listening to the drumming rain, their worried eyes shifting, minds racing. Kim had told Ben she was going shopping.

Suddenly nervous, Kim turned to the side table, reached for her phone and quickly shot off a text to Ben.

"*Stuck in the storm. Will be home soon.*"

Kim threw back the sheet, got up and reached for a cigarette. She slipped into one of Derek's long sleeve shirts and padded across the floor to the patio. The low ceiling of clouds obscured the sea, but she could hear the waves thundering in, like a warning. She flicked her lighter and lit the cigarette, watching the hard rain wash and punish the world.

When Derek came up behind her, she felt his stiffness against her. She shivered.

"Still want more?" she asked.

He gently kissed her neck. "Always. You're my drug."

Kim leaned back, enjoying his kisses. "I'm going to tell him tomorrow," she said. "Tomorrow at breakfast. I can't stand it any longer. I can't keep dodging him, avoiding his questions. I can't keep looking at myself in the mirror. I don't like what I see."

"What do you think he'll do?" Derek asked.

"I don't know. I really don't know. Maybe he'll be relieved. He'll probably just throw me out right then."

"Then you'll come here."

She turned and kissed him. "Yes… Where else?"

Derek touched her cheek, then turned and started for the kitchen. Kim was confused by his abrupt exit.

She took a long drag from the cigarette, blew a plume of smoke out the door, turned to find an ashtray and screwed it out.

In the kitchen, Derek was pouring two mugs of coffee.

"Something wrong?" she asked.

He turned and faced her boldly, handing her a mug of coffee. "Yes… I'm going to be blunt, Kim. I'm going to be honest. I'm not really the marrying type. I'm a loner, and I'm not looking for what most people think of as a long relationship. I've never had one and I don't want one. What we've got is good. That's all I want. That's all I can give."

Kim's chin tipped up in wounded defiance. "What am I supposed to say to that? That's just fine? I'm so happy about that? I'm about to tell my husband I want a divorce because I've fallen in love with another man and all you can say is, I'm a loner and I don't want a relationship? What the hell is that?"

"I'm just trying to be honest," Derek said, looking down and away.

"Well then don't be so damned honest," Kim said, angrily. "I don't give a damn about honesty. Lie to me. Tell me you love me, and that you'll do whatever it takes to have me, including marrying me. I'm about to break into pieces, Derek, so shut up about honesty. I love you, okay? How's that for honesty?"

Derek stared into her hurt, burning eyes. He audibly sighed. "You're driving me crazy, okay? Every day you drive me crazy, because I can't keep my mind and my hands off you. I've never had to deal with that, okay? I don't know what the hell to do with that."

He tugged on his ear, staring into space.

Kim searched his eyes for the truth. He looked away as if the distance held some answer. Her icy stare stayed glued to him.

"Now that's more like it. See, you're a good liar when you want to be."

He seized her arm and pulled her into him. She fought him, spilling her coffee, but he forced his lips on hers and kissed her deeply.

She broke away.

"I'm not lying, Kim."

Kim slammed the coffee mug down. "Bullshit! And you killed that kid," she said bluntly, wanting to attack him.

Derek's jaw tightened. "I told you. They tried to run me off the road. They tried to kill *me*. It was self-defense. Yes, he's dead. Anita called just before you got here.

How did you hear about it?"

Kim's stomach knotted. She turned her head left, lowering her eyes, folding her arms tightly against her chest. "The local news."

"The other kid talked, Kim. He said I ran them off the road for no reason. The father of the dead kid is on the town council of some town nearby. I assume he's going to file charges."

Kim avoided his eyes. "So the police will come for you?"

"Of course."

"… And?"

"And I'll deny it. There weren't any witnesses. There was a UPS truck, but the kids nearly smashed into him. They ran him off the road. There was a Mustang, but the driver didn't see me. He was focused on the accident. It's the kid's word against mine. They've got no case."

Kim sat down at the kitchen table, listening to the static of falling rain, hearing static in her head.

Every single thought that shot through her head was painful: Ben, Derek, her infidelity, the dead kid. She was living a nightmare.

Kim raised her glaring eyes on Derek. Their eyes connected.

Kim sensed there was some wound inside him that had never fully healed—maybe some childhood thing; maybe it was something that had happened to him when he was in combat. Maybe she was just kidding herself. Maybe he was just another Ben, struck down by something that broke him into bits, and those bits could never be put back together again to make a whole man, a complete man, a man who could love her the way she wanted and needed to be loved.

"I'll get my own place," Kim said, resigned.

"Why?" Derek asked.

"Why? Did you hear what you just said? You obviously want to be alone. Look, the lie was good but I'm a girl who can face facts. I'm all grown up. Okay, fine."

"Don't do that."

Kim shot up. "What?" she said, with an obstinate hand on her hip.

"I was open with you."

"Well whoop-de-doo for being open. How admirable."

"I want you here, Kim."

"No, you don't. You want me in your bed. Okay, fine. I'm fine with that. In fact, I love it. You're the best lover I've ever had. Okay, so no vows. No strings. Nothing except good sex."

He went to kiss her, but she turned her head aside. "Leave me alone."

"I can't."

They locked eyes, emotions high.

Kim felt some of the fight drain out of her. She was tired. So damned tired.

"Don't shut down, Derek. Don't shut us down before we begin."

He lifted a hand and touched her lips, his eyes tender and warm. "I want you to leave him, Kim. I want you here with me. Let's go back to bed."

"I can't. I've got to go. I'm already late. I don't want Ben to know about us until after I've told him."

Derek searched her eyes. "Do you really think he doesn't know? Look at you. You're gorgeous. Your eyes, your mouth, your skin. You glow, Kim, like a big hot summer sun, and you weren't glowing before we met. You have sex written all over you, like a lusty spring flower."

Kim narrowed her troubled eyes on him. "I'll tell him tomorrow. I'll call you afterwards and let you know what happened."

"I'll be waiting. I'll get to you as soon as I can."

After she left, Derek sat hunched in the kitchen chair, sipping coffee, eating a dry piece of wheat bread. He was not typically a worrier—he let things take their course because he knew they never went the way you thought they'd go anyway. Combat had taught him that. Do what you can, prepare, then keep it simple. Don't worry over what you have no control over. Respond and adjust as the situation unfolds. That's the way he'd been trained, and that's what had kept him alive in combat.

But Kim worried him. She was getting to him. Every time he made love to her something snapped loose inside, and he didn't know what the hell it was. His body simply ached for her, and whenever he thought of her, he ached. His only release from that ache was to make love to her. And then, soon after, that damned ache arose again, and he craved her again—had to have her again—just like the first time.

He thought his desire for her would burn itself out. It always had before. He'd had many lovers and always before, after a few days or a week, he was finished with them. The desire diminished, the fire just fizzled out.

But his desire for Kim hadn't diminished. It seemed to expand and grow. The more they loved the more he wanted her. And afterwards, some cold and icy thing inside his gut would grow warm and start to melt. It was a little-by-little thing, like the slow drip from a melting icicle. It was a slow thawing that brought warmth and peace.

Derek got up, showered and dressed. He sat down at his desk to look over some invoices, but he couldn't concentrate on them. He didn't believe Ben Maxwell would take Kim's plea for a divorce gently or lightly. Derek had seen Ben's face—a hard face—the face of a fighter. Derek was certain that Ben knew Kim had a lover. Did he know it was Derek?

CHAPTER 13

That same evening, as darkness settled in, Derek was working on the same invoices when he heard a car crackling across his gravel driveway and come to a stop. He stood and entered the front room, peeled back a curtain and peered out. It was a late model black BMW. Derek lifted a surprised eyebrow. The car easily went for $150,000—more if it was fully loaded.

Derek watched a tall, beefy driver emerge, dressed in a dark suit and tie. He stepped around to the trunk. He opened it and heaved out a wheelchair. He closed the trunk and brought the chair to the back passenger door. The door swung open, and the man helped lift Ben Maxwell up and out. He gently lowered him down into the chair.

Derek looked on in mild surprise as the man servant pushed Ben along the concrete walkway up to the front door. Ben had guts, Derek thought. Yep, he certainly had guts.

At the first ring, Derek opened the door.

Ben Maxwell was cheery, with all white teeth and cold, steady eyes. It was the expression of a happy predator. Derek had seen other bad guys like that—in the service—

in Afghanistan. They were fake carnivorous smiles—like a shark's.

Derek feigned surprise. "Yes?"

"I'm Ben Maxwell. I would like to talk to you if I may."

Derek didn't budge.

"May I… have a talk with you, Mr. Gray?"

Derek leveled his eyes on him and then on the man servant. The man servant's eyes were a flat dark lake, seeing nothing. Derek was sure the man couldn't hear either. He was getting paid not to.

"Okay…" Derek said, stepping away from the door. "Come in."

The man servant rolled Ben into the modest living room and parked him near the couch and coffee table. After completing his duties, the driver turned and left the house, closing the door quietly behind him.

The room was quiet and lit only by the pale light of a floor lamp that stood by Derek's desk. The two men appraised each other, like fighters about to meet in a ring.

"Can I get you anything?" Derek asked.

"Not a thing," Ben said, smiling that sharky smile again.

Derek eased down in an arm chair to Ben's right and waited with rising nerves and rapt curiosity.

Ben glanced around the spare room, feeling the occasional draft of wind from an oscillating fan. His eyes focused on the framed color photo of a soldier that sat on Derek's desk. The soldier was wearing his dress blues Marine uniform. Ben stared at the soldier, who looked back at him with a meaty, military face and the determined eyes of a warrior.

Ben pointed. "Is that your father?"

Derek nodded. "Was. Yes."

"Is that why you joined the military? Because of him?"

Derek waited. Ben had come prepared. He'd done his homework, and that was impressive. But then Ben had the money to pay for information, didn't he? Maybe he'd hired a private investigator.

"Maybe because of him," Derek offered.

Ben inhaled a breath, folding his hands in his lap. "I won't waste your time, Derek… can I call you Derek?"

"Why not?"

"All right then, I'll get to the point."

Derek stared, expecting Ben's threats to be harsh and final. He expected Ben to threaten him. He expected Ben to say he'd destroy him and his business unless he left town and vowed never to see Kim again.

"Your father was a staff sergeant in the Marines," Ben said, matter-of-factly. "He was also a drunk. He went on to be a Brooklyn cop. Right?"

Ben watched to see if Derek would react to the harsh description of his father. He didn't. Ben continued.

"He died from complications of pneumonia when you were fifteen years old."

"I was sixteen," Derek corrected, "And he died from cirrhosis of the liver. Pneumonia just helped take him out."

"Okay, sixteen and cirrhosis," Ben said, nodding. "Your mother worked two jobs, selling women's clothes and working as a bookkeeper in Manhattan, in the Garment District."

"I know all about my family, Mr. Maxwell."

Ben spread his hands. "Please, call me Ben… Well, anyway, then you have a sister who doesn't stay in touch. It seems she took after your father and has drug and alcohol problems."

Derek stood up. "Mr. Maxwell, sir, you're wasting my time. Let's level with each other: why are you here?"

Ben's face stayed cheerful, though there was a slow burn in his eyes. "Sit down, Mr. Gray," he said, waving him down with a hand. "Please, sit down."

Derek sat.

"I just wanted you to know that I have checked you out thoroughly for a good reason. I don't come to decisions impulsively or lightly. I'm careful."

Derek stared into Ben's cool, distant eyes, struggling to read him. He couldn't.

"Derek, this is a new town of sorts. It's coming into its own—it's growing—and the town board wants the right people to grow with it."

"And I'm not the right people to grow with it?" Derek asked.

Ben laughed. "Oh, on the contrary, you *are* the right people, Derek. You're exactly the right people. You're my kind of people. You know what you want and you don't mind going after it and knocking some heads together if they get in your way."

Ben's icy, challenging eyes took Derek in, and then he smiled darkly. "And you have knocked some heads together… haven't you, Derek? So the rumor goes."

Derek squared his shoulders. "If someone tries to kill me, I protect myself. If somebody tries to hurt my people, I'll hurt them," Derek said, evenly, without emotion.

"Of course," Ben said, slapping his knee with the flat of his hand. "That's just what I'm talking about. You are my kind of people."

Derek was confused. He needed time to think—to try to figure out what game Ben was playing.

"Sorry about the no air-conditioning," Derek said. "I usually get a good ocean breeze. Do you want a beer, some whiskey or something?"

"Beer's good," Ben said. "Perfect for this weather."

Derek got up, went into the kitchen and reached in the refrigerator for two beers. He closed the door and paused, unmoving, unblinking. What was Ben up to?

Back in the living room, Derek screwed off the two beer tops and handed a beer to Ben. Derek tipped the bottle back and swallowed half down. Ben held his by the neck, waiting, as Derek lowered himself into the chair.

"Derek, are you perceptive enough—smart enough—to grab a good opportunity when it comes your way?"

"That depends," Derek said.

"Of course it depends. So I'm going to tell you what the opportunity is. Now, I know you don't know much about me, but as you now know, I've done a lot of research on you."

Derek was measuring Ben's every word.

Ben took a swig of his beer, holding Derek's interested gaze.

"Derek, I want you to work for me."

Derek was still, his eyes narrowed, calculations going on behind them. He was astonished, but he didn't show it. He kept his voice low and calm.

"Work for you?"

"Yes. I have a job for you—a good job. A fantastic job."

Derek took another swallow of beer. He had not seen this coming and his mind was cluttered with confusion and speculation.

"What kind of job?"

"Managing my beach-front properties on Scorpio Beach. You'll be my beach guy. I have four properties already and I'm going to be building some condos down where that old broken-down motel used to be. I've already bought the beach front and the motel. We'll start knocking down and building in about a month."

Derek knew there was something wrong, but he couldn't find it or put his finger on it.

"I've never managed properties, Mr. Maxwell, except this one and I don't own it. I rent it."

"You're smart, Derek. And from your military record, which I checked out, by the way, I see you have a very high I.Q., and you're a fast learner. You were an Army Ranger sniper, a Team Leader and a Senior Weapons Sergeant on a Military Free Fall team. After all that, I don't think managing beach properties will be much of a challenge for you."

It was a very long moment before Derek spoke. "Thank you, sir… I don't think it's right for me. I have my business, and it's going well."

Ben's stern expression looked him over. "I'm sorry you feel that way. You disappoint me, Derek. I thought you were an ambitious man."

"In my own way, sir."

Ben set the beer bottle down on the 70s-style walnut finish coffee table. He nodded, his eyes shifting about the room.

"Derek… The Sheriff will be by to talk to you about that car crash out on Fairview Road. One kid is dead. The other has testified that it was you who ran them into that telephone pole."

Derek's back straightened.

Ben continued. "The more prominent people of this town will not tolerate this kind of activity in their town—a town that is rapidly growing—a town that is drawing big Wall Street and Hollywood money. Nobody wants this kind of publicity. It could kill business and growth before they get started."

Derek's mind was galloping—working to comprehend Ben's point of attack. Derek drained the last of his beer.

"I don't know anything about that accident," Derek said, glancing away toward the window.

"The kid says different."

"It's my word against his."

"Maybe, but there was a witness who said your truck went speeding past the scene."

"Hearsay. Not provable, unless the witness got my license plate number."

"You're missing my point here, Derek. Think. You're a smart guy. What if the paint on that old Chevy that you allegedly swiped matches the paint on your truck? What if the witness did get your license plate? And let's just say, for argument's sake, that someone on the scene accurately describes you. Well, you know how surprises can pop up when you least expect them."

Derek was getting the picture. Ben had the influence and the power to produce evidence, or to be more accurate, to tamper with and create evidence. Ben was blackmailing him.

"Yes, Derek. You'll have to hire an attorney and it will cost you dearly. You'll most likely go broke defending yourself. Your business will fail because, I can tell you, your phone will start ringing very shortly after I leave. The clients you currently have will call to cancel. They do not want to be involved in your mess. They are here for summer fun in the sun, not some turf war—pardon my pun—and not to be involved in a manslaughter lawsuit. Do you understand me, Derek?"

Derek did… at least part of it. He still couldn't connect all the dots. Surely, Ben had more cards to play.

"Are you blackmailing me, Mr. Maxwell?"

"Oh, no, no, no, Derek. I'm protecting you."

Derek got up again and went to the front door. He opened the door and gazed out into the night. Ben's driver swung open his door and got out, thinking he was being summoned. Derek waved him back as he listened to the ringing sounds of the insects.

Derek pulled the door shut and turned slowly to face Ben.

Ben gripped the neck of the beer tightly. "I can offer you protection, Derek. And I can offer you a good job."

"Why?" Derek asked.

Ben smiled, but it didn't reach his eyes. "Because I need a good, steady manager."

"I don't get it. You can find good managers anywhere. You're worth millions. You can get the best, the most experienced."

"Perhaps, but I can tell you from vast experience that most of that kind are not hungry. Or they're simply 'Yes' men or women. Others don't have your sense of aggression and your experience with, let's say it because it's accurate, combat."

"Are you sure you know me so well, sir?"

"Are you hungry?" Ben asked, indicating with his hands. "Don't you want more than this little beach rental? Otherwise, why are you fighting to establish a business in a tough, growing town? Answer me that."

Derek didn't speak.

"Derek, I started out with $20,000. I never went to college. I fought my way up. Clawed my way up. Kicked ass on the way up. Broke a few heads on the way up and I never, not once, looked back with any regret."

"How much are you worth?" Derek asked boldly. "Ten million?"

Ben let out a laugh. "Oh, my, yes. Millionaires are a thing of the past, Derek. Think big. Think billions."

For the first time, Ben saw a flicker of surprise and hunger in Derek's eyes. He wanted to grin with triumph, but he didn't.

"I started out like you, Derek, with a small business. I bought some real estate and then I made it pay. Now I own two tech companies, an upscale bar or two, and many condos, much commercial real estate, office buildings, luxury homes and beach front properties."

Derek looked down at his hands. He felt a little shaky.

Ben continued. "I live in a little beach house up on a cliff about a mile from here. I bought it two years ago. Could I buy better? Yes, but it has sentimental value. My wife, Kim, loves it. I bought it for her."

Derek's eyes came to Ben's. Each man studied the other for reaction. Neither reacted. It was a stalemate.

Ben glanced down at his watch.

"It's getting late. Please ask Victor to come in."

Derek hesitated. "How much?"

Ben fought another smile of satisfaction. It worked every time. Money always won the day. Never failed.

"How much for what, Derek?"

"For the job?"

Ben glanced about as if it hadn't occurred to him. "Oh, let's say, $300,000 to start."

"That's a lot of money," Derek said.

"You'll earn it, Derek. And I tell you what. I'll give you a starting bonus of, let's say… Oh… Let's say, $50,000."

Derek paced to the edge of the living room and back to the front door. "And the Sheriff won't come for a visit?"

"He might, but it won't mean anything. After all, who's going to believe a drunken kid's word against my property manager and a veteran of the Afghan war with a

Purple Heart?"

Ben shook his head. "Nobody, Derek. And if they do, I have some of the most expensive and effective lawyers money can buy."

"When do you want my answer?" Derek asked.

"Right now. It's now or never."

Derek inhaled through his nose. "I have people working for me. They have families."

Ben looked at him with unsympathetic eyes. "Let the Latino lass have it. She can run it. I hear she's a good little business woman herself."

Derek was very impressed with Ben's knowledge. He'd surely hired a private detective.

"She'll help calm things down, Derek. Nobody's going to get upset about a chubby Latino gal riding around on a power mower."

Derek lowered his eyes, despising Ben Maxwell even more—if that was possible.

Ben spread his hands. "Well, Derek, what's it going to be?"

CHAPTER 14

On Monday, the morning dazzled with bright sunlight and cooler temperatures. Although the public schools weren't out for another week, the beaches were swarming with crowds by 9 a.m., and the main roads were clogged with traffic, crawling toward Scorpio Beach.

Kim sat nervously at the dining room table, sipping coffee. The room faced east and was filled with scintillating light. It had an array of windows, tall floor plants, hanging ferns and a splendid view of beach and sea.

Ben had texted Kim at 7 a.m., saying he wanted to have breakfast with her. He had something very important he wanted to discuss. Kim had stared at the text for minutes, struggling to read between the lines, straining to decode its true meaning.

What the hell did he want to discuss? They never had breakfast together, at least not since the accident. They seldom had dinner together. So what had happened?

And there was the woman in the kitchen, cooking breakfast. Kim smelled the bacon as soon as she stepped out of the shower. Her name was Rosa Sanchez, a short, thin, middle-aged Latino woman, with warm dark eyes, a shy expression and silky long black hair tied from behind by a yellow ribbon.

"Mr. Maxwell hired me yesterday," she said smiling, as she smoothed her snow-white apron. "I work very hard. I'm on time, always. Nice to meet you, Ms. Kim."

Kim blinked away astonishment as she took the coffee pot and wandered into the dining room. She wore a sleeveless, V-neck, yellow sun dress that exposed her cleavage, and a pearl necklace with matching pearl drop earrings that Ben had given her on their first anniversary. Her hair was loose and touching her shoulders, her make-up light, her lipstick a deep red, Ben's favorite.

Kim was anxious. Did Ben know about her affair with Derek? Was he going to call her on it? She sipped the coffee, absently, trying to think it through, her mind tangled with thoughts. Did it really matter? Ironically, this was the morning she was going to ask him for a divorce anyway, so even if Ben did know about Derek, what did it matter? Well, it didn't matter—or did it?

Their marriage was dead. It had died long ago, when Ben tried to kill himself because of his stupid jealousy, a jealousy totally unfounded at the time. She'd been faithful to him. She'd always been faithful to him… until she met Derek.

But why did Ben want to meet with her now? It was weird. She'd been about to text him—she was only minutes away from it—when his text had arrived. He'd beat her to it.

Kim had just finished her second cup of coffee when she heard the hum of Ben's wheelchair as he left his office and rode into the dining room. He was beaming, his gray-green eyes dancing, his whole demeanor polished with happiness. The blue blazer, white shirt and gray slacks suggested the old Ben. The Ben Kim had known when they'd first met: the passionate, optimistic and vital man she'd fallen in love with.

"Good morning, Kim!" he said, with booming enthusiasm.

Kim was gently startled. "Good morning."

Ben rolled up to the opposite side of the table, snatched his folded napkin, snapped it out and spread it on his lap. "I am ravenous."

Kim rose, reached for the coffee pot and poured him a cup. "I went to the kitchen to start breakfast, and I saw…"

He cut her off. "Forget about all that. You're not cooking anymore. I hired Rosa Sanchez yesterday. She's in the kitchen right now making breakfast and she'll bring it out when she's finished. I ordered scrambled eggs, lox, bagels, plenty of crisp bacon and a bottle of Roederer Cristal, 2004. It's dry, full-bodied and toasty, with cherry overtones. You remember? We had a bottle to celebrate our first wedding anniversary."

"Yes, I remember," Kim said, feeling her nervousness rise along with her blood pressure.

Just then, Rosa entered, carrying a silver wine bucket that held the bottle of champagne and two crystal champagne flutes. As she'd been instructed, she set the bucket down before Ben. She removed the two flutes and set them on the table near Ben.

"Ah yes, Rosa, thank you. Now let's have that breakfast as soon as it's ready."

"Yes, Mr. Maxwell," she said, giving a little bob of a bow before withdrawing.

Ben extracted the champagne from the bucket and peeled back the foil.

"I feel reborn today, Kim. Like a brand-new man."

Kim glanced about, unsure. She swallowed away apprehension. "Has something happened?"

Ben twisted the cork. It popped, and he swiftly filled the glasses. "Yes, Kim. Yes. Something has happened. That's why we're celebrating."

Kim watched the champagne foam and bubble. "Are you going to tell me?"

"Of course. Of course I'm going to tell you. But let's just relax, drink our champagne and enjoy our breakfast."

Kim stood, accepting the glass from Ben. They touched glasses.

"To rebirths and second chances," Ben said, leveling his eyes on Kim, catching her worried gaze.

They tasted the champagne and Kim sat.

"Ah… this is heaven," Ben said, staring at his glass. "It's like drinking bubbling gemstones, don't you think?"

"Yes… it's very good."

And then Ben talked about his new beach properties, and how he'd received six million dollars for one he'd sold just a mile up the road.

"He's a Hollywood producer. Lives in Malibu most of the time. But he loves it here in the summer and fall, or so he said."

Ben rambled on about his new condos and the new beach front property.

Kim couldn't take the suspense any longer. She was certain he was toying with her, and she'd had enough.

"So tell me why we're celebrating, and why you feel… reborn?"

"I've hired a new man. He's going to manage all my properties here in Scorpio Beach. It will take a lot of the pressure off me."

Kim stared, warily. She knew Ben was up to something, but she had no idea what it was. All she could do was wait.

Minutes later, Rosa entered, pushing a silver cart that

held silver plate covers. She served the breakfast with careful, steady hands, and poured more coffee. Ben closed his eyes and inhaled the aroma of bacon, lox and eggs.

"Wonderful, Rosa. Simply wonderful. Thank you for your excellent service."

Rosa gave a pleasant smile and a little demure bow before leaving the room.

Ben dove in, delighting in every bite, eating faster and with more vigor than Kim had seen him eat in months.

Kim ate slowly, uneasily, waiting for Ben to drop the bomb she knew was coming.

"Is that all? I mean, it's good news that you won't be working so hard, but I'm sure you're holding something back. Tell me. I'm on pins and needles."

Ben swallowed a bite and then laid both hands on the table, composed and serious.

"Kim… I've been a fool. A complete ass. I've been sitting in that damned office for months brooding over spilt milk—bitter and angry about things I cannot change and, as a result, I nearly destroyed the one thing that I prize over everything else: you and our marriage. Well, yesterday it hit me like a flash of lightning. I woke up, Kim. I had a kind of religious experience, and I felt so bad and so good at the same time. Can you imagine?"

Ben stared directly into Kim's eyes. "I want you to forgive me, Kim, if you can. Forgive me for the ass I've been these last months. Can you forgive me? Can we begin again? Can we fall in love all over again and be the ecstatically happy couple we once were? Can we, Kim?"

Kim stopped eating. She went rigid, her eyes round with surprise. She felt an astonished agony and couldn't speak.

Ben leaned back, folding his hands. "I've been hard

on you, and you didn't deserve it. You stayed here with me, faithfully, when most women would have left long ago. Most women with your looks and smarts would have just walked away. But not you. You stayed. Good and faithful Kim."

Unpredictable silence hung in the air. Kim heard singing birds. She heard the rushing sea and watched the wind billow the yellow curtains.

Ben continued. "Okay, so now I want to give you something back for all your faithfulness and sacrifice. I'm going to buy you that yoga studio—the one you talked about—and you can do whatever you want with it. You just tell me what you want and you'll have it. In addition to that, I'm going to open a joint account and fund it with two million dollars. It will be yours—all yours—and you can spend it anyway you want. It's yours, free and clear. Now, what do you say? Can we fall in love again? Can we, Kim?"

Kim left his words hanging in the air. She looked down at her shaking hands and then closed her eyes. It was as if she'd just experienced a great inner explosion. She wanted to cry and laugh at the same time. This was a comic nightmare.

"I know this is all a big surprise, Kim," Ben said, tenderly. "You remember Dr. Eaton said it would take some time. Well, he was right. It took a little over eight months. But it's happened. I feel like the old Ben again—even better—even stronger—even more dedicated to our marriage."

Tears trickled down her cheeks. She didn't want the tears, and she wasn't sure why they'd come, but she couldn't stop them. They just pumped out of her.

"It's okay, Kim," Ben said, softly. "You just let it all come out. Let the tears flow and let the whole damn thing come out. Let's let the whole nightmare pass and move on with our lives."

Kim opened her eyes and stared, with blurry vision. "You don't know how long I've waited for you to come back to me."

And then there was a rush of a fragrant wind, and the whispering sound of the sea.

Later that afternoon, Kim shot Derek a text.

"We're finished. I can't see you again. I'm breaking it off for good. Please don't even respond to this. Let's just move on."

But Derek did respond, within minutes.

"We have to talk—in person. ASAP."

Kim was on the beach, strolling, confused, scared, trying to recover from her shock at Ben's declaration.

"No, Derek. We can't meet. Never again. It's over."

"Kim… A private investigator has been watching us."

Kim was frozen to the spot, her mind spinning.

"It doesn't matter anymore."

"Yes, it does. More than ever. We HAVE to talk. I will come for you. I will find you."

Kim shut off her phone, dropped it into a pocket and wandered under a blazing sun, confused, fighting panic. She roamed until she felt her bare shoulders sting and sweat trickling into her eyes.

She paused at the crest of the dunes, staring, straining to put it all together.

Was it true? Was Derek telling the truth? Had Ben hired a private investigator to follow her? To watch her?

A slow, crawling terror arose, lodging in her throat. Then he knew about the affair. He must know. Had it been responsible for Ben coming back to her? Did he truly want to start again? Was he truly in love with her again?

CHAPTER 15

Two days later, Ben gave Derek a tour of his local properties, finally stopping at the dingy, two-story motel that sat on the far end of Scorpio Beach. Derek strolled along next to Ben's electric wheelchair as they traveled across the abandoned parking lot. There were dunes on one side of the motel and, on the other, a jetty stretched out like a rocky royal carpet, surrounded by a bright expanse of sand and sea.

"I bought the whole thing for eighteen million," Ben said. "Beach front and motel property. No investors. I'll eventually make three times that—maybe more."

"What are you going to do with it?" Derek asked, dressed in jeans, a blue T-shirt and sunglasses.

"It's going to be condos and a private membership beach club. I'll get the twenty-and thirty-somethings in stilettos and Polos, and the late-model Porsches and BMWs crowds. The town's ready for it—crying out for it."

"Some don't like change," Derek said. "They like things to stay the way they are."

"They're the old hippies. The suckers. The old surf crowd who's been coming here for twenty or thirty years.

They don't have any money and they don't spend money."

Derek kicked at the clumps of grass that had poked through the pavement. He scanned the area, seeing rust stains streak down the motel and the crumbling concrete swimming pool. He also noticed a couple of bare-chested, sinister-looking men in bright swimming suits, glaring back at them from the edge of the tide. They were tattooed, had sagging bellies and deep tans. One wore an old sweat-soaked red bandana and was clutching the neck of a bottle of beer. He scowled back at Derek and Ben and spat a stream of spit into the sand.

The other man looked like an antagonist from a bad movie. He was bald, had a bandito mustache and small, impudent eyes. If looks could kill, Derek and Ben would be face down in the sand, dead.

"Aren't they trespassing?" Derek asked.

Ben dismissed them with a wave of his hand. "Yes, but we'll leave them alone for now. Once we start bulldozing, we'll sic the deputies on them. That will be your department."

"They don't seem to like us being here," Derek said. "Do you know them?"

"I've seen them around. To hell with them. They're part of the losers that sank this place."

Derek took in the spread of beach and land, seeing the possibilities. "It's a beautiful spot," Derek said.

Ben shaded his eyes with the flat of his hand. "The old owners let the place go to shit. They were losing money. Imagine losing money with a place like this. They charged $220 a night. They had bonfires going and wild parties, and losers like those two clowns over there, who just wrecked the place."

Ben looked up at Derek. "I want you on this project

day and night, Derek. You'll be in charge: the contractors, architects, the town board and the protestors. There'll be lots of them. Think you can do it?"

Derek nodded firmly. "I can do it."

Sitting next to each other in the backseat of Ben's BMW, traveling back toward town, Ben turned to Derek.

"I want you to come to my place for a late lunch. You'll meet Kim, my wife."

Derek's jaw flexed.

"Any problem with that?" Ben asked, seeing the tension rise to Derek's face.

Derek hesitated. "No, no problem."

"I need to catch you up on some other issues and introduce you to some of my other employees. Speaking of property, have you been looking around for a new place?"

"Not yet."

"Get out of that old run-down cottage, Derek. You can afford it now. Find a good beach house up on the cliffs. I've got just the one for you. I'll even give you a break on the rent. I can't have my property manager living in a beat-up old cottage on the other side of the tracks."

Derek was lost in thought. "Yeah… Yeah, sounds good."

Minutes later, they'd arrived at the house and Victor helped push Ben up the ramp to the front door. Derek followed, and as they entered the living room, Derek glanced about uneasily.

"Let's go on into the dining room," Ben said. "Rosa will serve us lunch there."

Ben called for Kim, and Derek looked away, his hands restless in his pockets.

In the dining room, Ben drew up to the table and Derek sat to his left with his back to the windows. Derek had no idea whether Kim knew Ben had hired him or if she knew he was coming for lunch. She had not responded to any of his texts. He'd wanted them to meet face-to-face to talk things out—to tell her what had happened to him and to learn what had happened to her, because something dramatic had happened to her or she wouldn't have ended the relationship so abruptly. They needed to have a discussion, but Kim had refused.

Now, as Derek felt tension constrict his muscles, waiting for her entrance, he wished he had texted her and told her everything he knew. But then again, what if Ben got ahold of her phone and read all her texts and emails? Had he already?

If Kim didn't know about Derek becoming Ben's property manager, then Derek was afraid of Kim's reaction. Would she give them both away? Is that what Ben was up to? Derek was positive that Ben knew more than he was letting on. He was orchestrating something but, for now, Derek had to wait and bide his time. He had to wait for the accident and the death of that drunken kid to blow over.

Kim strolled down a short entrance way, down a short, carpeted staircase and into the dining room, where her eyes were fixed on Ben. Derek held his breath.

Kim looked stunning in a peach-colored sundress with spaghetti straps. It hugged and accented her long legs and perfect figure. She wore light beige, one and a half-inch sandals that gave her a sexy grace and stature. Her blonde hair, shimmering in the sunlight, was combed smooth and straight, falling to accent her tanned face, her bright red lips and her crystal blue eyes.

Derek swallowed away a huge lump as he stood to meet her.

"Kim, finally you're here," Ben said. "This is our

guest, Derek Gray. He's also my new property manager."

Kim turned and smiled a greeting. She came over, reached and shook his hand. She was cool, her face closed and mechanically friendly, her eyes steady, betraying nothing. But inside, her stomach did a flip- flop, and she was nauseous with fear.

"It's nice to meet you, Mr. Gray. Ben told me he'd hired a new manager."

"Call him Derek, Kim," Ben said.

"Yes, call me Derek."

Kim flashed a frosty smile. "Okay then, Derek it is."

Kim settled into her chair opposite Ben and reached for her napkin.

Ben sat back, watching the lovers, examining their eyes, mouths and expressions. He was impressed, they didn't reveal anything. But, of course, Kim had been an actress and a dancer on Broadway. She was skilled at pretend and make believe. Was Derek? He'd faced death many times, no doubt, so he didn't scare easily, and Ben had to admit that Derek had a good poker face. He was stoical and cool.

Still, Ben was enjoying his little game. He'd have them squirming in no time. In the coming weeks, he'd enjoy watching them struggle to hide the heat, the lust they felt for each other. He'd seen photos, thanks to his private investigator. He'd seen them kissing and touching. He hadn't actually caught them together having sex, but it was only a matter of time.

One thing he had to admit. They were pretty lovers—handsome lovers. Hell, he got turned on—if only in his head—at those white-heat-hot photos. Yes, they were pretty lovers, and Ben was going to make sure they would pay for every moment they spent together.

Rosa deposited the lunch of cold salmon, salad and

white wine. They ate for a time in silence.

"So what have you been up to today, Kim?" Ben asked.

Kim ate slowly, her eyes avoiding Derek's. "I went to the yoga studio, and I met with your accountant."

"Good… Very good."

Ben turned to Derek. "Kim's going to take over the yoga studio in town and improve it. I'm going to buy out the woman who owns it. She's an airhead who hugs trees and kisses dolphins. Anyway, we're going to make good money with it. Now, there's nothing wrong with that, is there, Derek?"

"No, sir," he said, glancing over at Kim.

Kim avoided his eyes.

She was giving off perfume and Derek picked it up. It was the same she'd worn once before. Her scent had lingered on his pillow for days. Derek felt his pulse rise. He remembered that night. How juicy she'd been. How wild and lovely she was.

"So, Derek," Ben said, shaking Derek from his vision. "I want you to help Kim with this yoga studio thing, you know, look into it and make sure everything's going smoothly."

"Okay, whatever you say."

"Don't go crazy, just check in on Kim now and then. I'm always so damned busy with everything."

Ben looked up at Kim. "Are you okay with that, sweetheart?"

Kim didn't look up. "Sure, why not?"

Ben lowered his half-hooded eyes in dark amusement. This was so much fun, he thought. This was the most fun he'd had in years.

He saw Kim squirm in her seat.

He thought, "*Squirm, you unfaithful bitch. Squirm away.*"

CHAPTER 16

In the month that followed, Kim managed to avoid Derek, and he seemed to avoid her. But she sensed he was watching her and knew when she was at the beach or in town. It was an intuitive feeling, something visceral.

He had dropped by the yoga studio twice, as Ben had instructed him to do, but she hadn't been there either time. How did he know? She spent a lot of time there, as the wood floors were replaced, the massage rooms constructed, an office expanded, and a new wing added for the dance studio.

Most early mornings, Kim stood at the dining-room window, hoping to catch sight of Derek tossing a ball or a stick for Colin to fetch. When she did see Derek's lithe, graceful body slowly drift along the tide, she was aroused by a strange little tickle that gathered in her chest, and she would long for him. She'd never felt that warm excitement with any other man.

Derek had awakened her to a love and passion that heightened everything and touched every part of her life. The tempting allure of him upset and thrilled her, and as the days rushed by, she wrestled with her emotions to push him away and out of her life.

She worked to redirect all her love away from Derek and back to Ben, her husband. She struggled to forgive herself for her infidelity and to be, once again, a faithful and supportive wife.

After Ben's new declaration of love and commitment, Kim recommitted herself to make the marriage work, helped by reviving the memories they'd made before Ben's accident. She and Ben had shared so many good times together. Yes, she believed they could pick up where they'd left off and begin again. At least most of her believed that.

She was pleased that Ben had returned to his former self—the pleasant, generous Ben, the spirited, humorous man, who complimented a new hairstyle or a new outfit, who commented on her skill at over-seeing the yoga studio renovations.

But as the month ended, Kim began to feel a subtle change in Ben—or maybe she'd grown more aware. Certain cracks in his enthusiasm began to appear. There was an emptiness to his gushing compliments. They smacked of artifice. The laughs often seemed forced. The conversations overly solicitous.

His touch was not as gentle, his eyes not as soft and warm as they'd once been. When he took her arm or caressed her leg, she nearly recoiled. It was as if a strange, passive/aggressive man was handling her.

And she'd never been comfortable with the fact that Ben hired Derek. The more she thought about it, the more she felt it had been contrived. If she'd learned anything during their marriage, it was that Ben was an expert at contrivances.

Derek had not moved to a new beach house as Ben had requested. He said he was happy in his little private cottage and, when he found the right place, he would buy it.

Ben mumbled his disapproval, but he didn't force anything. He didn't demand that Derek move.

On a late Sunday night in July, Kim left the house for the beach. There was the sliver of a quarter moon riding through purple clouds. She wandered and kicked at the sand, thinking about the yoga studio which would open for yoga, dance and massage the next day, on Monday. She was pleased and satisfied. It would be *her* business, and she'd always wanted to own her own business. Had she managed to push aside her qualms over Ben's new commitment to the relationship? Her qualms about his hiring Derek? Yes, she had, almost.

Kim clasped her hands behind her back and rambled, her mind recalling her father, a tall, hulking man, who had little humor or imagination. He was a coarse man—handsome once, Kim's mother had said, but he was loud and brooding, and he ran around with whores and low-lifes and gambled away most of his paycheck.

Kim's eyes darkened at the thought of him. What would he say to her now—now that she had two million dollars in the bank and her own business to run? As Ben had promised, he had transferred two million dollars into a joint account.

She, Kimberly Ryan, from Binghamton, New York, was a millionaire, and not just once, but twice. The little girl who'd danced for her father on the faded and curled linoleum floors, longing for her father's approval and attention, was a millionaire. What did he used to say to her?

"You're too skinny and clumsy to be a real dancer, Kim. You'll never make it."

But Kim did make it. She'd danced in eighteen Broadways shows since she was nineteen years old; and eight more on national tours. She'd had speaking lines in some and she'd danced at both Lincoln Center in New York and the Kennedy Center in Washington, D.C. She'd even filled in for a time as a Rockette at Rockefeller Center.

How Kim wished her father could see her now. She had more money than he, or any of her friends or family would ever have. She'd made it—escaped from that lousy neighborhood and shabby house, where her mother struggled to pay the rent and keep food on the table for her and her brother. Her mother had been the one who sacrificed so she could pay for Kim's dance lessons when she was just a girl, until Kim got a job waitressing, so she could pay for them herself.

Kim would make sure her mother had plenty of money now, and she'd live in a big clean house with a gigantic TV. She'd have the best smart phone and a new car.

She thought of her father, and she spat at him into the sand. She spat at his irresponsible, loveless life. She spat at him because he'd abandoned them all for a cheap woman he'd met at some bar. She spat at him because she hated him.

Kim paused, turned and gazed into the distance toward Derek's cottage. Was he there? Was he out working? Was he watching her?

She stood there, shivering. Derek's body—his heat, force, size and touch—had changed her. She couldn't deny that, and her body had gone into a kind of withdrawal since she'd broken off their relationship.

But why shouldn't she have ended it even if Ben hadn't recommitted himself to the marriage? Derek wasn't interested in any kind of long-term relationship. There was no future there. Their relationship had been a sexual, destructive and selfish one. She'd been okay with that in the beginning. She was a big girl, and she knew what she was getting into. And it was fun and sexually satisfying. There was no doubt about that.

Kim faced the sea, lifting her face into the rushing wind. She shut her eyes, and she saw Derek's face and powerful body.

She considered their relationship. Somewhere along the way, just as everything had changed and they broke it off, something had shifted.

She sensed there was more to him than just a big, sexy animal who gave her pleasures she'd only imagined. She'd begun to feel there was something warm and trapped inside, fighting to get out. It was the way he touched her, kissed her and moved her. The way he looked at her while he was making love.

There was his gentle touch after sex, when his voice dropped and his energy softened. He didn't abruptly pull away or leave the bed as he had the first couple of times. Not after their third time together. He stayed close, stroking her, whispering sexy words, playing with her hair and kissing her eyes. She sensed a protective authority, and that had really turned her on.

And when he loved her a second time, as he always did, she often felt the hard aggression gradually grow tender. She sensed a wounded man who was struggling to heal hurts and pains, but he didn't know how. She could see and touch the outer wound. But what about the inner wound? Would it ever heal? Could she help him heal that inner wound?

Kim stood there in a trembling contradiction. She wanted her marriage to last. She wanted the yoga studio. She wanted the two million dollars. God help her, and she wanted Derek. She wanted him so badly that she felt physical pain in her stomach and in her loins.

Kim turned back toward her house and saw one light on. It shone like a tiny fire. It was Ben's office window. Was she still being followed by a private investigator?

She'd made a vow never to see or be with Derek again. It was over, and it had to be over. It would require her entire discipline and focus. Eventually, over time, her persistent desire for Derek would fade. Everything faded over time. Everything.

Kim started back to the path that led to the house.

Suddenly, she was grabbed from behind, a strong arm wrapping her waist, jerking her back, a tight hand over her mouth.

Her first thought was that it was Derek, scaring her as he had before. But the sour body odor, the fat belly and stale beer breath said otherwise.

"Hey, pretty woman. Don't scream or I'll slit your throat."

Kim tensed up with fright, every muscle on alert.

"Now you listen to me, pretty woman. We're going up the beach a-ways to my car. You scream or call out, you're dead, okay? Nod if you understand me."

Kim swallowed hard. She nodded, her eyes bulging.

"Okay, now, let's go."

CHAPTER 17

Under pale moonlight and lingering shadows, Kim and her attacker slowly advanced across the sand, the man just behind, gripping her left arm so tightly he'd cut off the blood, and her entire arm was throbbing. Twice he'd nudged the tip of a knife into her back, to let her know it was there and to boost his threat.

Kim calculated place and distance. She was not going to give up without a fight, no matter what happened to her, and she knew she had to act before they reached his car. Once in the car, he'd probably rape her and then what? Kill her? She wasn't taking any chances.

Though terrified, she fought to clear her mind, so she could plan an attack strategy. Kim had dated a black hip-hop dancer four years back, and he'd taught her Krumping. It's a popular street dance, and they'd danced it in clubs and on the street in Harlem. It's a free style dance, expressive, exaggerated and highly energetic. African-American kids saw Krumping as a way to escape gang life and to release rage, aggression and frustration positively, in a non-violent way. But it was a very aggressive dance, and she'd loved it.

Kim's attacker shoved her toward a narrow path that

she knew led to a secluded side road that was abandoned at night. Surely his car was up there. She didn't have much time. The knife blade dug into her back. Fear kicked in her chest, her heart loud in her ears.

She shut her eyes to think. There are four primary moves in Krump: jabs, arm swings, chest pops, and stomps. They entered the path, Kim's eyes shifting from side to side. They strolled past dune grass along the path, moving into darkness. Was Derek around? Had he forgotten her?

The man's foot slipped sideways on uneven sand. He stumbled. This was Kim's chance. In her head, she heard drums—hard-core beats exploding in her brain. She ducked right, twisted, and in a wild motion, she used the leverage of her attacker's grip to swing right-to-left, wrenching herself free.

In her head, Kim heard the hard beat of a bass guitar, reverberating through the soles of her feet, into her stomach. She saw the man now—his heavy silhouetted body. She felt raw, savage anger.

Kim attacked, in a series of jabs and arm swings. She caught him in the head and chest. He back-stepped, grunting out surprise. Stunned, he dropped the knife, frozen. Before he found his balance, Kim braced, inhaled and gave him a jumping drop kick to the center of his face. He shot backwards, tumbling into the dune grass, a wounded animal rolling about, groaning.

She boiled over to him, pressing her attack, her body taut and on fire.

"Get up, you piece of shit!" she yelled. "Get up!"

He backed away, covering his bloody face with a shaky hand, his nose broken. "No!" he shouted. "No more!"

"Get up!" Kim repeated, breath coming fast.

He struggled to retreat, his ass dragging across the

sand, hands and feet working backwards, a crab trying to flee the beach.

From Kim's immediate left, she saw a figure emerge from the dark and dart down toward her. She spun, ready for the attack. Derek stopped five feet in front of her, his hands raised in surrender.

"Take it easy, Kim. Easy now. It's just me."

Kim squinted at him as he stood in the dim moonlight. "*Now* you come," she said, angry.

Derek turned to see her attacker push to his feet. Derek flicked on his flashlight and swung the shaft of light into the man's terrified face. His eyes were wide circles of shock, his nose gushing blood. He back-stepped, wiping his nose, hand up, blocking the sharp, stabbing light.

"Hey, asshole," Derek said. "I saw you at the old motel the other day, didn't I?"

The wounded attacker glanced back over his shoulder, ready to bolt.

"Don't even think about running. I'll catch your ass and beat you into the ground."

"Let me go," the attacker pleaded. "I didn't mean nothing, man. Let me go. I didn't mean nothing."

Derek shot a glance at Kim. "Do you have your phone?"

"Yes…"

"Call 911."

"No, man!" the attacker said. "I tell you, I didn't mean nothing. I wasn't going to do anything."

"Of course you weren't," Derek said, "because she kicked your ugly fat ass all over the beach. What a piss poor excuse for a man."

Derek noticed Kim hadn't moved. "Is there a problem with the phone?"

Kim waited. "Let him go."

"What?" Derek asked.

"Let him go. He won't bother me again, will you, asshole?" she shouted at him.

"No way. No way. I won't bother nobody. Please don't call the police. Let me go."

Derek stared at her, baffled. Then he swung his attention back to the attacker, the beam of the flashlight still full in his terrified face.

"If I ever see you around here again, I'll kill you. Get the hell out of here," Derek shouted.

The man turned, ran, stumbled, fell, got up and scampered away into the darkness.

Derek slowly turned to Kim, shining the beam of light on her. He studied her, the fire in her eyes, the rise and fall of her breasts. Her scattered hair. Derek thought, "Those eyes are spectacular. She's spectacular."

Kim turned from the light, deflecting it with her hand. "Get that damned light out of my face."

Derek shut it off, smiling.

"You think all this is funny?" she asked, with heat.

Derek was silent.

"Do you? Where the hell were you? You show up *after* it's over?"

"Take it easy. You wouldn't have reached that car. I was about to move in. But, hey, I didn't have to. You took care of it. I was impressed. That was one helluva drop kick. That's Special Forces stuff."

"Do you know who that asshole is?" Kim asked.

Derek made a small frown of concentration. "Yeah, I know him. I've seen him hanging out by the old motel a couple of times, before we knocked it down. He has a brother. They're both worthless. Why didn't you call the police?"

Kim drew a breath. "Too many questions. There would be way too many questions, and forms and interviews and some goddamned reporter or two. I don't want to be in the papers and on the internet for the rest of my life. At least, not that way. Anyway, he'd tell the cops that you just happened to appear out of nowhere. You just happened to be around at the right time. Who knows what else he might say… anything to clear himself."

They stood there, evaluating each other.

"You have experience with this kind of thing?" Derek asked.

"I dated a cop a few times. Women almost never win, despite these enlightened times. Something always goes wrong. People talk. Ben would get suspicious, especially about you. So would others. I don't want it. Any of it."

"Kim, Ben's already suspicious. Hell, he knows about us. You know that. He's toying with us. He's got something planned. I don't know what it is, but he's planning something for both of us. For all I know, he hired that guy to attack you."

"That's bullshit," Kim said, but she was conflicted, not sure.

Derek stepped closer to her. "Kim… the only reason I agreed to be Ben's property manager is because he blackmailed me. It was either take the job or I was going to be prosecuted for killing that kid out on the highway. I'd be screwed… my business, everything. I can't afford a lawyer. Ben knew that. So, I'm just waiting…"

Kim stared at him, and in the dim light, he saw her spooked eyes and heard her heavy breathing. When she spoke, her voice was shaky. She shifted the weight of her feet.

"Waiting for what?"

"Waiting for him to make his move."

"Ben's not like that. I know him."

"Do you?"

"Yes."

"Then you're deluding yourself. That's not what you told me back in the good old days when you and I were lovers. You said he was devious, aggressive and manipulative. Remember?"

Kim stared hard.

"What else did he give you besides that yoga studio?"

"That's none of your business."

"Then he did give you something else. Was it money?"

Kim folded her arms in defiance.

Derek nodded. "Okay, it *was* money. Okay, so be it. You play it any way you want to play it. I'll play it my way."

"What does that mean?" Kim asked, a little shaken. "Play it your way? What the hell do you mean?"

Derek leaned and kissed her. She drew back. He seized her shoulders and pulled her into him. Their faces were close, breathing staggered, eyes hard and searching. Adrenalin was still pumping through Kim's veins.

"It means, I want you back, Kim," he said, low in his throat. "It means, I want you to leave him and come live with me. He's no good for you. He's playing us both for fools."

Derek tightened his grip on her shoulders, drew her in and kissed her again.

Kim wanted to resist. She'd made a vow to be faithful after Ben had recommitted himself, but Derek's magnetic pull was too great, his energy too seductive. She wriggled, trying to free herself, but Derek was too strong and too insistent. He knew she wanted him as much as he wanted her. Kim gave up struggling, feeling the allure of him, caught by the smell of him, feeling him harden against her. She backed away, gulping air, staring at him, wanting him, panting for him. There was no backing away. She had to have him.

A cool wind poured over them as they shuddered and gradually awakened to the reality of time and place.

Derek released her and they lay close on the bare sand, her head resting against his shoulder, her body still quivering and warm. The sound of the sea rose and fell, lulling them both into a dreamy contentment.

He gently kissed her ear and cheek, her closed eyes. He wiped sand from her face and neck, feeling peace, feeling he'd come home.

"You kill me," she whispered. "What the hell am I going to do with you?"

He pressed his cheek to hers, whispering in her ear. "You're beautiful. You're perfection. Let's get out of here, Kim. Leave him. Let's leave this town and run away where no one will ever find us."

Kim's eyes were still shut. She sighed, still wanting more of him. She thought, "*It's impossible. Impossible to want him so completely and relentlessly. Impossible.*"

Kim drew in a sharp breath, her muscles finally beginning to relax "… And where will that be, Derek? We'll just be running from ourselves."

"Bullshit. We'll get the hell out of here and away from Ben. I have some money. Let's go to Central America. I have some friends there… a couple of old Army buddies moved to Costa Rica. We can go there and start all over."

Kim sat up, pulled on her top, and looked him full in the face, unsure. "I don't know. I don't think so…"

"Why?"

"I have to finish this."

"Finish what?"

"I'm married. I have to finish that. I can't run away from that. If I do, I'll never forgive myself."

Derek was incredulous. "Kim, you *have* run away from it. You've already left him. You're here with me. We're together. We fit together. We go together. That's it. Finished. Your marriage is over. Can't you see that? What crazy daydream are you living in? This isn't some Broadway show where everybody sings and dances and lives happily ever after. This is the real world, and the real world is the world Ben lives in."

Kim gave him a long, searching look and then she stood up and finished dressing.

"Okay, then, I have to end it, officially. I can't run away until I end it. I'm not going to run away like my father did. I can't. He was a coward. He was a son of a bitch. Okay, maybe I'm no better than my father was. Maybe I'm just a whore, but I'm not going to run away. I'll face Ben, and I'll tell him the truth about us. I'll finish it."

Derek stood, knocked the sand from his body, and pulled on his shorts. His eyes held questions, but he kept silent. "Okay… so finish it."

He took her hands and held them. She looked away.

"… And?" Derek asked, trying to find her eyes.

"And… it won't be easy."

"Do it, Kim. Let's get out of here before it's too late."

"Too late for what?"

"Before Ben makes his move—and he will make a move."

Kim retracted her hands and turned toward the sea. She thought about the yoga studio and the two million dollars. It had all come so swiftly. Ben's change had been so sudden and complete. She sighed. "Until this moment, I hadn't realized how scared I am of him. He's different. He's been different and changed for a long time. Maybe I've always been scared of him."

Derek moved behind her and took her shoulders. "He knows about us, Kim. Believe me. You know it, too. Finish it and let's get out of here."

Kim chewed on her fingernail. "Okay, I'll finish it."

She turned and faced Derek, her eyes taking him in, fully, honestly, lovingly. "I can't stop seeing you. I tried. I did try, but I can't. I love you."

"You'll never get away from me, Kim. Never. We belong to each other."

CHAPTER 18

On July 29, Kim nervously paced her room, the outside patio and then the beach, planning what she'd say to Ben. He'd been in his office all morning and most of the afternoon, working with his accountant. He said he'd meet her for dinner.

At 6:06 p.m., Kim was sitting at the dinner table, waiting for him. She was anxious and perspiring. Rosa had already delivered the roast chicken, new potatoes, green beans and fresh corn, as per his instructions. Ben was supposed to join Kim at six o'clock sharp, and he was always on time.

But he was late. Kim poured herself a glass of Chardonnay but didn't drink it. She glanced at her phone. It was 6:10.

She had her speech memorized. It was going to be short and sweet. She was going to leave him. It would be that simple. Yes, short and sweet. He could arrange for the divorce, or she would. She would return the two million dollars. She'd find somebody to take over management of the yoga studio. It wouldn't be difficult. Not after all the renovations and the hard work she'd put into it. She already had someone in mind. She was also a professional dancer and a yoga instructor from New York. That wouldn't be a problem.

Kim drummed a finger on the table, waiting, wondering what was going on in that office.

Could she really give up everything and run off with Derek? Yes, she could. She reached for her wine and took a sip, feeling a warm, helpless glow expanding in her when she thought about him. Could Derek sustain a relationship? First things first. Divorce Ben and then take her chances. What else could she do? She loved Derek.

Kim was startled from her thoughts by shouts coming from Ben's office. She saw Ben's office door burst open and Ben's nurse, Lois Carson, emerge. She rushed over, her expression grave.

Kim shoved her chair back and shot up as Lois approached.

"What's the matter?" Kim asked.

"Ben's had a heart attack," Lois said, her voice shaky.

"What?"

"He was talking on the phone and his head just fell to the desk. Mr. Walker and I got him to the bed, and I gave him CPR. His pulse is very weak. An ambulance is on the way."

Kim stood staring, trying to grasp the impossible moment. She started for the office, but Lois firmly grabbed her arm.

"Don't go in there," Lois commanded. "Don't disturb him."

Kim wrenched her arm away and hurried to the office. Rosa stood outside the room, her trembling hands to her mouth, her eyes filling with tears.

"Is he all right, Mrs. Maxwell?" Rosa asked.

Kim didn't answer. Inside, she saw Ben lying on his back on the double bed he'd had moved into his office only the month before. He was dead still. His face was as white as paper.

Howard Walker, Ben's primary accountant, dressed in his usual dark suit and tie, stood at the foot of the bed, frightened and anxious.

Lois whisked back into the room, shouting for everyone to get out.

Kim ignored her. She was immobile, thoughts and emotions rolling, colliding. She heard the ambulance approach, its siren wobbly and piercing. It reminded her of the awful day Ben smashed his car in the trees, paralyzing him. This was another kind of nightmare.

Lois seized Kim's arm again, to force her out of the room.

Kim yanked it free. "Leave me alone! I'm staying! Just leave me alone!"

Stunned by Kim's outburst, Lois stepped back.

A moment later, Lois went to Ben and re-checked his pulse.

"There's no pulse! He has no pulse!" she exclaimed.

Lois immediately went to work pumping Ben's rib cage, breathing, pumping, working to restore his heartbeat.

Kim whirled and left the room, running to meet the EMS paramedics.

Minutes later Kim led the paramedics into Ben's office. They met Lois, and she summarized his condition. They inserted a breathing tube down Ben's throat and took over with compressions.

Kim watched, shaken to her very core. She stared at Ben's placid, white face and thought, "You're too tough to die, Ben. You're just too damn tough and mean to die."

She watched as the paramedics shocked him with a defibrillator to restore his pulse. Then they eased him onto a stretcher, carried him downstairs and loaded him into an ambulance.

Kim climbed into the rear of the ambulance and sat next to him, sunken in despair and guilt.

The next few hours brought dizzying action. Ben was rushed to the Southampton Hospital ER, where the ambulance was met by two doctors and a nurse, who whisked him inside. Over the years, Ben had attended fund raisers in Southampton and had donated money to various charities. Once, Kim had accompanied him to the yearly hospital gala. Ben was well-known by many of the staff and doctors.

Kim paced the waiting area, glancing up frequently, especially when a door swung open or a doctor or nurse hurried by. Her mind played through all the scenarios: if Ben died, what would she do? If he didn't die, what would she do? If he survived, there would undoubtedly be a long recovery period. What would she do? There was no question: she would stay and see him through until he had recovered one hundred percent. She would have to. Her conscience wouldn't allow any other possibility. She was still his wife.

Kim stalked back and forth, recalling bits and pieces of conversation regarding Ben's health during the past few weeks. He'd had a physical only six weeks before, and the doctor had pronounced him healthy and strong, although he did have heart issues. What were those issues? Her mind was a blank.

Kim strained to remember. In the last week or so, she recalled him complaining about having headaches and some dizziness. He'd even complained about shortness of breath a couple of times and she had suggested that he go back to his doctor.

"I've already seen the doctor, for God's sake!" he'd bellowed. "He gave me a clean bill of health. Said my heart was doing better. I'm not wasting any more time going to see him."

Kim had mentioned the symptoms to Nurse Carson, but she got defensive and snippy. She said Ben was just working too much and that he needed more rest. She said she was monitoring his diet and his blood pressure.

When Lois Carson and Howard Walker arrived, Kim had no news for them. The three of them sat apart, waiting, each pondering their own thoughts.

It was late afternoon when a forties something, heavy-faced doctor approached Kim. He had deep set, grayish-green eyes, thinning brownish hair and a bit of a paunch.

Lois and Walter stood at attention nearby.

"Mrs. Maxwell, I'm Dr. Klein. Can I see you in private?"

He led Kim down a long, polished hallway, past a medical laboratory, to a set of offices. Dr. Klein opened the door and allowed Kim to enter before he quietly shut the door behind them. He offered her a seat in a black leather chair and he sat behind a tidy, modern, cherry wood desk.

Kim sat very still, focusing for a time on the photograph of the doctor, his wife and two smiling teenage girls that sat prominently on the right side of his desk.

Dr. Klein sat, folded his hands and fixed Kim with a pointed gaze.

"Ben has suffered a mild heart attack but, as of now, we believe he will recover."

Kim sighed with relief. "Mild heart attack?" she asked, hoping for clarification.

"Yes… At this point, we think it might have been brought on by some substance."

"I don't understand," Kim said.

Dr. Klein leaned back. "We're going to be speaking with Nurse Carson to find out what medications he's taking. They could have been a contributing factor. We just need to get a list of all his medications to determine if one, or a combination, helped induce the heart attack. We'll also be sending blood work to toxicology. That should help us as well."

Kim stared down at the gray carpet. "Yes, well… Nurse Carson would know more about his medications than I."

Kim lifted her eyes. "I used to know," she said, somewhat defensively. "I mean, before Nurse Carson, I knew most of what Ben's medications were. What kind of drugs can cause a heart attack?"

"It can be a number of possibilities. Sometimes prescription-strength doses of non-steroidal anti-inflammatory drugs are involved. Even over-the-counter meds like Advil and Voltaren can, in some cases, contribute to a heart attack. But often, increased heart attack risk is highest in those with a previous history of heart disease, high blood pressure or high cholesterol. We'll be looking into Ben's medical history and speaking with his doctor."

Kim held his stare. "He had been complaining of headaches and dizziness, and some shortness of breath. I told him he should go see his doctor. Maybe Ben was taking something for that."

Dr. Klein rose to his feet, signaling the end of the conference. "Well, I wanted to bring you up to date."

"Can I see him?" Kim asked, standing, clutching her purse tightly, unaware of the tension.

"Not just yet. We're going to be carefully monitoring him through the night and into tomorrow. You can see him first thing in the morning."

Howard Walker gave Kim a ride back to the house. They spoke little, both repeating how grateful they were that Ben would recover.

As they drove along Beach Road, Kim turned to Howard. "Did Ben complain of headaches or dizziness to you, Howard?"

"He told me yesterday that he wasn't feeling so good. It was after you brought him his green tea."

"Did you tell Lois?" Kim asked.

Howard kept his eyes on the road. "No… No, I didn't. I'd heard him tell her a week or so ago that he was feeling dizzy."

"What did she say?" Kim asked.

"She told him to get more rest."

The road curved right and, as Kim glanced out the window, she saw lights from the bungalows and cottages that lay along the dunes. Derek's cottage was only a quarter mile away.

Kim dreaded having to text him. Everything was changed again. Everything was wrong. What would he say? What could she do?

CHAPTER 19

Kim was at Ben's bedside the next morning, but he was in and out of sleep. He was in a private room, on an IV drip and a heart monitor. A nurse came in frequently to check on him and the equipment. Dr. Klein had come by, but he spoke only briefly to her, and during that short conversation, he had not looked her in the eyes. He seemed uncomfortable, as if he were hiding something. He seemed distant and aloof. Kim had passed it off as lack of sleep or a preoccupation with other patients, or maybe his lack of bedside manner. Still, it had unnerved her.

When Ben's eyes fluttered open, and he saw her, he smiled. He mumbled something, but Kim couldn't make out what it was.

"You just sleep now, Ben. Just rest. Don't try to talk."

Kim sat there for long minutes, her mind wandering and distracted. She shut her eyes and saw, in her mind, Derek's response after she'd texted him the night before.

"I don't care *what* happened to him. This is just another one of his tricks."

She stood up and drifted over to the window, staring

out into the late morning sun. She smiled ironically. Fate had taken charge again. Again, she could not end her marriage with Ben. Maybe he would need her more than ever. Maybe they would truly grow close again. Maybe it was all for the best.

Kim watched the bright sunlight glint off the windows of parked cars. She watched patients come and go. She watched a nurse smoking at the far end of the lot and Kim wished she could join her.

Just then, the door to Ben's room opened and a tall, thin, middle-aged man entered, dressed in a blue suit and gray tie. Kim turned as he approached. Dr. Klein also stepped in, his dark face turned aside.

The man's ruddy face was impassive, his eyes steady and focused on her. He had the expression of someone who hadn't laughed in a long time. Dr. Klein remained near the door, like a guard.

"Hello, Mrs. Maxwell, I'm Detective Sergeant Saunders. I'm with the Scorpio County Police Department."

He reached into his inside pocket, took out his badge and held it up for Kim to see.

Kim blinked at it and then at him, inquiringly. "Yes?"

"Dr. Klein has agreed to let us use his office. I'd like to ask you a few questions concerning your husband, Mr. Maxwell."

"What kind of questions?"

Detective Saunders turned back toward the doctor. "I'd rather we speak in the doctor's office, if that's okay with you. My partner is already waiting for us."

"Partner?"

"Yes, Detective Holder."

Kim's eyes slid from Dr. Klein to Detective Saunders. "Is something wrong?"

Detective Saunders cleared his throat and indicated

toward the door. "I can answer all your questions in the doctor's office, Mrs. Maxwell."

Kim nodded, uneasily, and they left the room.

Detective Holder was a stocky man in his thirties. He wore a brown suit and a solemn, frank expression. His face was blunt, his nose was blunt, his manner was blunt, and he was smoothly bald.

After Kim sat down, Detective Saunders closed the door softly. Detective Holder introduced himself and then he moved away to the corner of the room while Detective Saunders brought the doctor's chair from behind the desk and placed it a short distance from Kim. He sat and managed a tight smile that didn't fit his humorless face.

"Mrs. Maxwell, I…"

Kim interrupted. "Call me Kim, please."

"Kim… I'm going to ask you some questions. You are under no obligation to answer them. You're welcome to call your attorney and have him present while we ask the questions. Do you want to call an attorney?"

Kim rearranged herself in the chair, licking her dry lips. She studied both men, trying to understand.

"I don't need an attorney," she said. "Just come to the point."

"Yes… all right. Dr. Klein called us this morning to report the lab's findings regarding your husband's toxicology report."

Kim waited, feeling cranky, trying to anticipate where the detective was going.

Detective Saunders fixed his eyes on her. "Kim… toxicology found traces of cyanide in your husband's system."

Kim leaned forward as if she didn't hear him clearly.

"What?"

The detective repeated the sentence.

Kim stared, not comprehending.

The detective continued. "Kim, cyanide is a poison."

"I know it's a poison," Kim said sharply, immediately wishing she'd waited before speaking. "Of course I know it's a poison. How… why… how…?" Kim couldn't find the words to form a coherent question.

"That's what we are trying to determine. That is, under what means did your husband ingest the cyanide, when did he start taking it and for how long was he taking it?"

Kim bristled. "Are you saying Ben was trying to kill himself?"

The two detectives exchanged furtive glances. "Either that, or there is the possibility that someone was deliberately trying to poison him and did, in fact, poison him."

"What!?" Kim said, breathless, bewildered.

Detective Holder spoke. "Do you have any knowledge of this?"

Kim snapped her head toward him. "Knowledge? What? No, of course I don't have any knowledge. What kind of question is that? How in the hell would I have any knowledge of this?"

Detective Saunders softened his voice. "Kim, did your husband ever mention taking cyanide?"

"No. Never. Ben wouldn't deliberately take poison. He's not the type. He's a fighter."

Detective Holder turned away.

Detective Saunders lifted his chin a little. "Did he ever discuss with you that he wanted to take his own life?"

"No. Of course not. I told you, he's not the type to take his own life."

Detective Saunders took out his pocket black leather

notebook. "Kim… About nine months ago, Mr. Maxwell was involved in an auto accident. Isn't that correct? In fact, he is paralyzed from the waist down because of the accident. Isn't that correct?"

Kim swallowed. "Yes… but…"

The detective continued, giving a quick summary of the accident report. "I read the police report, and I noted that…" Detective Saunders flipped through some pages. "You stated that, quote, 'Ben was trying to kill himself.'"

Kim straightened herself up. "I was upset. I was angry and confused."

"But you did believe your husband was trying to kill himself because, as you stated in the police report, he thought you were having an affair with another man. Isn't that right?"

Kim shook her head. "Detective Saunders… if you read further in the report, you'll see that I also said I was *not* having an affair."

Detective Holder slanted her a look. "But according to your statement, you did believe that Mr. Maxwell did try to kill himself because *he* believed you were having an affair. Is that right? He had even produced photographs."

Kim's jaw stiffened. "So what are you both getting at? Just get to the point. Do you believe Ben tried to poison himself? Kill himself?"

Detective Saunders' eyes were flat but direct. "He was either trying to kill himself or, as I said, someone else was poisoning him. Dr. Klein believes he was taking, or was being administered, low doses of cyanide over a period of weeks. This would account for the poison having a more gradual onset of symptoms. Dr. Klein also stated that, conversely, an acute ingestion would have a dramatic, rapid onset, immediately affecting the heart and causing a sudden collapse. According to Dr. Klein's statement, it would logically seem that if Mr. Maxwell wanted to kill himself, he would most likely have taken some kind of pill or taken a more aggressive dose of the poison. So we are looking into all possibilities. We are trying to ascertain the facts, and one of those possibilities is that someone was poisoning your husband."

Kim blinked with anxiety. "Poisoning him? Someone?" Her words seemed to drop into the floor. Her eyes searched the walls for answers.

"Our investigation is just in the beginning stages, Kim. We are hoping you can help us… help us straighten all this out. I'm sorry to have to ask you these questions at a time like this."

Kim gazed at him without focus.

The room filled with a long, chilly silence. The two detectives kept their firm attention on Kim, who was struggling to process the explosion of information.

"It doesn't make sense," Kim said. "It just doesn't make any sense."

Detective Saunders rose to his feet. "All right, Mrs. Maxwell, that's enough for today. Our investigation is ongoing, and we will keep you informed."

He reached into his pocket and handed Kim his card. "Meanwhile, if you remember anything or hear anything, please call me day or night."

Kim stared at the card, lost in a fog of disbelief and confusion.

She looked up at him. "Have you spoken to anyone else? Have you spoken to Ben's nurse, Lois Carson?"

Detective Saunders stood a little taller. "We'll be in touch, Mrs. Maxwell. Thank you for your time."

Kim promptly returned to Ben's room, her face the color of white powder. Inside, she slowly wandered over to Ben's bed, staring at him. She sat down beside him and stared into his broad, sleepy face. She heard the beep of the monitor. She heard the chop of a helicopter drift over the building and then fade into the distance. Her eyes lifted to see a blank TV monitor perched high and angled down, and she saw her own reflection. She looked scared.

A sudden sense of danger struck her in the gut. As she continued staring at Ben's face, he made a sound, without opening his eyes, some dream fleeing by.

"Ben," she whispered. "What is going on?"

CHAPTER 20

At eight o'clock the next morning, Kim called the hospital to check on Ben's progress. She was told by a nurse that he'd slept well; he was improving, and he was currently having an MRI.

After a shower, Kim found Rosa in the kitchen, weepy and distressed.

"I didn't know if I should come today. No one said."

"It's okay, Rosa. I'm glad you came."

"How is Mr. Maxwell?"

"He's improving, Rosa. He'll be back before you know it. Did Nurse Carson come in?" Kim asked.

Rosa's eyes were red-rimmed, her face weary. "No. She didn't come. Mr. Maxwell is such a nice man. Nice to me. Gave me this job. A nice man. I hope he comes back to us," she said. "This house is so empty. He was always so nice to me, Miss."

"He'll be back soon, Rosa. I just talked to the hospital. He's much better."

"Thanks God," Rosa said, folding her hands at her chest prayerfully. "Thanks God, he comes home soon."

Kim gave her a little hug.

"I'll fix you breakfast, Miss Kim," Rosa said. "I have

coffee made for you."

Kim took a mug and walked into the dining room. She stared out the window, seeing an overcast day and lowering clouds. Two surfers were paddling out to sea, searching for good waves. Seagulls wheeled and shrieked. Kim ventured a look up and down the beach but there was no sign of Derek and Colin. She hadn't heard from him since his text yesterday. Would he come to the house? Who was in charge of Ben's businesses now that he was in the hospital? She didn't know. Howard Walker? Ben's attorneys? She should know these things, but she'd never given it any thought.

Kim sat at the dining room table sipping her coffee. She'd slept fitfully, waking sharply from nightmares about dogs chasing her, waves engulfing her and dark shadows creeping in all around her. She couldn't shake the conversation she'd had with the detectives the day before or make any sense from their information that Ben was being poisoned by cyanide. It was too incredible—too absurd. She was sure it was a mistake. The hospital had mixed up something—the medical records or the toxicology report. She half-expected to receive a call from Dr. Klein or the detectives telling her the whole thing was a big misunderstanding and to forget it, with their apologies.

Rosa delivered scrambled eggs, rye toast, chicken sausage and orange juice. She lingered at the table until Kim looked at her.

"Everything okay, Rosa?"

"Should I keep coming, Miss Kim?"

"Of course, Rosa. Of course keep coming."

"I have a little boy. My husband's out of work. Mr. Maxwell's been so nice to me."

"Don't worry, Rosa, he'll be back any day now."

"Thank you, Miss. I do the rosary for him. I pray for him."

Rosa bobbed a bow and left.

Kim ate a few bites of the eggs and then pushed the plate away. She reached for the toast and swabbed some butter on the corners. After a few bites, she laid it aside.

What if the hospital did not make a mistake? What if Ben was being poisoned? By whom? Why? Kim sank a little, feeling an exhausted sense of dread.

She heard the front doorbell, and Rosa's footsteps advancing toward the door. Kim heard voices. Rosa's voice rose in protest. The male voice grew loud and threatening.

Kim shot up and walked briskly across the dining room and down the stairs. Before she reached the bottom, she saw Detectives Saunders and Holder, standing in the foyer, with Rosa blocking their way.

Rosa turned back to Kim, her face pinched in distress, her hands twisting. "Miss Kim, they say they are the police."

Kim took a little breath. "Yes, Rosa, let them in. It's okay."

Rosa lifted her chin in defiance but moved out of the way.

"You can go upstairs, Rosa."

Rosa lowered her head and started up the stairs as Kim descended, standing before the two detectives.

"Good morning, Kim," Detective Saunders said, his face as hard as stone.

Kim nodded. "What's this about?"

Saunders held up a piece of paper. "We have a search warrant to search the house, including all the computers, and to remove the hard drives."

Kim froze. Had she ever emailed Derek? No.

Texted? Yes.

Kim noticed there were two people standing behind Detective Holder, a young black female cop wearing a blue police uniform, and a man with a starched face wearing a suit.

Kim projected a calm bewilderment. She stepped back, indicating the house with a sweep of her hand.

"Okay. Search away."

Holder's eyes lingered on her for a moment. Kim sensed he was noticing her for the first time. Her hair was piled up, somewhat carelessly. She wore a blue, V-neck T-shirt and tight white shorts. She was barefoot, and since she wasn't expecting guests, she wore no makeup.

Holder's gaze slid down as he quickly studied her slim, well-formed legs and her red toenails.

"I suppose I have to be here while you search?" Kim asked.

"No, Kim. You don't."

"So I can go to the hospital and see my husband?"

"Yes," Saunders said.

"Can we get started?" Holder said, all brisk and businesslike.

Saunders straightened. "Yeah… Okay. Let's go."

While they worked, Kim took her coffee and went out on the patio. She slouched in an old canvas chair she'd found at a yard sale, and slipped on sunglasses, basking in the weak morning sun that was fighting to break through gray, moving clouds.

Kim felt a storm building in her chest. So there was no mistake. The toxicology report was correct. The hospital had not mixed up Ben's records. Either Ben had been purposely taking cyanide or someone was coldly trying to kill him.

Even though the wind was humid and warm, Kim shivered. She wanted to call Derek to hear his voice and to get his advice, but she was frightened and confused. The police were searching the house. What would they find? Did she have anything to hide? If the investigation led to a possible attempted murder case, everything about her and Ben's lives would be open to investigation. Everything! That would include the private investigator's report and possible photographs.

Kim exhaled, suddenly feeling a rising panic. She had to do something. She grabbed her phone and called Howard Walker.

"It's Kim, Howard."

His voice was soft and hesitant. "Yes, Kim?"

"The police are here, searching the house."

Silence. Then a fearful, "Oh, God."

"I need to get in touch with Ben's attorneys. I don't have the number and the police are in Ben's office right now. Can you call them and tell them what's going on?"

Again, silence.

"Howard? Did you hear me?"

"Look, Kim. I don't want to get involved with this."

"Howard, you are involved. We're all going to be involved, okay? So give me the number and I'll call them."

More silence.

"Dammit, Howard. Give me the goddamned number!"

"Kim… they've already been called."

Kim turned in place, her face flushing with fear.

"Who called them?"

"Ben."

"Ben? He's barely conscious. He can't even talk. Yesterday, he was mumbling. I don't think he even knew I was there."

"He's conscious. I've talked to him."

"When?"

"A few minutes ago."

"Well, how is he? What did he say?"

"I've got to go now."

"Howard… Howard?"

But he was gone. Kim immediately called him back, but he didn't answer.

Kim called Ben's cell phone, but she didn't get an answer. She called the hospital and asked to speak with him.

A stern sounding nurse answered. "I'm sorry, Mrs. Maxwell, Mr. Maxwell does not wish to be disturbed at this time."

"Will you tell him it's his wife, please?"

There was a long pause.

"Hello?" Kim shouted, irritated and scared. "Hello, are you there? Hello!?"

Kim was stunned when she heard Lois Carson's stilted voice. "Kim, this is Lois Carson. Ben doesn't want to speak to you right now. He also told me to tell you not to visit him."

Kim's voice took on force. "Lois, I want to speak to Ben, and I want to speak with him now. I have nothing else to say to you."

"And I have nothing else to say to you," Lois said, imperiously.

After Lois had hung up, Kim stood paralyzed with rage, confusion and terror. She didn't know where to turn. In a panic, she called Derek.

He picked up on the second ring.

"Kim… hang up. Come and see me at my place. Now."

Before she could speak, he was gone.

Kim left the house, descended the stairs to the patio and rushed toward the path to the beach. It was already crowded and bustling with kids, volleyball games and kite flyers. The clouds parted, and the sun came slamming down, burning her bare head and shoulders.

As she hurried across the foaming tide, she glanced back over her shoulder to see if she was being followed. No one. Her heart was hammering in her chest, her temples pounding.

As she approached Derek's cottage, she saw him walking toward her. She relaxed a little, finding a friend, at last.

"I need to talk to you," she said, breathless.

"Not here," he said.

He took her arm at the elbow and led her away toward the beach cottage. But they bypassed the cottage, and he ushered her to his truck.

"Get in."

She did. He slid behind the wheel, cranked the engine, threw the truck in reverse and backed out onto the narrow asphalt road. He turned left, taking Dune Road. It skirted the beach and more isolated beach cottages, and an old crab house that sat near the water.

"I'm scared," Kim said. "Something is happening."

"I know," Derek said. "I heard about the whole thing."

"What did you hear?" Kim asked, her expression tense.

"I've been informed that I'm fired."

"What?"

Derek glanced at her. "Do you know about the poison?"

"Yes. Of course, I know."

"Kim… I know a good attorney. Her name's Maggie

Stone. She was a JAG in the Army. She started her own law firm in Albany, New York about five years ago."

"What are you saying? What's a JAG?"

"A Judge Advocate Officer—an attorney. You'll need one."

Kim swallowed, the full awful truth slowly dawning.

Derek stole another look at her as he whipped the car right and then drew up under the spreading shade of trees and stopped.

Kim heard the sound of an airplane. She looked up through the windshield to see a single-engine plane pulling an aerial banner over the beach. It read THE DOCK CAFÉ SCORPIO BEACH.

Kim's mind went numb. She'd suspected something dark, but she hadn't let herself follow the logical evil steps to the truth.

"Kim… Ben has made his move. I believe he has created this whole thing just to get back at us both, but especially you."

"But it doesn't make sense," Kim said. "He wouldn't poison himself and risk his own life, just to get back at me. I don't believe it. He's not that crazy."

"For God's sake, Kim, he drove his car into a tree a few months ago and paralyzed himself because he thought you were having an affair. Does that sound like a sane man? Either he took the poison himself or somebody helped—I don't know which, but I don't think he gave a damn if he lived or died, although I'm sure he preferred to live just to see you go to jail."

Kim turned away, absorbed and worried. "Jail?"

"Listen to me. We have to be ready. I don't see any way around it. You're going to be charged with attempted murder, and I'm going to call Maggie Stone and hope she takes the case."

Kim stared at Derek, and the coldness grew inside her.

Two days later, in the morning, Detectives Saunders and Holder came to the house and arrested Kim on one count of attempted first-degree murder, after allegedly trying to poison her husband. Kim was accused of planning to poison and poisoning Ben with small doses of potassium cyanide that she added to the green tea she served him every afternoon. The evidence included a small bottle of cyanide found in Kim's room, and a teapot with traces of the cyanide found in Ben's office.

Kim was read her rights, handcuffed and then led away to a dark sedan where she was taken to the Scorpio Beach Sheriff's Department. She was booked, fingerprinted and placed in a holding cell.

Twenty-five hours later, Kim's first appearance in court was before the Magistrate Judge Thomas Brown. Since Derek's attorney of choice, Maggie Stone, had not yet been secured, Kim was appointed a lawyer to represent her.

Kim was read the charge: one count of attempted first-degree murder, after allegedly trying to poison her husband, Ben Maxwell, with potassium cyanide. Her attorney entered a plea of not guilty. Bail was set for two million dollars.

Kim stood before the judge with sad, suffering eyes. It was a living nightmare. She didn't seem properly anchored in her skin. The surrounding scene was some absurd fiction. Who was this person, Kim? Who were these people? How had all of this happened?

She'd also learned that Ben had withdrawn all the funds from their joint account, leaving her with no means of posting bail. No one she knew had anywhere near that kind of money. When she mentioned the joint account to her assigned lawyer, he avoided her eyes and told her he'd look into it. When she asked him if there was any way he could speak to the judge about reducing her bail, he said he'd look into that as well, but there was no conviction in his voice.

It took several attempts before Derek was able to speak with Maggie Stone and explain the details of Kim's situation. Maggie listened quietly, without asking any questions. She made some notes on a legal pad and told Derek she'd call him after she had looked into it.

The next morning, Maggie called Derek and told him she'd take the case. She'd be on the first plane to LaGuardia, rent a car and be there sometime the following afternoon.

Meanwhile, Kim was transferred to a larger facility, the Green Township County Jail, ten miles away. Her case would be presented to the Grand Jury within five days, on August 10.

With less than ninety thousand dollars in a private account, and less than twelve hundred in a checking account, Kim was helpless to free herself while she awaited the decision of the Grand Jury. Bail was so large, even a bail bondsman was out of the question.

Kim entered the Green Township County Jail after dark, was processed and finger printed, and then escorted down a long, harshly lit hallway to a narrow, dimly lighted cell. Inside the cell, she watched the barred door slide shut with a loud metallic click. She stared out of the grill of iron bars, feeling sick with fear and nausea.

Her roommate was asleep on the top bunk, a quiet gray bundle under the sheet. The room smelled of mold and some sweet lemony cleaning fluid. The walls seemed to close in on her, as the hellish nightmare expanded into a black, horrific reality.

Kim was immobile for a time, unable to think or

move. With all her energy and spirit drained, she sank down on the hard mattress and began to sob.

From above, Kim heard her bunkmate whisper. "That ain't gonna do you or me a bit of good, girl. Shut up."

CHAPTER 21

Margaret Harris Stone, or Maggie as she was called, was short, thin, quick and clever. Her graying hair was a stylish spiky cut, her jaw set in determination, and her chipped, icy green eyes were always flickering about, looking for a challenge.

Major Maggie Stone's military career started when she graduated in 1990 from Ryan Point. She was commissioned as an officer in the Advocate General's Corps and did personnel and human resource management. She was later selected for the Army's Funded Legal Education Program and went to law school. From there, she was sent to Fort Bliss. For a time, she was chief of military justice for the criminal law division, supervising ten trial counsel, in addition to being a special victims' prosecutor. She was, essentially, the district attorney for Fort Bliss.

She left the military because she and another female JAG officer decided they wanted to start a practice of their own outside the military. They did so, and Maggie never looked back. Maggie gained some notoriety for defense cases that involved abused and battered women.

Her most famous case was that of a woman who had been violently abused for four years and finally shot her husband five times. Prosecutors claimed it was because her husband had another woman and the murder was about jealousy and revenge.

Maggie Stone presented evidence that revealed a history of persistent abuse and then stated in her closing argument that her client believed her husband was going to kill her. Her client acted in self-defense, a right of every human being. The woman was acquitted.

Maggie was known to be tough, terse and lucid. She ran five miles four times a week, ate a high protein diet and had been married once for one year, when she was 26 years old. With regard to her marriage, she had gone on the record to say, "I would have been a lot better off if it had never happened."

She'd moved to Albany and opened her practice there, because that was her home town and she had some connections. She was forty-seven years old.

Nearly overnight, Ben's and Kim's story became a media sensation and the lurid details were splashed across the internet, in newspapers and on television. Photos of Kim and Derek in suggestive photos—photos taken by Ben's private investigator—were leaked as well, along with the suggestion that the two of them might have conspired to kill Ben for his money.

The D.A. had considered charges against Derek, but he had found no clear evidence that could directly link him; therefore, he didn't pursue it. On the other hand, the search of the Maxwell house did turn up damaging evidence against Kim, and the media played it up in dramatic headlines:

Leggy Blonde Dancer Charged with Poisoning Real Estate Magnet Husband

Real Estate Magnate Allegedly Poisoned by Blonde Dancer Wife

Blonde Dancer Wife Arrested for Allegedly Poisoning Rich Husband over Hunk

Broadway Dancer Wife Allegedly Poisons Rich Hubbie for Love and Money

Blonde Broadway Bombshell Wife Alleged to Poison Rich Hubbie for Ex-Soldier

Broadway Baby Allegedly Poisons Rich Hubbie for Soldier Hunk

Maggie met Derek on the steps of the Greek style Scorpio Beach Courthouse, near the solid Doric columns. She wore a light gray business suit and low heels and held a brown leather brief case.

They had met only once, three years before, when one of Derek's Army buddies was involved in a rape case.

Derek saw Maggie appraise him with her eyes. He wondered what she was thinking.

Maggie had remembered Derek's sexy macho attractiveness. But she'd forgotten just how powerful his chest and shoulders were. She hadn't remembered his piercing blue eyes, his sharp jaw and his warrior face, hard as stone and as rugged as a Montana cowboy's.

Maggie informed him that she had a hearing scheduled with Judge Brown and the D.A. in ten minutes, and that was her first priority.

Derek was tense and angry and ready to fight. He fired questions at her, but she deflected them all.

"The first thing I've got to do is stop Ben Maxwell from leaking information and photos to the press. I've hired a private investigator to look into Lois Carson, Howard Walker and Rosa Sanchez, and anybody who's been coming and going in that house. He's also going to be looking into the police report, toxicology report and Ben Maxwell's medical records and emails. We've got to move fast on this. I want as much information as I can get before the Grand Jury convenes in 4 days. Then I want to go see Kim. I have a lot of questions for her and for you. Will you come with me?"

Derek nodded. "Of course I'll come with you. I'll do anything you need me to do. Is there anything you can do about Ben transferring the entire two million out of Kim's account? She can't post bail. It was her money too."

"I'll approach the judge about that during the hearing. So meet me back here in an hour."

Derek watched Maggie ascend the remaining stairs, pull open the heavy oak doors and enter the dimly lit courthouse. As he watched her fade away, he thought "*I'm glad she's on our side.*"

Maggie was escorted to the Judge's chambers by a tall, long-striding bailiff, who inspected her purse, something that surprised her. Inside, Judge Thomas Brown stood up from his impressive oak desk and came around to meet her. He was short and stocky, with graying hair, a thin gray mustache and an affable smile. To Maggie, Judge Brown looked more like a bartender than a judge. And, as she shook his meaty hand, she thought she could use a straight rye whiskey right about then.

The D.A. had been sitting in one of the two burgundy leather chairs arranged in front of the Judge's desk. He stood and turned to welcome Maggie.

He took her hand, limply, his voice smooth and caressing.

"So good to meet you, Counselor. We've been waiting for you."

Maggie nodded her greeting. She'd done her homework on the D.A., Mr. Baxter M. Cahill, *googling* him and finding articles in old Long Island newspapers. She read about his past cases and she found a few attorneys' personal impressions of him, as well as some newspaper articles. Baxter Cahill was an imposing man, with exceptional trial skills, a brilliant mind, and a sturdy 6-foot 2-inch frame that carried a belligerent stomach.

In one article, she read that *"The current D.A. of Scorpio Beach, Mr. Cahill, carries his stomach like a battering weapon to his enemies, cutting a path through any crowd with assurance and purpose. But when he's laughing with friends or a jury, he holds that same stomach like a bowl full of jelly, jollily shaking and patting it like a pet."*

"There's nobody like Bax," friends reported.

"There's nobody like Bax," his enemies said.

At forty-six years old, Baxter was married and had three sons. He also had political aspirations.

Maggie took the chair next to Mr. Baxter as Judge Brown returned to his desk, sat, folded his hands and lowered them easily onto the desktop.

Maggie came straight to the point. "Your Honor, I request that all confidential information and photos in Ben Maxwell's possession be seized immediately. It is obvious that he's trying to influence the investigation and gain public sympathy."

Baxter spoke up. "I can assure you, Your Honor, and Counselor Stone, that I have recently spoken with Mr. Maxwell and he disavows any knowledge of any leaking of information or photographs. I have advised him, in the strongest terms, to refrain from any practice of speaking about this case to anyone, especially to the press. He assures me that he will abide by my wishes and he apologizes for any inconvenience."

Maggie drew in a suspicious breath, but she held her tongue.

Judge Brown narrowed his eyes on Baxter. "Yes, Ms. Stone. Mr. Cahill and I were discussing that very thing when you arrived. It's a very serious matter and one I will not tolerate. I'll take Mr. Cahill's word that we will have no more of these kinds of unfortunate incidents."

Maggie could have said many things, but she didn't. She needed time to learn about the county, Judge Brown and the case.

Maggie lifted the flap on her brown leather Coach briefcase. "Judge Brown, I would also like to ask that you reconsider bail review and reduction in this case."

Maggie drew out her Motion. "I have here a Motion to Reconsider. My client has no prior arrest record, and she is not a flight risk."

Maggie stood and presented Judge Brown with the Motion. He took it. When she returned to her seat, he glanced at it. He lifted his eyes and squinted a look at her.

"You realize, Counselor, that your client is charged with attempted murder in the first degree. This charge requires premeditation or a willful act. If your client is convicted, she could be sentenced to life imprisonment. I will look your Motion over, but this court has already been lenient in allowing any bail, based on the evidence from the D.A."

Maggie nodded. "Yes, thank you, Judge. Your Honor, I also note that Ben Maxwell has liquidated all the funds from a joint account, thus preventing my client from posting bail. As you are aware, when two people hold a joint account, they each have an equal right to its balance. It is obvious that Ben Maxwell has acted out of presumed guilt and anger in liquidating all joint funds, therefore preventing my client from necessary living expenses, which include posting bail. Therefore, I request a court order reinstating the joint account funds."

Judge Brown considered her request, staring at her curiously. His eyes slid over to Baxter Cahill.

"Do you have anything to add, Mr. Cahill?"

Baxter pursed his lips and narrowed his eyes. He briefly shut his eyes and shook his head.

"Very well, Counselor," Judge Brown said.

"Thank you, Your Honor."

Judge Brown went into a brief summary of Grand Jury procedures for the Eastern District of New York and Maggie listened, politely, anxious to conclude the hearing.

After he'd finished, Mr. Cahill turned to Maggie.

"Will your client be testifying before the Grand Jury, Ms. Stone?"

Maggie didn't face him. "At this time, I don't know. I'll consult with my client and let you know."

The Judge stood, indicating the hearing had concluded.

Maggie quickly studied each man. Both men's expressions were politely guarded, confident and patronizingly solicitous. She concluded she was going to have a real battle on her hands.

CHAPTER 22

Kim sat in her narrow gray and white cell, waiting for the guard to come and escort her downstairs where she was to meet her attorney and Derek. She felt claustrophobic in the little cell with a toilet, a sink and an undersized desk. She longed to see Derek—to see a familiar face, a lover's face—her lover. She sat on the edge of her single lower bunk bed, fighting despair and depression. Her bunk mate was off to the lounge watching TV or surfing the internet.

Kim's case was to go to the Grand Jury in two days. Derek had promised he'd find an attorney, and he had found one. Kim hoped the woman was competent, and that she would truly believe that Kim was innocent. Derek said Maggie Stone was one of the best, and that she only took cases that she believed she could win. Derek also told Kim to stay optimistic and not give into fear.

"We'll fight this thing together," he said. "I'll never leave you alone."

Kim was strengthened by Derek's words because she knew he meant them. Despite the awful events, Kim had seen a stark change in Derek and in their relationship.

The hard edges of his personality had softened around her. And even though his anger over what he believed Ben had done was at times explosive and seething, Kim knew she could rely on him more than she'd ever relied on anyone else. That's what kept her from collapsing into hopelessness.

Kim longed to be in his bed. She longed for his kisses. She wanted to wake up with him in his little beach cottage and realize that this whole raging nightmare was just a horrible dream.

Kim pushed up and paced the little space. She couldn't think about that now. The focus of her thoughts had to be on staying positive and calm. But that was easier said than done. Terror rose in her chest in bursts of heat every few minutes. She was terrified at what might happen if the Grand Jury indicted her. Since she couldn't post bail, she could be in jail for months before the trial. And what would happen if a jury found her guilty? She'd tried to discuss this with Derek, but he grew moody and silent, refusing to tell her what Maggie Stone had said when they'd discussed the issues of the case.

But Kim had done her own research on the internet.

She had been arrested on a first-degree attempted murder charge. First-degree attempted murder requires planning and is usually reserved for those who kill or try to kill their spouses. If Kim's research was correct, then the only sentence available for attempted murder in the first degree (a class A-I felony) was life imprisonment, with parole eligibility fixed at no less than fifteen years and no more than twenty-five years.

Kim gulped in air, suddenly struggling to breathe. She sat back down on the bed and put her face in her hands. God! How had this happened?

She still had difficulty believing that Ben would set her

up as Derek firmly believed. Would Ben really voluntarily take poison over a period of time, risking his own life, just to frame her for attempted murder? Just to get back at her because he'd destroyed all the love she'd had for him? Was he really capable of that?

Kim just couldn't fathom it. She thought it was more likely that someone else was trying to kill Ben and that they had placed the poison in the tea. Maybe it was Lois or Walter or someone else. But why? What was their motive? Hatred? Money? Maybe they were in it together? Maybe there were others?

Just then, the husky female guard came walking heavily down the hallway. Kim lifted her head, wiped her wet eyes and took a deep breath, bracing herself. The guard's footsteps echoed loudly, as if some giant were approaching.

The guard led Kim down the long hallway that was lined with pastel green/black trim doors; a hallway that seemed to stretch into shadowy infinity.

Minutes later, Kim was escorted into the small, square, private meeting room that contained a brown Formica table and four plastic chairs, two gray and two orange. There were surveillance cameras on either side of the room, and a picture window where a guard could always see in. The room was filled with harsh light and it smelled of disinfectant and fear. Yes, Kim could smell fear. Fear and despair filled every square inch of the place. It reeked of them.

Kim entered, contritely, her hair tied into a ponytail. She was wearing an orange jump suit and hard plastic sandals. She'd been able to keep her white bra, white underwear and white socks because they were white. Wearing any color was against the rules. Normally when in her cell, the lounge or cafeteria, she wore t-shirts and sweatpants, but if she left the cell to meet visitors, she was required to wear the jumpsuit.

Derek and Maggie were sitting at the table waiting for her. They both climbed to their feet when she entered.

When he saw her, Derek's eyes flashed anger and frustration. Anger at what Ben had done to her, and frustration that she had to stay in this asshole of a place because he didn't have the money to post bail. He gently hugged her. His touch brought stinging tears to Kim's eyes. The two lingered for a minute while Maggie waited, not taking her eyes from them. She studied Kim in every detail.

Kim was a beautiful woman. Maggie observed a natural seductive quality about her, a fascinating allure that could pose a problem in a courtroom, especially if Derek was sitting close by. He was achingly sexy. No wonder the press had latched on to them, posting old photos of Kim in a tight sexy outfit, when she'd danced in the Broadway musical *Chicago*, and a photo of Derek wearing his Army Ranger camouflage, complete with his Ranger's patch clearly visible. Derek looked like a hero. Kim like a star.

They were the perfect shining couple for this modern, sex-drenched culture. Maggie would have to confront, honestly, the fact that Derek and Kim had been involved in a sexual affair. Kim had committed adultery. Derek was one of Ben's employees.

One could easily presume that Kim—with her lush blonde hair, sexy body and pretty face—had men sniffing after her from every corner of town. If Kim was indicted, and the case went to trial, which Maggie was sure would happen, she would have to reduce Kim's attractiveness and mute her glamor. Maggie did not want the press presenting Kim as a vampish mantrap who exploited men, Ben being one of her victims. Maggie would have to disarm Kim's sexy aura to keep the women of the jury from being jealous of Kim's looks, jealous and judgmental of her affair with Derek, and critical of her marriage to Ben, and her subsequent lack of gratitude for her lavish lifestyle and wealthy prestige.

The D.A. would no doubt portray Ben as a victim and Kim as an ungrateful, selfish and wanton slut. Maggie knew that, if most women were honest, they would have thrown themselves into Derek's arms any day of the week. Some might have even considered the many ways they might rid themselves of the older and unfortunate Ben Maxwell while inheriting his money and running off to live happily ever after with Derek.

Maggie watched Derek hold Kim at arm's length, as she slowly raised her eyes to meet his gaze. Her face was pale and drawn, her eyes vague and bloodshot from lack of sleep.

"We're going to get you out of here, Kim. I promise," Derek said. "Maggie filed a motion with the Judge to reduce your bail. The court will also order Ben to reinstate the joint account funds. As soon as that goes through, we'll find a way to get the rest of the money to get you out of here."

Kim looked at him with a blank, entranced expression. She was relieved and thrilled to see him, though weary and weak from fighting fear and despair.

Maggie stepped over, extending her hand. "Hello, Kim. I'm Maggie Stone."

Kim released Derek and gratefully took Maggie's hand. "Thank you. Thank you for taking my case."

"Sit down," Maggie said. "We don't have a lot of time and I have a lot of questions, so let's get started."

Kim and Derek sat next to each other across the table from Maggie. Maggie reached into her briefcase and extracted an iPad, a digital recorder, a yellow legal pad and several pens.

Maggie looked up. "I'm going to tape this interview. Any problem with that?"

Kim shook her head. "No…"

Maggie switched on the recorder and documented place, time, date and those present.

Maggie looked at Kim pointedly. "Kim, I'm going to ask you directly. Did you ever, at any time, knowingly, willingly and repeatedly make a pot of green tea, place cyanide powder into that pot and then bring the tea to your husband, with the intent to kill him? Yes or no."

Kim swallowed. "No."

"Have you ever purchased cyanide in any form at any time in the past? Yes or no."

"No."

"Were you aware or did you have any knowledge of anyone else in your home, placing potassium cyanide in the teapot that was meant to be served to your husband? Yes or no."

"No."

"To the best of your knowledge, did anyone else in the house, other than you, ever make green tea for your husband and then bring it to him? Yes or no."

"Yes."

Maggie straightened, and Derek leveled his eyes on Kim.

"Who?" Maggie asked.

Kim's voice was tight in her throat. "Rosa."

"Rosa Sanchez?" Maggie asked.

"Yes."

"How many times?"

Kim thought. "I don't know."

"Approximately," Maggie pressed.

"I'm just not sure. I prepared the tea most of the time. His doctor said it would be good for him. He said it would help lower his cholesterol and relax him."

Maggie continued. "If you were aware that Rosa Sanchez brought him the tea, then you must have some idea of when she brought him the tea."

Kim's eyes moved as she searched for the answer. "I went shopping some afternoons, or to the yoga studio. When I did, Rosa would make the tea and take it to him."

Maggie nodded, making notes on her legal pad.

Kim studied Maggie as she worked, making mental notes. Her hairstyle was precise and artful, black hair streaked with gray; her gray suit and white blouse were crisp like a uniform, her movements clean, her eyes clear and a little hard. Kim thought Maggie was probably a lesbian, and she reminded Kim of a general.

Maggie glanced up from her writing. "Kim, did you ever witness Rosa making the tea before she took it to your husband?"

Kim thought. She lit up with a memory. "Yes. Yes. Once."

"Did you brew the tea with tea bags or was it loose tea?"

"Loose."

"Did you notice if Rosa Sanchez put anything into the tea other than the loose tea?"

"... No."

"Did Rosa ever witness you brewing the tea?"

"Yes, many times."

Maggie nodded. "Did she watch you carefully or was she doing other things?"

"I don't recall, really. We would talk. Sometimes the TV was on or there was music playing on the Alexa Echo. Sometimes we were checking our phones."

"Okay, Kim. Good. Now, did you ever know of—or witness—anyone else in that house making the tea for your husband?"

Kim licked her lips. "I think Lois Carson did once or twice. Rosa told me Lois made it, but I don't remember how many times. Rosa would know that."

Maggie leaned back into her chair and made a steeple with her hands, holding them up to her lips. Her eyes held questions. She switched off the recorder. The room fell into a hard silence. Kim was aware that a guard was standing near the picture window, peering in now and then, probing the room. She heard a siren off in the distance. She waited.

Maggie took in a thoughtful breath. "Kim, the most damaging evidence the prosecution has is that when they searched your house, they found a small bottle of potassium cyanide in your lower underwear drawer, pushed way in the back and wrapped in a pair of red satin underwear."

Kim looked away. Derek heaved out a frustrated breath. "That's bullshit," he said bitterly.

Maggie held up her hand to stop him, and then she continued. "Kim, have you ever purchased potassium cyanide?"

"No, I don't even know what it looks like or what it is."

Maggie lowered her steepled hands. "It's colorless crystalline salt, similar in appearance to sugar, and it is highly soluble in water. So, to be clear, you did not purchase the cyanide?"

"No."

"And did you put the bottle of potassium cyanide in your lower underwear drawer?"

Kim's eyes widened in resentment. She shoved back

her chair and shot up. "No. No, of course not. It's ridiculous. This whole thing is completely stupid and ridiculous. Of course I didn't."

Derek rose, reached for her hand, and drew her back down to her chair. He settled back into his.

Maggie watched them, showing no emotion.

Derek spoke up. "So who planted that cyanide in Kim's drawer? That's what we must find out! Was it somebody in the house? Did the police do it because Ben is so well connected in that town?"

Maggie sat quietly, appraising them both.

Derek sighed audibly. "Can Kim take a polygraph test? Would that help?"

"Polygraphs are inadmissible in New York," Maggie said.

"Will the Grand Jury indict me?" Kim asked nervously.

"I believe they will, yes."

"Should she testify before the Grand Jury?" Derek asked.

"I see no advantage in Kim testifying. The prosecutor will present the evidence and the detectives will corroborate it. They'll say that, basically, Kim was allegedly having a sexual relationship with you, Derek, and that the cyanide bottle was found in Kim's drawer. They'll infer that Ben is paralyzed and is a victim. All Kim can say is, I didn't put the cyanide there and I don't know how it got there. Who is the Grand Jury going to believe? The police or Kim? No, what we need to focus on is bail reduction and the trial."

Kim felt the return of panic. She swallowed hard. "How can we prove that I didn't put the cyanide in my drawer?"

Maggie blinked slowly. "Kim, if you didn't poison

your husband, and if you didn't put the bottle of potassium cyanide in your drawer—and I believe you didn't do either—then we have to try to find out who did. At the very least, we must force the D.A. to prove—beyond any reasonable doubt—that it was you, and only you, who could have poisoned Ben Maxwell. We must convince the jury that there is reasonable doubt that you were not the only person who had the opportunity to poison Ben, regardless of motives."

Kim stared soberly, feeling deflated.

Maggie continued. "We know there were other people in the house who could have put poison in the tea, after the tea was made, and brought it to Ben. Someone else could also have easily planted that cyanide bottle in your drawer. Interestingly, there were no fingerprints on the bottle. None. They seemed to have been wiped clean. Okay, so we will establish a reasonable doubt in the jury members' minds."

Maggie's mouth formed a little wicked smile. "That will be our challenge. And we will make the D.A. jump through a few hoops along the way, because he thinks this will be an easy case."

Maggie shook her head. "No. It will not be an easy case, for any of us."

Kim and Derek exchanged worried glances.

Maggie looked at them sternly. "If bail is posted and Kim is free before the trial, I do not want you two together at any time before the trial. Is that clear? I don't want anyone to see you together. I don't want photos, and I want to minimize the news stories. As far as anyone knows, you have split up. If I can be so blunt: you are dead to each other. Understand?"

They both nodded. Kim's face grew sad and dark. She knew she was just beginning a long nightmare.

CHAPTER 23

On a hot Monday in August, Kim was indicted for the attempted murder of her husband, Ben Maxwell. Judge Brown denied Maggie Stone's motion for bail reduction and so the bail remained at two million dollars.

Now that the Maxwells' joint account had been restored, Kim had one million to post. She didn't have access to more, so she was returned to the Green Township County Jail, where she was to await her trial or stay until she could post the additional one million dollars. Maggie told her not to give up, that if there was any way to raise the one million, Derek would do it.

Derek tried to raise the necessary funds by borrowing from the bank that had helped fund his landscaping business. All the negative publicity, and no doubt Ben Maxwell's influence, had a decisive impact on the bank's decision. Derek was turned down.

Struggling with depression, Derek called Anita and asked her to meet him at The Dock Café for a late lunch.

As they entered the mostly crowded cafe, patrons' eyes immediately locked in on Derek. Conversations died. The music seemed louder. Derek glared boldly into curious faces while some heads lowered and some glanced away. He saw a few smiles of encouragement, one being from the bartender, Skip. Skip waved, and Derek waved back.

Unfortunately, Derek was a local celebrity, and he hated it. Anita and Derek slid into an empty booth, each pulling out their cell phones and scrolling through messages.

Natalie came over with two foaming mugs of beer. She set them down with a firm nod. "Hey Derek. Hey Anita. These are on me."

Derek slanted a look up at her. "You don't need to do that, Natalie."

She glared at him, putting a sassy hand on her hip. "Don't tell me what I need to do. You've got lots of friends around here. Don't forget that."

Derek's eyes softened on her. "Thanks, Natalie. How's Mike?"

"He's been calling you. You haven't been taking his calls. He wants you to know he's your friend no matter what."

"Tell him I don't want my friends involved in all this shit. Tell him, thanks."

Anita took a long sip of the beer. "What have you been hearing, Natalie?"

Natalie leaned in, lowering her voice. "Like most things, it's about half and half." Natalie focused on Derek. "Most people I've talked to don't believe you were involved, Derek. They think it was Kim."

Derek's eyes blazed anger. "Natalie, she was framed. Ben framed us both. He knew we were shacking up, so he set us up. A perfect set-up. The good and generous husband gives his wife two million bucks and a yoga/dance studio. What does this ungrateful slut do? She screws his property manager and tries to murder him with poison, so she can have it all. He got us both, Natalie. That's what he set out to do, and he did it. I've got to hand it to the son of a bitch. It took smarts and guts."

Natalie straightened and placed a gentle hand on his shoulder. "Does she have a good lawyer?"

Derek stared into his beer. "Yeah. The best. But if it goes to the jury… well, who knows."

After they ordered, Natalie moved away, and Derek and Anita got down to business.

"How many clients have we lost total?" Derek asked.

"All but six."

Derek sighed. "Damn. Not good."

"But the six we've got are good," Anita said. "They told me they're staying with us no matter what."

"I got your text about this guy, Matthew Oliver," Derek said. "You said he called yesterday and wants us to do all his landscaping?"

"Yeah. I called him back, and he was like, really direct and blunt, you know. He said, 'Does Derek Gray own this business?' When I said, yes, he said he wants us to do all his landscaping."

Derek slid his hand across his scratchy, day-old stubble. "Isn't he the guy who was tried and acquitted for allegedly killing his wife a couple of years back?"

"I don't know," Anita said.

Derek grabbed his phone, *googled* his name and found hundreds of listings. He tapped on one. "Yeah, here it is. Matthew Jason Oliver was tried for first-degree murder for allegedly drowning his wife. He claimed it was a boating accident. They had been drinking and arguing. He claims he left her and went below. When he returned to the deck, she was gone. He claims she had accidentally fallen overboard. He said he climbed into the tender and searched everywhere for her. Her dead body was found later by the Coast Guard."

"Wasn't there some famous actress who died like that? That woman who did the movie *West Side Story*?" Anita asked.

"Yeah, I forget her name."

"Natalie something," Anita said. "Like Natalie the waitress."

Derek looked up. "Yeah, so anyway, did you go meet the guy?"

"No, he wanted everything done online or over the phone. It's a big property. It's a good account. It will help make up for the ones we lost."

Derek dropped his eyes back to the phone and read aloud. "Oliver was a big hedge fund guy. Paxton Associates. He sold out after the trial and moved here. He seldom leaves his place. The press was hard on him. They beat him up pretty bad."

Derek scrolled down. "Damn… the guy's salary was $640 million. His estimated worth is 3.8 billion dollars."

Derek looked up thoughtfully. Anita appraised him, nodding.

"I think I know what you're thinking, boss," Anita said.

Derek winked at her.

About an hour later, Derek drove his truck in light traffic up Fairview Road. It was another hot August day, and the sun brought record heat and record crowds to Scorpio Beach.

Derek took a right onto Windham Road and drove for a half mile until he came to a secluded area, sheltered by trees. A sign at the entrance of the drive read PRIVATE DRIVE, PRIVATE PROPERTY.

Derek ignored the signs and turned into the driveway. Slowly, he crept ahead until he came to a security gate.

He stopped, stepped out and strolled leisurely to the gate. He noticed a security camera and the cable gate box. He stood there, feeling the weight of the sun on his back and shoulders.

The security camera moved, making a little buzzing sound. Derek stared at it, waiting. He reached for his phone and checked his messages. He had texted Matt Oliver back at The Dock Café to ask if he could come and see him. Oliver had not responded.

Derek waited. The security camera whined as it moved gently from side to side. A moment later, the gate clicked and swung open. Derek quickly jumped behind the steering wheel and drove through the gate. He parked in the circular drive and climbed out.

Matt Oliver's luxury beach house sat high on the cliffs, with a commanding view of the ocean. There were wrap-around stairs, a side patio, decks and skylights. Derek estimated it to have six bedrooms.

He advanced toward the front door and rang the bell. It was a good minute before the door slowly opened and a tall man in his late forties, with short, chestnut brown hair, stood looking back at Derek with suspicious almond eyes, and a cold expression. He wore white Bermuda shorts and a yellow Izod Polo shirt. He seemed reluctant to move.

"What do you want, Derek?" Matt said, in a low business voice.

Derek took off his sunglasses. "I need your help."

The skin tightened around Matt's eyes as he took Derek in. "My help?"

Matt was a good-looking man. A man you associated with the country club set, the polo set, the privileged set, where money flowed as readily and easily as fine wines at a billionaire's wedding. At least, those were Derek's thoughts.

"Yes. Can I talk to you? Just a few minutes. No more."

Matt was motionless while he considered this. Finally, he backed away and Derek entered.

Derek took in the high ceilings, the wrap-around windows with stunning views of the ocean, and the polished wood floors. Matt stood rigid, not offering Derek the opportunity to sit.

"What can I do for you?" Matt asked.

Derek was a proud man. In his entire life, he'd never asked anyone—other than his Ranger buddies—for anything. He fortified his courage with a breath.

"You called my landscaping company. You spoke with Anita."

Matt nodded.

"Maybe you know that I'm losing business because of…" Derek stopped, swallowing. He tried again. "I'm losing business because of the negative news."

Matt didn't speak.

"*You* called. Not one of your employees. You called, when most of my other clients are bailing out, canceling their contracts. People like you don't call landscapers. You have your hired people do it."

"Is that why you came, Derek? To find out why my hired staff didn't call you?

"I'm sure you know my story, Mr. Oliver."

Matt made a dark, sad smile. "I know your story. I don't go out much, but I keep informed about what's going on around here."

"Okay, then I came to thank you. I need the business."

"You're welcome."

Derek struggled with words. His forehead knotted into a frown. "There's another reason I came. I came because… well, because I need money. I need a loan."

Matt stood expressionless, his eyes steady, revealing nothing.

Derek felt the weight of the moment, just as he had before he was going into a hostile environment in Afghanistan. He sensed he'd made a mistake. It had been a stupid, desperate act, but then it was the only tactic, the only action he could think of. He had to get Kim out of that damned jail.

Matt turned and left the room. Derek waited, perplexed. He glanced about at the sun-heavy room. A few minutes later, Matt returned with a crystal whiskey glass, partially filled with a sun-brown liquid. He handed it to Derek.

"Drink it down. It's good. It's Blanton's, a single barrel Bourbon."

Derek took the glass, uncertain. "You're not having one?"

"No, I stopped drinking. I've had the bottle for a couple of years. It's still good and I need to get rid of it. Go ahead, drink it straight down."

Derek downed the whiskey in one quick swallow. It was sharp and warm sliding down his throat. Matt took the glass, staring at it.

"How much, Derek?"

Derek paused. "I need to get her out on bail. Kim. I need to get Kim out of jail. The bail is two million. We have one."

"So you need a million dollars?"

Derek met Matt's eyes, unblinking. "Yes, sir, that's what I need. I went to a bail bondsman. They want ten percent. That's a hundred thousand dollars. I can't even raise that. The bank turned me down, but then they would, things being what they are."

Matt sniffed the glass. "I used to drink a lot of this bourbon, Derek, before my wife died. But that seems so long ago. A lifetime ago. Maybe more than a lifetime ago."

Matt smiled, and it was curiously unpleasant. "I had drunk too much that night. So had she. Della. I always loved her name, Della. You don't hear that name anymore. I called her by her full name sometimes. Delphine. That's a nice name, isn't it?"

Derek noticed that Matt was staring at something far away. His voice was low, almost at a whisper.

"Yeah, that's a nice name."

Matt's attention seemed to return to the room. "Well, anyway she drowned. Did I already tell you that?"

"No, sir. But I read about it before I came over."

Matt nodded. "Yes… well it was big news back then. Like yours is big news today, and will be big news for a long time. And then it will pass, people will move on to another sensational story and it will mostly be forgotten. So goes the world."

Matt looked into Derek's eyes. "And when you read about Della and me, what did you think? Guilty? Innocent?"

"I'm no judge. If I judge you, I have to judge myself. I don't want to do that."

Matt raised his glass as if to toast. "Good answer, Derek. Della and I had both drunk too much that night. In fact, we drank too much most nights."

Derek listened, feeling acid pool in his stomach. If Matt didn't post the bail, he had nowhere else to turn. Matt seemed lost in his own personal hell.

Matt canted his head to one side. "Is she worth it, Derek?"

"You mean Kim?"

Matt's gaze was direct. "Yes. Is Kim innocent?"

"Yes, sir. She's innocent. She's being framed."

Matt considered that. "And you want to save her?"

"I want to free her. Help her. Yes."

"How many tours in Afghanistan did you do?"

"Three."

Matt lowered his eyes. "I've never done anything quite so noble. I read that you received a Purple Heart, among other medals."

"Yes…"

Matt waited for more, but Derek didn't offer more.

"Do you have a good attorney?"

"Yes. She's good."

"Do you love Kim?"

Derek was startled a little by the question. He glanced away, considering it.

"Do you have to think about it?" Matt asked.

"Yes, sir, I do love her, and I can't stand to think of her in that damned jail."

Matt turned and left the room again. This time, he returned with two glasses of whiskey. He handed one to Derek. Staring at the one in his hand, he shook his head.

"First drink I've had in two years. I've been secluded in this big old beach house like a hermit for too long. And you know what, Derek? I haven't done one damned good thing for anybody in a very long time."

He raised his glass, and Derek touched it with his.

"Let's drink to women, Derek. They're wonderful and mysterious, and they break our hearts. But we love them, don't we? Yes, we do love them."

Each man swallowed the whiskey down. Matt winced. "Wow… that's better than I remember."

He looked at Derek pointedly. "You'll have your

money, Derek. Kim will post her bail, but I don't want anyone, ever, to know where the money came from. Do you understand? No one."

Derek nodded. "No one will ever know. I promise… Thank you… Thank you, sir."

CHAPTER 24

Kim was released on bail two days after Derek's meeting with Matt. Her bail instructions included her living close to Scorpio Beach, with the police having easy access to her at all times. She could not leave the state for any reason, and she had to report any travel within the state, listing phone numbers and names.

Kim found a modest, one-bedroom apartment in Brandy Beach, a small town five miles from Scorpio Beach, and settled in, living a quiet, simple life. Her trial date was set for February 24 of the following year. She met with Maggie on several occasions during the fall and winter, while Maggie slowly worked the case, gathering evidence, taking depositions and sifting through countless pages of evidence and testimony.

Derek did not contact Kim, and she stayed away from him. Kim lived off the money from her own private account, leaving her apartment only when necessary, for groceries, a doctor's visit, and twice to go to the movies, the last show of the night.

Autumn came with sharp gusts and storms, blowing the birds and gulls to seek shelter inland, away from the beach. Winter brought snow and bitter cold winds that moaned and rattled her windows. Kim read, watched TV and paced. Each minute seemed endless, each hour lonely, each night, punishing, as if she were awaiting the steady footsteps of an approaching executioner. Her dreams were filled with dark, foul-smelling jail cells and mad women screaming for help. Ben was in most of her nightmares—he rose from his wheelchair in one dream, dancing about and laughing manically, jabbing a sharp, accusing finger at her, shouting that she was going to die.

On a few occasions, her dancer friends came by and they laughed, smoked, got drunk and stumbled and tumbled while doing some old routines. Those were the best days and nights, and Kim always looked forward to them.

Some nights Kim drove for hours, to nowhere, struggling to calm her nerves and clear her head. One bitterly cold night, she drove through Scorpio Beach and was amazed at the quiet, solemn emptiness of the place. It appeared like the exterior set for some Hollywood movie, waiting for the actors to take their places. When she drove past the yoga studio, her heart sank. It had closed. Then she had to pull over because her eyes had filled with tears. It was as if her entire life had been closed down and she was waiting for the end of things.

On New Year's Eve, Maggie called her.

"How are you holding up, Kim?"

Kim was sipping a glass of cheap champagne that her friend, Denise, had brought over. Kim had been invited to a number of parties, but she just couldn't get up the energy to go to any. She felt like a part of herself was dying.

"I'm on hold, as always," Kim said.

"Don't lose hope, Kim. We've got a good case. We'll be ready for trial by February 24. Kim, I know we've discussed this before, but I need to contact your old family friends. I want them at the trial. I want them dressed conservatively and I want them sitting close to us. Now, have you spoken with your mother again? Did you convince her to come?"

"She said she'd come, but I told her not to. I told her I couldn't stand for her to sit there and watch all the shit that's going to come down on me. She's so broken up already, Maggie. She's had a difficult life and then this."

Maggie pressed on. "She needs to be in that courtroom... and your brother. Kim, both need to be there. It is very important. Please, tell them to come."

"She's not well, Maggie. I've told you. She has a bad heart. If things go wrong, I'm afraid it will kill her."

Maggie took a breath. "I respect that, Kim. I do... But..."

Kim cut her off. "I'm not going to ask them, Maggie. My brother said he could come for some of the trial. But he has to work. He has a family. I have friends who want to come, my dancer friends."

"No, Kim. Listen to me. Neither the jury nor the press needs to see an entire row of your sexy Broadway dancer friends. That will work for the prosecution, but not for us. We need your mother and brother."

Kim shrank a little. "Okay... I'll call some of my mother's friends. Maybe I can get them to come."

"Okay... Okay. Do what you can... and don't worry. We are going to give the D.A. a fight he's never seen, so hang in there. And happy new year!"

"Yeah... you too, Maggie. Happy new year."

It was just after two o'clock in the morning when Kim jerked awake and raised up. She heard a noise—a foreign sound. It wasn't the wind. It was a creaking sound. Fear burned her chest. She swallowed slowly, straining her ears. Nothing.

Her phone "blinged," and it was loud in the silence. She flinched. The phone lay on the night table next to the bed. She reached for it. To her surprise, it was Derek.

"It's me. Don't be scared. I'm here. I'm coming into the bedroom. Don't turn on the light."

Kim felt a desperate relief. A sudden exhilaration.

Then there he was. A large silhouette framed in the doorway. He slowly advanced toward her, stopping at the foot of the bed. Kim waited, feeling life pumping up through her loins and chest, feeling unsteady and thrilled.

Neither spoke. The room was alive with quiet. Kim could hear her breath. Derek slowly began to undress. His gloves, ski cap, his heavy coat. When he was naked, he drifted toward the side of the bed. In the pale glow from the night light, Kim stared at him, desire rising.

"Lotion?" he whispered.

She leaned over, opened the top drawer of her night table and took out a plastic bottle. She handed it to him. Derek squirted a worm of it into his hands and rubbed them together, building heat.

"Turn over," he told her.

She did so. Kim felt the bed give as Derek eased onto it, swung a leg over her ass and straddled her. He pulled the sheet down to her lower back and squeezed out more of the lotion into his hands. He rubbed his hands, building the friction, and then gently began to knead the muscles of her back and shoulders and the nape of her neck. Kim sighed, as the tension began to melt under Derek's strong, clever fingers.

Derek's soothing hands both stroked the tension from her and built a sexual stress that stirred her passion.

And then she turned over and they kissed, their

mouths changing and yielding with soft, heated sighs.

They made love, tenderly, nothing rushed or urgent.

Later, they lay close, hands clasped, breathing softly, not speaking, as a night wind whispered around the house and Kim fell into a relaxed, easy sleep.

When she awoke, she glanced at her night clock. She'd been asleep for only a half hour. Derek was next to her, his breathing easy, his body warm next to hers. She kissed him awake, and they played and laughed.

Kim swung out of bed, slipped into a robe and padded into the kitchen. She soon returned with two glasses of champagne. She handed one to Derek and sat down beside him on the edge of the bed. They touched glasses and drank slowly, their eyes meeting again and again, saying everything that needed to be said. Once the glasses were drained, Derek lay back, staring up at the ceiling, with an arm resting under his head.

"What were you like as a kid?" Derek asked.

"Skinny, shy. I ate lots of Snickers."

"The candy bar?"

"Yeah… I loved Snickers. Still do."

Derek laughed. "Who doesn't like Snickers? I ate a lot of them overseas."

Moments later, Derek placed an arm over his forehead. "You must have had guys falling in love with you right and left," he said, tilting his head and looking up at her as she stared down at him.

Her hair was mussed, her breasts firm and lovely in the dim light.

"Actually, I was sort of ugly. Skinny, with glasses and crooked teeth. Boys called me spindle legs, and bug-eyed alien."

"Really? I don't believe it."

"I took dance lessons two days a week, but I never had

a boy to dance with until Kent Powell moved to town. He was fifteen, and he was openly gay, even then. We did dance routines together and became friends. He's a choreographer on Broadway now. Does a lot of the big shows."

"Who was your first boyfriend?"

"I was in love with a guy named Bobby. Bobby Harmon. He played on the little league baseball team. He wouldn't even look at me though."

Derek pushed up on elbows. "What happened to you?"

"I was an ugly duckling. When I turned thirteen, my body began to change. My mother saved her money and got braces for my teeth. I got contacts, and I started filling out in all the right places."

Derek nodded, smiling. "Oh yeah. You definitely filled out in all the right places."

"When I was sixteen, Bobby Harmon came strutting down the hallway and, just as he was about to pass me, he stopped flat. He was a year older than me and one of the most handsome and popular guys in school. He looked me over and said, 'Hey, Kim Ryan, what happened to you? You're gorgeous. You've got to go out with me.' I looked him over, lifted my chin, made my face look superior and I said, 'No thanks, Bobby, I've got better things to do than to go out with you.'"

Derek laughed again. "Good for you, Kim. Good for you."

After their laughter died away, Kim drifted down and kissed Derek. She hovered over his face, studied it. The shape, the eyes, the lean jaw.

"And what were you like as a kid?"

Derek turned thoughtful. "Got into trouble a lot. My father beat me, that is, when he was home. I stole things from stores, just for the fun of it. Started drinking when I was fourteen years old. Took drugs for a while until a friend of mine overdosed and died. Then I never touched the stuff again. Dated the bad girls, just to piss my mother off, until I found out she didn't care. Hated school. Grades were bad."

He looked at her pensively. "I wasn't a very nice guy, Kim. I got a woman pregnant when I was sixteen. She was ten years older, and she was married. I ran around with a lot of married women. I didn't care. I looked older, and I wasn't bad to look at."

Kim stroked his hair and traced the bridge of his nose. "Such a bad boy… Derek. Certainly not bad to look at. But definitely a beautiful bad boy."

"Then I joined the Rangers. They kicked the living shit out of me. They pushed me to the max. For sixty-one days I survived on one meal a day and a few hours of sleep a night. I lost twenty-five pounds. It was intense. Only about a third of the candidates made it. I thought I was tough, but I barely made it. I just kept thinking about my father kicking me around and my crazy mother running around with some loser. I knew I couldn't go back to that, and I wasn't about to fail. So I made it. I got the Ranger Tab. After that, I took a Special Forces Sniper Course. Then I went into combat."

"Did you kill many people?"

"That was my job. They were the bad guys. Some had slaughtered women and children. Some were terrorists."

Kim lightly touched his scar. "Did it hurt when you were wounded?"

"Yeah, it hurt."

"What did you think about?"

"After I was hit?"

"Yes."

"Not much. I thought I might die."

"Did it scare you?"

"No… I was strangely calm. I just thought about my buddies. I didn't want to let them down. I wanted to be there for them. I wanted them to live. They had become my family, the only real family I'd ever had."

"How long were you in the hospital?"

"Weeks… It seems like a bad dream now."

Derek shut his eyes, as if suddenly tired.

Kim kissed him gently on the face and lips.

"Derek… I love you."

His eyes didn't open. There was a long, serene silence. When he spoke, his voice was soft and tender. "You're the best thing that's ever happened to me, Kim. The very best thing. I'm not going to lose you."

"No, my love. You'll never lose me."

Kim awoke when the first dim light of dawn crept into her bedroom window. She was immediately aware that she was alone. Instinctively, she felt for Derek. The sheets were cool. He'd been gone for a while. Surely he'd left before dawn, so there'd be no chance of anyone seeing him come or go.

Kim lay back and sank into memories of Derek, their love-making and their talk. Derek had been there for her when she'd needed him. He loved her. She knew now that he loved her. He'd somehow raised the money for bail, although he wouldn't say how he did it.

She also knew that he'd been watching her, and that he would always watch her and protect her, no matter what happened. If she had to go to prison, she knew he'd be there for her when she got out and, if there was any way to get her free, Derek would find a way.

Would he return before the trial? How awful she felt

when they weren't together. How lonely and isolated. She felt complete when he was with her, inside her, kissing her, talking to her; when they were lost in each other's bodies and each other's eyes.

Derek had opened her to a love that surprised, expanded and excited her. He had opened her to true love. How could she live without him? Would she have to?

CHAPTER 25

Monday, February 24, dawned clear, cold and calm. From the previous night's snowfall, a thin layer of snow etched the trees and gleamed off cars and lawns.

In his office, Ben Maxwell stared woodenly out to sea. His mind was filled with thoughts of sweet aggression, and he felt the satisfaction of inevitable revenge.

Maggie arose early, showered and dressed, ordered room service and read over her opening statement. She wanted it to be short and direct. The opening statement is often one of the most important moments in a trial. The jury gets to see you and hear you and form a first impression about you and the defendant. Above all, the jury must like you and be drawn into your outrage and your passion for the case.

Derek took a five-mile jog on the beach to calm his nerves. He wore a sweatshirt, ski cap and sweatpants, and kept his pace steady and close to the sea, where he watched waves arch, fall and spread across the sand. In the weeks leading up to the trial, he'd often kept watch over Kim's apartment. That morning he'd seen the reporters. He used binoculars to sweep the area just in case there were any nuts hanging around, but he hadn't seen any. He saw the police. Maggie must have called them.

As he ran, he felt the cold sea air burn his throat and lungs. He felt the sharp wind sting his face and the tops of his ears. He didn't care. His anger at Ben was acute. His hatred for the man's evil, unthinkable, malicious plan was unrelenting.

Several times Derek imagined himself with his M110 rifle and the sniper-spotting scope. He could set it up on the beach out of sight and wait for Ben to appear in his office window or out on the patio. The M110 has a semi-auto action and a 10 or 15-round magazine. But Derek would need only one shot. He'd be camouflaged and hidden. He would take Ben out in one clean shot right between his eyes.

After the shot, he'd slip away into shadows, leaving no footprints, no cartridges and no trace. He'd done it many times, both in training and in the field. There would be no witnesses and no murder weapon. He'd destroy the rifle, and no one would ever be able to prove he had killed the bastard.

Then he and Kim would be free. They would be free of that sick son of a bitch.

The cops would come for him, yes, but proof? Never.

Colin loped along beside Derek, his pink happy tongue flapping, his joyous open mouth puffing out white vapor. Derek thought, "*If things go bad, Ben is a dead man.*"

Kim paced her room, having managed to sleep for only two hours. Reporters were gathered outside, waiting to descend on her the moment Maggie's car arrived. In the past week, Kim had received over seventy letters, many from women supporting her, but there were many others from anonymous sickos, who wrote things like "Killer Bitch Die!" and "Devil Slut Dancer, Burn in Hell!"

She would have to move now that the trial was starting, and the online news and newspapers were once again hot for the story. Kim had packed a suitcase. Maggie had found a place for them both until the trial was over, and she had been guaranteed police protection.

As Kim envisioned the coming trial, she had difficulty breathing. She couldn't eat breakfast. She couldn't drink coffee. She drank a glass of wine and swayed unsteadily as if she might faint. She grabbed hold of the kitchen counter to brace herself. She prayed for strength to make it through the trial without completely breaking down. She prayed that her mother would survive the trial and that her brother, Scott, wouldn't go ballistic and wind up in jail himself. He'd told Kim before the wedding that he didn't like or trust Ben. Well, Scott had been right—not that he'd thrown it up in her face. His anger was directed only at Ben.

The Scorpio County courtroom had a classic quality to it, with wood-paneled walls and solid oak counsel tables, podiums and benches. All one hundred available seats in the audience were occupied. Seated in the front row were five of Derek's former Ranger buddies, two of whom were still in active service. They sat erect and stoic, wearing their dress blue uniforms, complete with the Ranger patch and various medals, including the Bronze Star for Meritorious Service, Medals for Valor and the Purple Heart.

Next to them sat Kim's mother and brother. Mrs. Mary Ryan was a fragile, snow-crested woman, whose sad eyes took in the surroundings with apprehension and fear. She sat proudly erect, struggling to project strength in the midst of the coming storm.

Kim's brother, Scott, sat in defiance, his thick arms crossed, his pale blue eyes locked ahead, waiting impatiently for the trial to begin. His short brown hair, rigid expression and strong face gave the impression of a formidable Irish street fighter.

Ben's friends were in the second row, the men stately and distinguished in their expensive suits, and the women in designer clothes, immaculately polished with expressions of superior blandness.

Next to them sat Ben's only daughter from his first marriage, Rachel Cox Kraft, and her husband, Dr. Edward Kraft. At 36 years old, Rachel was not a beauty, but her long toffee hair, glittering green eyes and regal manner added a look of intelligence and breeding. Dr. Kraft was an ENT, a short owlish-looking man who had the stern demeanor of a high school principal.

Kim had never met Rachel, nor had she ever spoken with her. Rachel did not attend the wedding and she and her father seldom spoke. When they did, the conversation was strained and formal. Rachel had sided with her mother during the divorce, considering her father a selfish, egotistical man and a lousy father.

So it was somewhat of a surprise that she'd appeared to show support for a father she had little respect for and hadn't seen in years.

Maggie attributed it to Ben's fortune. He had almost died. Perhaps if Rachel showed concern and support during this difficult time, he would remember her in his will. It was only speculation of course, but Maggie had seen this kind of thing before. She wasn't surprised, and she'd done her homework on Ben's two previous marriages.

The remaining audience consisted of additional friends on both sides, curious spectators and the press. There was a sedate hum of low conversation until Kim entered the courtroom, escorted by the bailiff. The room fell into watchful silence.

Kim had changed her hairstyle, based on Maggie's instructions. It was cut shorter in the front and longer in the back. It was pushed away from her face naturally, and it muted some of her natural sensuality. She wore a modest, charcoal gray, long-sleeve pleated dress with a high neck line, and low-heeled black shoes. Derek was surprised to see Kim wearing glasses, another of Maggie's suggestions. They were oval shaped, with copper/bronze frames, and they also helped diminish Kim's appeal, giving her a more intellectual appearance. Her make-up was light, lipstick faint, and she wore no jewelry. Kim sat beside Maggie at the counsel table. Maggie smiled at her, leaning, whispering something.

Maggie was wearing a smart black business suit, with a silver-gray blouse. Her hair was longer, and she wore it in a slightly layered bob that flattered and softened her face. Maggie made an effort to smile often and to appear cool and confident. She'd learned long ago that a smile did more for one's appearance than nearly anything else. A smile was good at the beginning of a trial. At the end, you presented a serious confidence.

Behind the prosecution counsel table was Baxter Cahill, his assistant, Marla Pelts, and Ben Maxwell, seated in his electronic wheelchair. Mr. Cahill wore a dark Armani suit, white shirt and burgundy tie. Marla Pelts, a very attractive 30-year-old brunette, appeared all attorney in her dark business suit, pert manner and designer black-framed glasses. They too had watched Kim's entrance into the courtroom. Baxter's expression was flat, Marla's curious, Ben's dark and brooding.

The twelve-person jury filed in and took their seats, glancing about the courtroom. There were seven men and five women, their ages ranging from twenty-three to sixty-two. Some appeared nervous, some preoccupied with their thoughts, others sat stiffly, waiting, their eyes shifting, feeling the pressure of the moment and the burden of their job.

When Judge Thomas Brown entered, dressed in his dark robe, the bailiff shouted "All rise" and the entire courtroom rose to its feet.

After the charges were read, Baxter Cahill stood, strolled toward the jury and began his opening statement. He stared into the distance, allowing all eyes to fall on him—and wait with anticipation. He licked his lips and turned his bold stomach to the jury.

Kim felt a network of nerves beginning to fray, and she inadvertently tightened her buttock muscles. And then she felt a rolling in her stomach, a queasy seasick fear. The nightmare trial was about to begin.

Baxter Cahill started it off. "Good morning, ladies and gentlemen. This case is about a greedy, selfish, unfaithful wife, who tried to poison and kill her generous, loving and wheelchair-bound husband, my client, Ben Maxwell. Why did she want to kill him? Simple. It's the oldest story in the world, ladies and gentlemen. It's easy to grasp and understand. The defendant, Kim Ryan, was having an affair with another man. She coldly decided to kill her husband to get him out of the way, so she could have her lover and Ben's money too. Sound familiar? Have your cake and eat it too? Yes. Simple. Greed and passion. Not difficult to understand, is it?"

Baxter Cahill moved in closer, with a solemn expression and the countenance of a minister. "Marriage is about love, honor and trust, isn't it? It's sacred. We, as a civilized society, honor marriage and we celebrate it. It is a special bond. It is a good and worthy partnership. It is blessed. It is a trust." Baxter turned to Ben. "Ben Maxwell trusted the wrong woman to share his life with."

Baxter faced the jury again. "On Thursday, July 27, Ben Maxwell almost died from a heart attack because he was slowly and willfully being poisoned with potassium cyanide. Potassium cyanide is a white, colorless crystalline salt, similar in appearance to sugar. Ben was being poisoned with small doses of cyanide that was being added to the green tea he drank for his health. His doctor had prescribed it. His doctor told both Ben and his wife, the defendant, Kim Maxwell, that it would help lower Ben's cholesterol and be good for his heart. The defendant heard all of this. The defendant, Kim Maxwell, followed the doctor's good advice, except for one small thing. She put potassium cyanide in the green tea. She placed it there so she could kill her husband.

"Now we are going to prove that it was the defendant, Mrs. Kim Ryan Maxwell, who not only brewed the green tea, but who also, regularly, over a period of days or weeks, brought the tea to him every afternoon, with the sole intention of killing him.

"During this trial, we will present evidence, motive, opportunity and access. We will prove, without a reasonable doubt, that the defendant, Kim Maxwell, did plan and execute the willful intention to kill her husband, by systematically poisoning him by placing potassium cyanide in his green tea."

Baxter looked each juror in the eyes. "You will have no doubt about this after we present the evidence and the witnesses. By the end of this trial you will have no doubts about the cold, willful attempt of the defendant, Kim Ryan Maxwell, to kill her husband because of greed and passion. You will have no doubts. Thank you, ladies and gentlemen."

After Baxter sat down, Maggie Stone slowly got to her feet. She stood behind the counsel table for a moment as if deep in thought. She gazed ahead, and all eyes stuck on her, waiting. Finally, she turned toward the jury.

"Good morning, ladies and gentlemen of the jury. My client, Kim Ryan Maxwell, would not, could not and *did* not place potassium cyanide in Ben Maxwell's, her husband's, green tea. She is not greedy because she has no reason to be and it is not in her nature. In fact, she was a self-sufficient and successful woman long before she met Mr. Maxwell. She made plenty of money, and she can continue to make plenty of money doing what she loves, what she has worked for and what she has been celebrated for. Furthermore, Kim has her own private accounts. If she is passionate, that is not a crime. Many consider passion to be a worthy attribute. Some say it is absolutely necessary in one's career and marriage."

Maggie left the table and approached the jury. "Ladies and gentlemen, there are two kinds of evidence: direct evidence and circumstantial evidence. Direct evidence is the testimony of persons who have seen, heard or felt the thing or things about which they are testifying. They are telling you something which they have observed or perceived with their senses. For instance, if a person came before you and testified that he or she saw the defendant drop potassium cyanide into green tea and hand it to someone to drink without their knowledge of the poison being in the tea, that is direct evidence; that points directly to the defendant and to the crime itself."

Maggie lingered, as if thinking it through herself. Actually, she was allowing the jury to rest their minds and take in the words. She clasped her hands behind her back as she continued.

"Circumstantial evidence is entirely different. Completely different. In this case, there is not one bit of direct evidence, from start to finish, against Kim Maxwell.

No one saw anything. No one witnessed anything. No one perceived anything directly with their senses. There is no connection, other than hearsay or speculation, that connects Kim to the poison in any way, shape or fashion. You will not hear one shred of direct testimony in this case connecting Kim with this crime. It is wholly and absolutely circumstantial."

Maggie turned away for a moment, focusing her hard eyes directly at Ben Maxwell. He glared back at her.

"To suggest that Kim is capable of this crime is, frankly, an injustice and an outrage."

Maggie whirled back to the jury. "Was Kim the only person in that house when Ben Maxwell was poisoned? No, she was not. People were coming and going all the time. Was she the only one who had access to the green tea, to the teapot, to the poison? No, she was not! Did she even have a motive to kill her husband? No, she loved him, as we will show. Is there a reason why Kim is singled out to be the only possible suspect in this crime?"

Maggie narrowed her eyes and let the silence and anticipation build. "Yes. Yes, there is. Now, as to the potassium cyanide. There is no evidence to connect Kim in any way to the poison. There is no evidence to support that Kim either bought the poison or at any time acquired the poison. It is all purely circumstantial. Circumstantial, ladies and gentlemen. It is not direct evidence. The case against Kim is a flimsy one, with flimsy, unsubstantiated evidence. Maybe it is easy, dramatic and convenient to try Kim for this crime, but there is no evidence, whatsoever, to support it. Please keep this in mind, ladies and gentlemen: the prosecution must prove—beyond any reasonable doubt—that Kim attempted to kill her husband by poisoning him. You have to be satisfied beyond a reasonable doubt… beyond *any* reasonable doubt."

CHAPTER 26

Kim sat stiffly, listening to the prosecution's expert witness discuss potassium cyanide. Her pulse surged at times. Her hands were cold and damp. She could only half swallow, and she had to take sips of water to relieve her dry throat and cool her nerves.

She had difficulty taking in the expert's words. He spoke with depth and dryness, each word coming at her like a rebuke, like an accusation.

Kim watched Maggie scratch notes on her legal pad. She watched the Judge lean and stare and shift in his seat. She watched the grim-looking female court reporter hover over her stenotype machine like a hawk, tapping out the endless flow of words. It all had a surreal quality to it, as if Kim were watching it on TV. She kept thinking of the highly politicized trial in the musical *Chicago*.

The cyanide expert was a tall, thin man with a long neck, beady eyes and a green bow tie fixed to his throat. He reminded Kim of a stage manager at the Ambassador Theatre, the Broadway theater where'd she danced in *Chicago*.

What was the stage manager's name? Yes, Calvin.... Chester Calvin. Yes, they called him CC. *"Good, Kim," she thought to herself. "Let your mind think of other things for a while and give yourself a break from this nightmare. You don't understand what the hell this expert witness is saying, anyway.*"

The expert slipped off his glasses, nibbling on the end of one stem, pensively, happy to be in the spotlight and blabbing out all his paid-for-by-the-D.A. knowledge.

"Potassium cyanide is a compound with the formula KCN. It is a colorless crystalline salt, similar in appearance to sugar, and it is highly soluble in water. Most KCN is used in gold mining, organic synthesis and electroplating. To a lesser degree, it is used in jewelry for chemical gilding and buffing.

"KCN is highly toxic. The moist solid emits small amounts of hydrogen cyanide due to hydrolysis, which smells like bitter almonds. Not everyone, however, can smell this; the ability to do so is a genetic trait."

Baxter Cahill was looking at the jury as he asked the next question. "Dr. Calvin, what is the lethal dose of potassium cyanide?"

Dr. Calvin did not hesitate. "The lethal dose for potassium cyanide is 200–300mg. Its toxicity when ingested depends on the acidity of the stomach, because it must react with an acid to become hydrogen cyanide, the deadly form of cyanide."

"And in your expert opinion, Doctor, how many doses was Ben Maxwell given before the onset of his heart attack?"

"That is difficult to say with any certainty. We have only the one sample from the teapot that was retrieved by the detectives. If we go by Mr. Maxwell's complaints in the week before his heart attack, those symptoms being weakness, headaches, perceived difficulty breathing, all culminating in cardiac arrest, a fatal dose for humans can be as low as 1.5mg/kg body weight. We found lower amounts of the cyanide in the sample from the teapot. So, I would say, Mr. Maxwell could have received the poison for as long as two weeks or as short as a few days."

On cross examination, Maggie approached him slowly. She let the silence grow.

"Dr. Calvin, based on your expert opinion and the analysis of the tainted green tea in the pot, could someone have administered the poison only once? I mean, could Ben Maxwell have had the near fatal heart attack with only one application of the cyanide in the green tea?"

Dr. Calvin twisted up his lips. "Well… that's difficult, again, based on the limited number of samples."

Maggie moved in on him. "But is it possible that that one single application of the potassium cyanide could have brought on Mr. Maxwell's heart attack?"

"Well, we did test Mr. Maxwell for his stomach acidity. It is quite high, which would suggest a more rapid onset."

"So, again, in your expert opinion, is it possible that one single dose could have caused Mr. Maxwell's heart attack? Yes or no."

Mr. Calvin cleared his throat and moved his lips. "Well, I suppose that…"

"Yes or no, Dr. Calvin?"

"Well, if you put it that way, I would say, yes."

Maggie pivoted. "Thank you, doctor."

Baxter sprang up. "Dr. Calvin, it is documented by Nurse Carson that Ben did have symptoms of cyanide poisoning at least one week before the onset. You saw that report, didn't you?"

"Yes."

"And as an expert, do you agree that Ben Maxwell's symptoms were consistent with potassium cyanide poisoning?"

"Yes."

"Thank you, doctor."

Kim whispered to Maggie. "What was that about?"

Maggie was blinking, her mind working. She whispered back. "I want to establish that anyone in the house could have poisoned Ben in one single dose and not over a long period of time. It helps broaden the field."

There were more experts, and when Kim gathered the courage to glance over at the jury, most seemed bored. Two broke into yawns. The experts droned on.

Maggie asked the experts only a few additional questions for clarification, preferring to listen and take notes.

By the end of the first day, Kim was exhausted. She and Maggie had to descend the courthouse steps, pushing through a swarming crowd of reporters who shouted questions and thrust video cameras, cell phones and digital recorders toward them.

Kim and Maggie piled into the waiting car, and the hired driver whipped the car away from the curb and sped off to a new, undisclosed location that Maggie had secured for them.

Kim's new home was a small, two-bedroom house, tucked away among trees and high hedges, with a clear view of the sea from the back windows. Maggie would occupy the lower floor and Kim the upper. Two policemen were posted: one at the entrance to the driveway and one at the house. Maggie did not tell Kim that she had received additional death threats. Maggie had received a few herself. It wasn't the first time in her career.

The living room was the most spacious room in the house, furnished with a worn paisley couch, an armchair, a recliner, and a rickety coffee table. It also had a functional fireplace with logs piled up beside it. Maggie built a fire and then unpacked and called out for dinner.

After a dinner of pizza, salad and wine, Maggie and Kim sat staring at each other from across the Formica table they had carried into the living room to be close to the fire. As it hissed and popped, Maggie leaned back and swirled her glass of wine.

"I tried to send your mother home, Kim. She wouldn't go."

Kim looked down. "No, she wouldn't. She told me nothing or no one could convince her to go. She looks terrible. So pale and scared."

"Your brother, Scott, is intense. I thought he was going to jump over the railing and punch old Baxter Cahill a couple of times."

Kim smiled. "We were very close when we were kids. He always stuck up for me."

"How do you feel?"

"Tired. Very tired."

Maggie took a sip of her wine, lifted her head toward the ceiling and gathered a thought. "Kim… the D.A. will put Ben on the stand."

Kim swallowed. When she spoke, her voice was small, child-like. "Yeah, I guess he will."

"They're going to play up your relationship… your affair with Derek. They have those photos that show you two kissing… touching."

Kim's head was lowered. She just nodded.

"Like I told you before, it will be ugly."

Kim continued nodding.

Maggie said, "Ben's first two marriages were rocky, at best. He was abusive to his first wife. Did you know that?"

Kim lifted her eyes. "No… He never really spoke about her."

"He slapped her around. Knocked her down. Threatened her. He often accused her of having an affair behind his back."

Kim's eyes held questions. "He only told me they weren't compatible."

"She was nineteen, and *he* was twenty-three. The truth was, he was having the affairs and then blaming her. That came out in a police report when Ben had beaten her so badly, she wound up in the hospital. He spent time in jail."

Kim's eyes widened. "I didn't know that."

"It was a pattern with him. The same thing happened to his second wife. There was abuse. I'm telling you all this for a reason. And you knew none of it?"

Kim sank in her seat. "No."

"Did Ben ever strike you?"

Kim hesitated.

"Did he?"

"Once, after he'd drunk too much. He accused me of having an affair with an old boyfriend. It all happened before the accident that paralyzed him."

"Do you know for certain he was trying to kill himself, or was it an accident that the car jumped off the road and hit the trees?"

Kim inhaled a painful breath. She shut her eyes. "I don't know, Maggie. I don't know anything anymore. I thought he loved me. I thought I loved him. I don't know. Everything is just so mixed up and crazy."

"Okay… never mind," Maggie said soothingly. "It's water under the bridge anyway."

Kim looked at Maggie intently. "Are you going to bring all this up at the trial? All this stuff about Ben's past marriages?"

Maggie stared frankly. "I was going to. I wanted to. The D.A. objected, and the Judge ruled in his favor.

Judge Brown ruled that it was not relevant to this case."

Kim's forehead wrinkled up in distress. "I don't understand. But it is relevant, isn't it? What Ben did to his wives. That he slapped me and knocked me down."

"But you never went to the police or filed a police report, did you?"

Kim shook her head. "No... he swore it would never happen again. I did threaten to leave him if he ever did it again. Jesus, how this all must sound. But he tried to kill me—or both of us—when he was driving like a crazy man; after he'd accused me of something I didn't do. I didn't do anything until I met Derek. I didn't want to fall in love with him, but I did. Goddamnit! Ben had pushed me away. He was so angry all the time and abusive. I was like his servant. He just wanted to punish me for something he did to himself. I kept thinking he'd come around or something. And then after I met Derek, I was going to leave Ben. Divorce him. I wish to God I had."

Maggie's voice was surprisingly calm. "I know, Kim. I know. It's okay."

Kim shook her head. "Oh hell, who am I kidding? I probably would have fallen in love with Derek anyway and screwed up my marriage. We're perfect together. We're meant for each other..."

Kim put her face in her hands as her voice fell into sorrow. "Look what I've done. God forgive me for what I've done."

"Stop beating yourself up, Kim. We're all human. Things happen. The point is, you didn't try to kill Ben. That's what we need to focus on. Save your energy for that, and that alone."

Kim dropped her hands from her face. "I still don't understand why the jury can't know about Ben's past marriages. About his abuse. Can't you question Ben about it?"

"Not if the Judge has ruled against it. It's inadmissible. My hands are tied. The jury will never know anything about Ben's past marriages or the abuse. Nothing."

Kim slowly pushed up from the table, still hunched over, struggling with the truth.

"I just don't understand."

"It's the way the law works, Kim. The Judge is a prosecutor's judge. He lives and works in Scorpio County."

Kim was dazed and limp. "How could I have been in love with Ben? It all seems so clear now, but why didn't I see it then? What the hell's the matter with me?"

"Kim, sit down. Please, sit down."

Kim lowered herself with an effort.

"I told you this, so you'd know where we stand."

"And where do we stand, Maggie? It doesn't sound so good to me."

"We are fine, Kim. Just fine."

Kim's jaw stiffened. "Are you going to put me on the stand?"

Maggie stared at her. "No… I don't think so. Baxter Cahill is a shrewd trial attorney. He would make it very uncomfortable for you. I'm not sure we'd gain anything by it."

Kim stared at Maggie with uncertainty. "Maggie, what if the jury believes Ben's story, regardless of whether the D.A. proves the case? What if the jury truly believes I poisoned Ben and tried to kill him? They could, couldn't they? They could believe him and say I'm guilty?"

Maggie's face tightened a little. Her voice was careful. "It's unlikely… but they could. You never know what a jury will do. But let's not get ahead of ourselves, Kim. Let's take it one day at a time."

CHAPTER 27

"Prosecution calls Mrs. Rosa Sanchez," Baxter Cahill exclaimed.

It was the second day of the trial and everyone was in place. The side door opened and Rosa entered, tentatively, nervously, her eyes two circles of wonder taking in the crowded room. She was led to the witness stand and sworn in. After she was seated and had gathered herself, Baxter rose.

He smiled his greeting at her as he approached. "Good morning, Mrs. Sanchez."

She swallowed and forced a smile, struggling to get comfortable in the chair.

"Good morning, sir."

"Mrs. Sanchez, please tell the court what your occupation is and who your employer is."

Rosa looked at Ben, smiled and nodded. Ben smiled back warmly. "I'm the cook and housecleaner for Ben Maxwell and Miss Kim. His wife, Mr. Maxwell's wife, Mrs. Kim Maxwell."

Rosa tried to look at Kim, but her gaze fell and drifted away, refocusing instead on Ben's encouraging face.

Maggie noticed. She scratched out an impression on

her legal pad. *R. Sanchez nervous. Won't look at Kim. Big smile at Ben.*

"When did you start working for Ben Maxwell?"

"On Monday, June 17."

Baxter took Rosa through a series of questions about her employment history, the length of her employment with Ben, her duties and the days and hours she worked.

"Mrs. Sanchez, do you consider Ben Maxwell to be a good employer?"

"Oh, yes, yes. Mr. Maxwell is so nice to me. He gave me a job. A very good job and he is so nice. Always so friendly and nice to me."

"And do you prepare all of his meals, that is, three meals a day, from Tuesday through Saturday?"

"No, not all. Mr. Maxwell doesn't always eat lunch, but he always eats breakfast and dinner. I prepare those."

"Did anyone ever help you while you prepared those meals?"

Rosa twisted her hands. "... Sometimes, Miss Kim... I mean Mrs. Maxwell helped me."

"Did she help you often—say more than five times—since you've been employed?"

"Sometimes she helped with breakfast... maybe two times a week."

"How did Mrs. Maxwell help you? What did she do? What did she prepare?"

"She make the scrambled eggs sometimes. She's a very good cook, you know. Sometimes she make the coffee or tea."

Baxter moved in closer. "On the days the defendant made tea, what kind of tea did she make for her husband?"

"Green tea. He doesn't like the green tea, but he drinks it because Mrs. Maxwell said the doctor said it was good for him."

Maggie looked at Kim, and Kim nodded. Maggie scribbled down a note.

Baxter continued. "Mrs. Sanchez, did you ever observe the defendant make the tea?"

"Oh, yes."

"As you prepared breakfast, how many times would you say you observed the defendant make the green tea for Ben Maxwell?"

Rosa tried to look at Kim again, and again she failed. "Maybe ten times."

"So from June 17 until late July of last year, to the best of your recollection, the defendant helped you prepare breakfast about ten times, and along with preparing Ben's breakfast, she also brewed green tea for him?"

"Yes."

Baxter turned to look at Kim as if gathering his thoughts for the next question.

"Now, Mrs. Sanchez, I want you to think very carefully about my next question. Take your time before you answer. Did you ever witness the defendant brewing the green tea at any other times?"

Rosa gave him an uncomfortable look. "Yes."

"And when was that?"

"Mrs. Maxwell always make tea for Mr. Maxwell in the afternoons. She told me the doctor said he should drink at least two green teas a day. She make that."

"That is, two cups of green tea a day, Mrs. Sanchez?"

"Yes, but Miss Kim always make a pot of tea for Mr. Maxwell."

"I see. The defendant, Kim Maxwell, always brewed a pot of green tea for Ben?" he restated.

"Yes."

Baxter looked toward the jury. "Thank you, Mrs.

Sanchez. Your witness, Ms. Stone."

Maggie shot up and walked aggressively toward Rosa.

"Good morning, Mrs. Sanchez. Did you ever prepare the green tea for Mr. Maxwell?"

Rosa tensed up. "…Yes. A few times."

"How many is a few times, Mrs. Sanchez?"

Rosa's mouth quivered. "Maybe ten or eleven times, I think."

Maggie narrowed her eyes on Rosa. "Mrs. Sanchez, you sound uncertain to me. Please try to think clearly and tell me if it was ten or eleven times or more?"

Baxter rose to his feet. "Your Honor, Mrs. Sanchez has already answered the question. Defense Counsel doesn't need to badger the witness."

Judge Brown leaned toward Rosa. "To the best of your recollection, Mrs. Sanchez, how many times did you prepare the green tea for Mr. Maxwell?"

Maggie glared at the Judge. "With all due respect, Your Honor, I would like to question the witness in my own way, if I may?"

Judge Brown ignored her. "Answer the question please, Mrs. Sanchez."

Rosa's eyes blinked rapidly. She trembled. "Maybe eleven or twelve times." And then Rosa began to sputter, fear taking hold, and she spoke rapidly, her accent growing more pronounced.

"I don't do anything wrong. I be a good worker. I do good work. I always on time. Mr. Maxwell is good to me. He always be nice to me. He's a good man. I work hard for him. He's a very good man."

Maggie's eyes were burning hot coals when she aimed them at Judge Brown. When she spoke, her voice was low and sharp.

"Thank you, Your Honor. Now, may I please proceed

with the questioning of my own witness?"

The courtroom buzzed with comment until Judge Brown slammed his gavel down. "Silence in the court. Silence."

Judge Brown glowered at her. "Yes, Ms. Stone, please continue, and do so without badgering the witness."

Kim twisted in her seat, glancing back toward her mother, whose face was white, her forehead wrinkled in distress.

Maggie took a little breath to cool her mind and refocus her thoughts. "Mrs. Sanchez, did you at any time ever witness anyone else brew the green tea for Mr. Maxwell? Now, just take a minute to think about it before you speak."

Rosa gave Ben an awkward glance. She stammered out her answer. "Sí… Sí, I mean, yes. I see Mrs. Carson make green tea."

The courtroom hummed and whispered. Again, Judge Brown hammered down his gavel, his bold eyes sweeping the courtroom.

"I said, quiet. If there is any further interruption, I will empty this courtroom." Then, with a little nod, he directed his gaze to Maggie. "Now proceed with your questioning, Counselor."

"All right, Mrs. Sanchez. You just stated that you witnessed Lois Carson, Mr. Maxwell's private nurse, prepare green tea for Mr. Maxwell. Is that correct?"

Rosa's voice quivered. "Yes."

"And how many times, to the best of your recollection, did Ms. Carson brew the green tea for Mr. Maxwell?"

Rosa began twisting her hands again. "I'm not sure."

"To the best of your recollection, Mrs. Sanchez."

"Maybe two or three times."

"Okay, maybe two or three times. And on those two or three times, why did she brew the tea for Mr. Maxwell and not you?"

"She said she not busy, and she would make it for him. I didn't like it that she brewed tea for him, because Mr. Maxwell hired me to do these things, but I don't say nothing. I don't talk to her and she don't talk to me."

"While Ms. Carson was brewing the tea, did you see her do anything unusual? Did she make the tea different from the way you made it, or the way Mrs. Maxwell made it?"

"She don't talk to me, so I don't look at her. I stay away from her."

"I see. Mrs. Sanchez, did you ever see anyone else brew the tea besides you, Mrs. Maxwell and Ms. Carson?"

She shook her head. "No. Never."

"And Mrs. Sanchez, after you brewed the green tea, did you take the pot of tea yourself to Mr. Maxwell?"

"Sometimes. Yes."

"You took a tray with the teapot, a cup and a little pitcher of milk to Mr. Maxwell's office?"

"Yes."

"Were there often people in Mr. Maxwell's office?"

"Yes."

"Did you know who they were?"

"Sometimes. Yes."

"Can you name them?"

"Ms. Carson was there. Mr. Walker, and sometimes others I didn't know."

Maggie stepped in closer, but she turned to look at Ben Maxwell. His right eyebrow was raised, his eyes intent, waiting.

"Mrs. Sanchez, on July 29, the evening that Mr. Maxwell had the heart attack, did Mr. Maxwell have green tea for breakfast?"

"Yes."

"Did you brew it and take it to him?"

Rosa hesitated. She looked at Ben, Baxter Cahill and then at the Judge.

Maggie's voice was firm. "Did you brew the tea and take it to his office, along with his breakfast?"

Rosa swallowed and nodded.

"Is that a Yes, Mrs. Sanchez?"

She spoke at a near whisper. "Yes…"

"And on that same afternoon, did you also brew the green tea and take that to him?" Maggie asked.

Tears appeared in Rosa's eyes. She began to cry.

Maggie turned to the bailiff. "Can we have tissues, please?"

They were brought, and Rosa blotted her eyes. "I don't do anything wrong. I don't… never."

Judge Brown cut in. "Mrs. Sanchez, no one is suggesting you did anything wrong."

Rosa whimpered on. "Mr. Maxwell good to me. Always nice to me."

Maggie drew in an impatient breath. "Mrs. Sanchez, please just answer yes or no. On the afternoon of July 29, did you brew a pot of green tea and take it to Ben Maxwell in his office, where he subsequently had his heart attack?"

Rosa wept into the tissue, nodding her head. "Yes… Yes. I was sorry. I was so sorry for him."

Maggie waited for the emotion to subside. She didn't want to leave the testimony hanging on Ben and Rosa being sorry for him, and on Rosa crying.

"Mrs. Sanchez, who was in the room when you delivered Ben's afternoon tea?"

"Ms. Carson and Mr. Walker."

"That is, Lois Carson and Howard Walker?

"Yes…" Rosa sniffed.

"Okay, Mrs. Sanchez, thank you."

Maggie walked back to her table, collected some typed pages and returned to the witness. "Just one final question, Mrs. Sanchez. When police detectives searched the house on July 31, they found the same teapot you allegedly delivered to Ben the afternoon of his heart attack. According to the inventoried items, they found the teapot and, I quote, 'in the right lower shelf of Ben's desk.' End quote. The teapot still had tea in it and it was from that tea that toxicology found the traces of potassium cyanide. My question is, Mrs. Sanchez, when did you *usually* retrieve the teapot and cup? Late afternoon? Evening?"

Rosa's face was strained and worried. She stammered. "I don't know it was there. I always go back in the evening after Mr. and Mrs. Maxwell is eating. I always clean up. I do good work."

"But you didn't collect the teapot that day, that is, the day Mr. Maxwell had his heart attack? And, in fact, you didn't collect it the next day either. If fact you never did collect the teapot because the detectives found it there two days later. Isn't that correct, Mrs. Sanchez?"

Rosa shook her head, beginning a new round of tears. "No… No… Everything crazy…. I just forget these things. I'm so sorry. So sorry."

"Thank you, Mrs. Sanchez. No more questions, Your Honor."

Judge Brown bent forward. "You can step down, Mrs. Sanchez. Thank you."

After Maggie had sat down, Kim whispered in her ear. "Did that go okay?"

Maggie leaned toward Kim's ear. "The Judge is a putz."

CHAPTER 28

That evening after a nap, Kim left her room and found Maggie in the living room, sitting by the fire, glasses on, going over her notes for the next day's proceedings. Maggie glanced up over her glasses and saw Kim had her coat, hat and gloves on.

"Going out?"

"I need a walk, Maggie, just down to the beach."

"Okay, let Officer Hanley know."

Maggie glanced down at her watch. "It's almost seven. Are you hungry? We can order from that little Italian restaurant… the only one open."

"I'm not very hungry, Maggie."

"You need to eat something."

"You sound like my mother."

"How is your mother?"

Kim held up her phone. "I'm going to talk to her as I walk. Scott said she's not holding up so well. I'm going to try once again to convince them both to go back home. There's nothing else they can do here."

Maggie peeled her glasses off. "Forgive me if I sound insensitive, but your mother and brother make a good impression—especially your mother. She has a kind of

Norman Rockwell appeal about her. The face of a strong but kind woman. I know it seems like a small thing having her in the courtroom, but it's the small things that sometimes help make the difference. Your mother looks at you often, and with great affection. The jury sees everything. They see things that attorneys will never see. They hear, feel and sense things that we can only guess about, and no matter how the attorneys try to shape and focus the facts, sometimes it's something visual, a feeling of sympathy or compassion, that can change the whole course of a trial."

Kim stared at Maggie, conflicted. "It's hard for me to have her here, Maggie. I know what's going to come, and it will be awful for her. It has been awful for her. She knows I'm not a saint, but… well I saw how she reacted to the prosecutor's opening statement. All the color drained from her face."

Maggie turned, staring into the gleaming fireplace. "I'll leave it to you, Kim. I'll let you and your mother make the decision. Have a good walk."

Kim found stocky and stoic Officer Hanley, stationed near the front door. She told him she was going for a walk down by the beach and he nodded, his gaze flat, his face impassive.

"Don't be gone long," he said aridly.

Kim strolled to the back of the house, found a narrow path and, with the light of a three-quarter moon, she blundered along until she arrived on the narrow, rocky beach. She stood gazing out on the dark velvety sea, watching the soft roll of the waves.

She retrieved her phone from her coat pocket and tapped her brother's number. She inhaled a breath and blew it back into the gathering wind.

Scott answered, his voice tense. "Kim… How are

you?"

"Been better. How's Mom?"

"She's here. I'll hand you over."

Moments later, Mrs. Ryan's small, shaky voice said, "Kim… Kim, how are you feeling, honey?"

"I'm fine, Mom. Really. I'm doing fine. I'm so worried about you. Have you eaten? Are you sleeping?"

"Well… how can a mother sleep?"

"Mom, you need to go home, please. There's nothing you can do here."

"Nothing? I can be close to you. I can see you, can't I? Is that nothing?"

"Mom, you know what I mean. Look, things are going to get a lot worse. They're going to say terrible things about me. I don't want you in that courtroom hearing those things."

"They'll say them whether I'm there or not, won't they? So why not be there? Anyway, I'm not leaving. I'm staying until this is over."

"Okay, look, Mom. I'll give you some money. The hotel's not cheap and I know Scott's taking too much time off from work."

"Don't worry about us, Kim. You just make sure that your attorney tells those people that you didn't try to kill Ben. It's just terrible what the papers are saying."

Kim took a quick breath. "Mom… yes, I know. Just don't read them, okay? Just don't read them. I wish you'd leave. Go home where you can sleep in your own bed."

"I'm staying, Kim. What kind of mother would I be if I left you now… in your worst hour? No, Scott and I are staying and that's the end of it."

After the call, Kim drifted along the beach, the cold wind sweeping up from the water and circling her. She ducked away and gazed up the beach into the shadowy distance. A figure was approaching, a dark silhouette. She frowned, hoping for solitude. She'd have to turn back to the house.

Something stopped her. It was a feeling, an instinct. Kim waited, and as the figure drew closer, she lit up when she recognized Derek's form. His tall, lean body and broad shoulders. In a rush, she ran to him. He gathered her up in his arms and bear-hugged her. They kissed, deeply, hungrily.

"How do you always know where I'm going to be?" Kim asked.

"I don't. I hang around a lot."

"Must be boring."

"You? Never boring."

They kissed again.

"Let's walk," Derek said, taking her hand.

They strolled for a time under the silver moonlight that dappled the sea and made ghostly shadows across the dunes, the trees, and the distant cliffs.

"How are you holding up?" Derek asked.

"Today was tough."

"Maggie's good, isn't she?"

"She's wonderful. She's like a mother hen. Thank you for finding her."

After a few moments of silence, Kim slanted a look at him. "How do you think it's going?"

"It's still early. I know Maggie wants to get at Lois Carson and Howard Walker."

"The whole thing makes me sick," Kim said, "especially when I think of Ben getting up there on the witness stand."

Derek was silent, but he dreaded it too. He put an arm around her waist. She hugged herself close to him.

"Derek… what will you do if they convict me?"

"They won't convict you."

"But if they do."

"Don't talk like that. Maggie will get you off."

Kim stopped. She faced him and, even in the dim moonlight, Derek could see the warmth in her eyes.

"Derek… It's so sad…"

"What's sad?"

"That this has happened to us now. It's sad that I thought I knew what love was… I thought I'd felt love—understood love. It's sad that now I could lose you forever, and I love you so much."

"Stop that, Kim. Stop it. Don't say that. You're not going to lose me."

Kim looked down. "Sometimes I think I deserve it."

Derek grabbed her shoulders tightly. "Look at me. Look at me, Kim."

She lifted her miserable eyes.

Derek's were burning with conviction. "You deserve to be happy. We deserve to be happy and we're not going to let that crazy bastard ruin it for us. It's not going to happen. Don't give up, okay? Don't."

Kim leaned into him, her face close, her body shivery, her lips moist.

Derek gently kissed her, and his soft kiss nearly broke her heart. For all of Derek's hard masculinity, there was a tenderness about him that melted her, especially when they made love.

"God, how I wish you could take me to bed," Kim said.

"My car's just up on the road. Come back with me. I'll cook us dinner. We can relax and get away from all this madness for a while."

Kim grinned in delight. "Oh, God yes. Let's go."

"What did you tell Maggie?"

"That I was going for a walk. That I was going to call my mother."

Derek looked up toward the house. He saw lights on. He calculated time and distance. He frowned. "We can't take the risk, Kim. If something happened and we got pulled over, it could look real bad for you."

Kim stared up at him. "Derek… If the worst happens, will you wait for me?"

Derek's face darkened. "If the worst happens, Ben won't live another month."

Kim recoiled, upset. "Don't say that."

"No one will know."

"Yes, they'll know. Of course they'll know. Don't even think about it."

"Okay… take it easy."

"Promise me you won't do anything crazy, Derek. Promise."

He shook his head. "I won't promise."

The sharp wind blew across them, stinging their faces.

Kim shivered. "Derek… if anything happened to you…"

"Nothing's going to happen to me, Kim. Nothing's going to happen to either of us."

Kim pressed her head into his chest, unable to release the inner darkness.

"I love you, Derek. I love you so much, and I hate this trial so much. I feel like we're both on trial, and our love is on trial. I hate what the papers say, and all that shit they put on the internet. Every stupid bastard has an opinion, and they think they know, when they don't know anything."

He held her there. "Stop reading it. It's all bullshit just to make money."

They clung to each other as the cold stars blinked and the night wind moved around them.

"I love you, Kim," Derek said, over the roar of the sea. "I love you. We're going to be together."

Derek's words warmed and healed her. She'd never heard such beautiful words.

Holding hands, they wandered along the beach, struggling up the steep, rocky path that led to a dark enclosure off a side road. Derek's truck was smothered in darkness, covered by tall trees, near a wall of shrubs. It was a road that fishermen used, but it was quiet and abandoned in winter.

They both glanced about to make sure they weren't being watched. Derek unlocked the doors and they slid in, Derek behind the wheel and Kim beside him. They shivered.

"Damn, it's cold," Derek said, cranking the engine and blasting heat.

Kim was already snuggling next to him. "I feel like I'm in high school again," she said, grinning. "I can barely see you. It's so dark."

Derek leaned over and kissed her nose, gently touching her face with his ungloved hand.

Kim drew back, laughing. "Oooh, your hands are cold."

"Should I stop?" he teased.

"Never."

"I like your short hair and your glasses," Derek said.

"Do they make me look more respectable?"

"Respectable and beautiful."

"What would your Ranger buddies say if they could hear you now?" Kim joked. "The tough Derek Gray, the romantic."

"They're all jealous of me. They wanted to know if

you had a sister. They're pulling for us."

Derek wrapped an arm around her shoulder and drew her close. They were dark shadows, two isolated lovers, suspended in the dark play of the world by events that could separate them, perhaps forever. Everything seemed heightened, immediate and terrifying. Neither stirred for a time.

Finally, Derek sat up and shut off the heat. Anxious silence filled the space.

"I want to marry you, Kim," he said, almost at a whisper.

Kim sat rigid, her eyes peering into the darkness, welling up with tears.

Derek felt her body tremble. He could tell she was crying. He reached and wiped her tears. "Don't cry, Kim. It's all going to work out."

"I'm so scared, Derek," she said, her voice choked. She was deeply moved and terrified at the same time.

"Let's get married as soon as this whole nightmare is over with," Derek said. "As soon as you can divorce Ben."

The darkness pulsed. They heard the faraway rasp of an overhead jet and the echo of a dog barking.

"What if I go to prison?"

"I don't give a damn where you go. I want to marry you."

Kim allowed the tears to trickle down her cheeks as she struggled to steady her emotions.

They sat in an intimate silence, their eyes searching the darkness for answers, for hope and for a miracle.

CHAPTER 29

The third day of trial focused on Ben's doctors, his health, his care, his medications and his diet. The testimony was long and tedious.

Ben's cardiologist and an old friend, Dr. Lawrence Eaton, droned on about the health of Ben's heart both before and after the accident. Ben had been taking medication for high blood pressure and stress for over ten years. Dr. Eaton stated that he had encouraged Ben to slow down and not work so hard. After the accident, Ben's heart was weakened, but it had improved with prolonged rest, less stress and reduced activity.

On cross-examination, Maggie asked Dr. Eaton about his examination of Kim after Ben's accident and his subsequent diagnosis of broken heart syndrome.

"Dr. Eaton, can you please tell us what the term means? Broken heart syndrome? You diagnosed Kim with this condition immediately following Ben's auto accident, didn't you?"

"Yes, I did."

"Can you tell us what that term means, please?"

Dr. Eaton looked like a doctor right out of a Hollywood movie. He had silver gray hair, a refined, pleasant face, a prominent nose and a confident, controlled manner.

"Yes, I can. Researchers noticed that many people with the condition were grieving because of the death of a loved one, a child or a spouse. When Kim arrived at the hospital where Ben was admitted, she collapsed and had to be taken to the ER. The ER medical report stated that she was in shock, her blood pressure had spiked, and she had hypothermia."

"Didn't the medical report also state that Kim had lacerations on her face from tree branches, and cuts on her feet from shattered glass, as a result of struggling to free her husband from the wrecked car?"

Dr. Eaton nodded. "Yes, that is correct."

Baxter Cahill climbed to his feet. "Your Honor, I object to this whole line of questioning. While it's fascinating and perhaps admirable, it has no bearing on this case whatsoever."

Maggie approached the bench. "Your Honor, if the Court will indulge me for just a few more minutes, I think I can satisfy the Court and Mr. Cahill as to the purpose of my questioning."

Judge Brown glanced over at the jury. They were fully engaged. His eyes swept over the courtroom. It was quiet, watchful. Kim sat on the edge of her chair. Ben Maxwell stared with contempt.

Baxter Cahill waited, his proud chin lifted in apprehension.

"Ms. Stone, I will allow you some leeway here. But come to your point quickly. Objection overruled."

Baxter Cahill stood there for a moment, coldly staring, before he finally lowered himself to the chair. Ben whispered something in Baxter's ear, but Baxter didn't respond.

"Thank you, Your Honor," Maggie said.

"Dr. Eaton, what happened to Kim as she was recovering from her injuries?"

"Kim was referred to me by her primary care physician. She had complaints of heart palpitations and severe depression."

"What was she depressed about?"

"She thought her husband was going to die. She was despondent because she thought she was going to lose him."

"Did she say that?"

"She said she loved him very much, and she didn't know what she would do if he died. Words to that effect."

"I see, and after your interview and examination of Kim, what was your diagnosis?"

"As I said before, after performing an echocardiogram, I diagnosed her with broken heart syndrome. Traumatic events can trigger one's sympathetic nervous system, which is also called your 'fight or flight' mechanism. The body unleashes a flood of chemicals, including adrenaline. This sudden flood can stun your heart muscle, leaving it unable to pump properly. So even though broken heart syndrome may feel like a heart attack, it's a very different problem that needs a different type of treatment. More than 90% of cases reported thus far have been in women. Kim was diagnosed and treated."

Maggie leaned in close to Dr. Eaton but turned to look directly at Ben Maxwell.

"And how did you treat Kim for this condition, Dr. Eaton?"

"I prescribed medicines to relieve fluid buildup and lower Kim's blood pressure. I prescribed additional meds to help prevent blood clots and manage stress hormones.

Once Kim realized that Ben was going to live, her condition improved markedly, and I discontinued the medication."

Maggie nodded. She turned to look at the jury.

"Doctor, does that sound like a woman who doesn't love her husband, and who would plot to kill him using cyanide poisoning?"

Baxter shot to his feet. "Objection, Your Honor! Counsel is leading the witness."

"Sustained."

Maggie turned back to the doctor. "Thank you, Doctor. No more questions."

Baxter continued. "I request that the last question be stricken from the record. This was an egregious trick, obviously made to mislead and influence the jury."

Judge Brown leaned over his bench to the court reporter. "Yes, strike that last question from the record."

The Judge glowered at Maggie. "Ms. Stone, I will not allow any more stunts like that in my courtroom, do you understand me?"

Maggie remained standing. "Yes. My apologies, Your Honor. It will not happen again."

She sat down, straining not to smile.

Kim searched Maggie's face, pleased.

The morning concluded with testimony from Detectives Saunders and Holder.

Maggie observed that one juror, a male somewhere in his 40s, viewed the proceedings with a marked lack of interest. He frequently yawned and his eyes searched the air, looking for something more interesting and engaging. Maggie made a note of him. This was Kyle Benton. She'd never been entirely sure about him, but there had been something there—a wild look, an independent air—that she liked. During jury selection, she could tell he disliked lawyers, but that didn't bother her. After she'd fired a few questions at him, she learned that he was married with two kids, he worked as a plumber and he'd grown up nearby. He'd also served in the Navy.

Baxter Cahill liked the local family man aspect. Despite that, Baxter also had some reservations about Kyle. There was something about him that was aloof and mysterious. Finally, Baxter and Maggie agreed to accept Kyle on the jury, Maggie because she felt he could be unbiased and make up his own mind. Baxter because Kyle was a local working man, who'd purposefully returned to Scorpio Beach after being in the Navy. Baxter also sensed that Kyle disliked Derek, even though Derek had also served in the military. But being a working man, Baxter suspected that Kyle resented Derek's intrusion into the local scene with his landscaping business.

Maggie believed there was more to Kyle than he presented, however. There was that indefinable thing about him that she couldn't quite put her finger on. He was a wild card to be sure, but what the hell, sometimes it's the wild cards that can sway a jury one way or the other. In this case, Maggie was hopeful it would sway Kyle over to Kim's side.

Maggie observed that the rest of the jury was struggling to stay awake as well. The detectives were thorough, without drama and, frankly, boring. She asked them a few questions, but they were mostly routine.

Kim and Maggie ate lunch in an isolated room in the basement. It contained a table, plastic chairs, a coffee machine, a microwave oven and an old Frigidaire refrigerator.

As they munched on ham and cheese sandwiches and potato chips, Kim pointed at the refrigerator.

"We had one of those in our kitchen when I was a kid.

My mother used to freeze everything: meat, bread, dessert. She was a good, practical mother. I'm so sorry she has to go through this," Kim said with dejection.

"Don't underestimate your mother, Kim. She's tough. We had a good talk the other day. She's got steel in her. I like her, a lot."

Kim's eyes changed. "What did you talk about?"

"You. The trial. She told me that when you were a little girl, you wanted to be a missionary."

Kim shook her head as she reached for her can of soda. "Oh, yeah, I did. I wanted to save the world from evil men like my father. I wanted to make the world a better place."

"What changed your mind?"

"When I was fifteen, I fell in love with Kenny Tanner. He kissed me, and I thought I'd die right there. He was seventeen and one of the bad boys in the school. So I guess he helped make me bad."

Maggie turned serious. "Don't go there, Kim. Your mother said you've always been a fighter."

Kim glanced up with malice. "I *am* a fighter—especially now. I woke up this morning, and I felt different. I felt strong and angry. It's the first time since I've been arrested that I feel the strength to fight back. I want to throw all the lies and the bullshit right back into Ben's face."

"Good," Maggie said, biting into half of her sandwich. "That's good. I thought you looked better this morning. I thought you seemed happier last night when you returned from your walk."

Kim grinned. "I am better. Derek wants to marry me."

Maggie looked at her with mild disapproval. "So, you two did meet last night? I thought so."

Kim looked at Maggie dubiously. "It wasn't planned."

"Don't do it again, Kim. Don't."

Kim stared down at her sandwich. "I won't."

"I can't protect you if you won't let me."

The corners of Maggie's mouth lifted, and her eyes brightened. "Congratulations."

They finished their lunch in silence.

The afternoon session began with Lois Carson. After she was sworn in, Baxter moved in. Lois Carson had a sharp, high-pitched voice that carried well in the courtroom. Her snippy manner was off-putting, and Maggie thought Mrs. Carson had the look of someone who was having issues with constipation.

She answered most questions with a simple "Yes" or "No."

Baxter took her through her work history and then brought her up to date with the description of Ben's care and the list of medications she oversaw or administered.

Maggie studied Lois, noticing the hard thrust of her jaw, her compressed mouth and the flat glare of her eyes.

Baxter looked directly at Maggie as he formed the next question. "Ms. Carson, Rosa Sanchez stated that you made green tea for Mr. Maxwell and I quote 'Maybe two or three times.' Is that correct, Ms. Carson?"

"I don't recall ever making tea for Mr. Maxwell, green or otherwise. Why would I? I'm a nurse, not a housekeeper. It's not my job."

Baxter faced her, his eyes narrowed. "So you never did, at any point, to the best of your recollection, ever make green tea for Mr. Maxwell and then deliver it to him?"

"Not that I recall."

"Did you ever personally witness seeing the defendant deliver green tea to Mr. Maxwell?"

"Yes, many times."

"How many times is many, approximately?" Baxter asked.

"Oh, I'd say 30 times, maybe more."

Baxter turned back to Maggie. "Thirty times or more. Ms. Carson, did you ever see anyone else make green tea for Mr. Baxter?"

"Yes."

"Who?"

"I saw Rosa Sanchez."

"You witnessed her actually make the tea?"

"Yes."

"In the kitchen?"

"Yes."

"Why were you in the kitchen?"

"I kept things in the refrigerator: fruit and sometimes my lunch."

Baxter thanked her and returned to his seat.

Maggie stood at the table, staring down at her notes.

"Just to clarify, Ms. Carson. You never, ever, not once, ever made green tea in the teapot for Mr. Maxwell?"

"Not that I recall."

"You never once ever took the teapot to Mr. Maxwell?"

"Not that I recall."

Rosa Sanchez was in the back of the audience. Her face flushed scarlet. Her eyes burned with anger. She touched her forehead and whispered *En el nombre del Padre*, touched her breastbone and said *y del Hijo*, touched her left shoulder and whispered *y del Espirito*, and touched her right shoulder and whispered *Santo*. Minutes later, her right hand was rapidly running the rosary through her fingers.

Maggie picked up a typed page and advanced to the witness stand. "Ms. Carson, I see here that you deposited two rather large checks, signed by Howard Walker. One is dated July 20 and the other dated July 27. One check is for the amount of fifteen thousand dollars, and the other is for twenty thousand dollars. That's a total of thirty-five thousand dollars in the space of seven days. What was that payment for?"

Lois sat up a little taller. "They were given to me as a bonus."

"Who gave the bonus and what was the bonus for?"

"Mr. Maxwell gave the bonus to me, for my loyal service to him."

"I see. Service to Mr. Maxwell. Have you ever received checks in similar amounts from any other patients you have treated?"

Baxter sprang up. "Objection."

"Sustained," Judge Brown said.

Maggie looked down at the paper again. "Ms. Carson, when reviewing your work history, I see that you were employed by a Mrs. Isabel Katz of New York City."

Maggie raised her eyes and stared directly at Lois. Her face was a dull blank page. "Is that correct?"

"If it says so on your paper."

"I'm asking you, Ms. Carson, not the paper. Were you the private nurse for Mrs. Isabel Katz?"

"Yes."

"I see from the medical report that she died from an overdose of narcotics."

Baxter moved to the edge of his seat.

"That's right, isn't it, Ms. Carson?" Maggie asked.

Baxter stood. "Objection, Your Honor. How Ms. Carson's former patient died has no relevance in this trial. Once again, defense counsel is trying to manipulate this witness and the Court."

Maggie spoke up. "Your Honor, I'm only trying to better understand the witness's background and work history, to better understand all the circumstances of this case."

Judge Brown frowned. "What Ms. Carson's duties were prior to this trial has no bearing on this case, Ms. Stone. Sustained."

Maggie looked at the jury. "Ms. Carson, have you ever been in Kim Maxwell's bedroom?"

Baxter leaped to his feet again. "Objection!"

Maggie turned to Baxter, her voice filled with impatience and irritation. "Mr. Cahill, it's a simple question that is relevant to this case. What can you possibly be objecting to?"

Judge Brown stiffened. "I'll decide what is and what is not relevant to this case, Ms. Stone. Not you."

"Yes, Your Honor."

All eyes were fixed on the Judge. For the first time, Kim saw Lois Carson shift in her seat. Her hard shell seemed to crack a little as she turned to face the Judge, waiting for his response.

"Overruled, Mr. Baxter. You may answer the question, Ms. Carson."

Lois Carson took in an uneasy breath. "No, I have never been in Mrs. Maxwell's bedroom. Again, I have no reason to be in her bedroom. I am not a housekeeper. I am a nurse."

"Not even once, Ms. Carson? Now think a minute before you speak."

"I don't need to think about it, okay? I have never been in Mrs. Maxwell's bedroom. Never."

Maggie waited, nodding. She strolled over to her table, dropped the page and picked up a photograph. She turned back to Ms. Carson and held it up.

"Ms. Carson, I have a photograph here. It was developed at the Rite Aid just outside town, and there's a date and time stamped on it. July 18 of last year at 10:15 a.m."

Maggie handed it to the bailiff, and he presented it to Ms. Carson. "Do you see it, Ms. Carson?"

Lois swallowed hard.

"Please tell the jury that you see the time/date stamp, Ms. Carson."

Lois bit off the words. "Yes, I see it."

Maggie faced the jury. "In the photograph that Ms. Carson is holding, there are three people standing in Kim Maxwell's bedroom. I have shown this same photo to Kim, and she confirms it's her bedroom. I have also shown this same photograph to Rosa Sanchez, who regularly cleans Kim's bedroom, and she also confirmed the location as being Kim's bedroom."

Baxter rose to his feet. "Can I see that photograph, please?"

Maggie took the photo from Lois Carson and walked it to Baxter. He examined it, his eyes unblinking. He handed it back to Maggie and then sat, his face passive, his expression bored.

Judge Brown requested a look and Maggie presented it to him. He studied it, nodded, and handed it back to Maggie.

Maggie continued. "The three people in this photograph are Kim, Ben Maxwell and you, Ms. Carson. Did you see yourself in the photograph, Ms. Carson?"

Lois Carson turned away, indignant.

Maggie moved in closer and held it up to Lois's pained face, pointing at Lois in the photo. "See… isn't that you, Ms. Carson?"

Lois's mouth twitched, and her eyes flared with irritation. "Yes, that's me."

"Do you remember the photo, Ms. Carson? Do you remember being in the photo?"

"If you say so."

"I'm asking you, Ms. Carson. Yes or no. Is that you in Kim's bedroom with Kim and Ben Maxwell?"

"Yes," Lois said sharply. "I said so. Yes."

"Do you remember the photo being taken?"

"I'm not sure."

"It's not so long ago, Ms. Carson. Try to think. Yes or no, do you remember?"

She sniffed, contemptuously. "Okay… yes. I remember now. I'd forgotten, that's all."

"Thank you, Ms. Carson."

Maggie turned toward Kim and then strolled toward the jury. "What was the occasion for the photograph, Ms. Carson?"

"I have no idea."

"Shall I refresh your memory, Ms. Carson? Please tell me if I'm wrong. Did Kim purchase the new oil painting?"

"I don't know."

"Didn't Kim want her husband, Ben Maxwell, to see it because she thought it might please him?"

"I have no idea."

Maggie returned to Lois, photo in hand. She held it up and pointed at the painting in the photo. "It's right there, isn't it, Ms. Carson? The painting. It's a seascape of Scorpio Beach, painted by a local artist. Kim loved the painting, and she wanted to show it off. So you, Howard Walker, and Ben Maxwell all went down to Kim's bedroom to see it. Kim hung it on the wall over her bed. Howard Walker snapped the photo using Kim's digital camera. So now, do you remember, Ms. Carson?"

"I said I did, didn't I? I just forgot, that's all. I can't be expected to remember every little insignificant thing, can I?" she snapped.

Maggie stared hard at her. "Thank you, Ms. Carson. Now, if I may just ask you once more… Since you could not remember being in the photograph, perhaps you also do not remember making green tea for Mr. Maxwell…"

Baxter shot up, angry. "Your Honor, please! The witness has already answered this question numerous times."

Judge Brown scowled at Maggie. "You are testing the patience of this Court, Ms. Stone. One more of these little stunts of yours and I'll hold you in contempt. Do you understand me?"

Maggie nodded humbly. "Yes, Your Honor. I do understand."

"I will not tolerate these kinds of tactics in my courtroom, Counselor."

"Yes, Your Honor. I would like to offer the photograph into evidence as Exhibit Four."

Showing annoyance, Baxter nodded. "No objections."

CHAPTER 30

The following morning, Howard Walker took the stand. Howard was a pale, jittery man, whose eyes couldn't stop moving. He confirmed that Ben Maxwell had indeed issued the checks to Lois Carson for thirty-five thousand dollars, as a bonus for her superlative work. When Maggie asked him if Ben Maxwell had ever given him a similar bonus for his superlative work, he said "No."

When Maggie asked him if he thought he did superlative work, he said, "Ben has always been supportive and generous. He's a generous, fair man."

When Baxter Cahill called Derek Gray to the stand, Kim began to perspire. She glanced over her shoulder at her mother and brother. Mrs. Ryan sat upright, like a soldier. Scott appeared anxious and uneasy.

Derek wore a dark suit, white shirt and dark blue tie. His hair was cut short, just long enough to manage a part. It was impossible to disguise his ruggedly handsome face, attractive breadth of shoulder, strong chin and piercing eyes.

Baxter stood and made a pronouncement. "For the record, Your Honor, the witness, Derek Gray, has been offered immunity from any prosecution in this case. Therefore, any answer he gives during his testimony cannot be used against him in a court of law."

"So noted," the Judge said.

Baxter approached Derek, his eyes boring into him.

"Have you and the defendant, Kim Maxwell, ever had sexual relations, Mr. Gray?"

Derek blinked slowly, his expression assured and honest. "Yes, sir."

"More than once?"

"Yes, sir."

"Many times?"

"Many, sir."

"Ten times or more?"

"I don't recall."

"Really. A smart guy like you doesn't recall a thing like that?"

Maggie shot up. "Objection!"

"Sustained," Judge Brown said.

"Mr. Gray, when you had sexual relations with the defendant, were you aware that she was married to Ben Maxwell?"

"Yes, sir."

"Did you have sexual relations with the defendant before Ben Maxwell hired you as his property manager?"

"Yes, sir."

"Did you have sexual relations with the defendant after you were hired as Ben Maxwell's property manager?"

"Yes, sir."

"Did that ever bother you, Mr. Gray?"

Maggie sprang up. "Objection. Requires an opinion."

"I'll withdraw the question," Baxter said.

Baxter circled the space and returned to Derek. "Mr. Gray… why did you accept Ben's position as a property manager?"

"The money."

"Anything else?"

"Not that I recall."

"When you and Ben discussed the terms of your employment, did the subject of an auto accident that occurred out on Fairview Road ever come up? An encounter that left one man dead and another seriously injured?"

"Not that I recall."

"Do you recall reading about it?"

"Vaguely."

"Mr. Gray, when you were in the military, did you ever have access to cyanide?"

"No, sir."

"Never? Ever know any soldier who had access to cyanide? Maybe a pill?"

"No, sir."

"During your sexual relations with the defendant, did she ever mention the possibility of wanting to kill her husband?"

"No, sir."

"Did you ever bring it up?"

"No, sir."

"Did she?"

"As I said before, no, sir."

"Did the two of you, that is, the defendant, Kim Maxwell, and yourself, ever discuss having a future together?"

Derek paused. "A future?"

"Yes, did you want more from the relationship than just sex? Or was your entire relationship based solely on sex?"

"We discussed Kim getting a divorce."

"Really? Why didn't she ever discuss this with her

husband?"

Derek thought carefully. "Mr. Maxwell changed. He had been somewhat cold and indifferent to Kim after the accident. After we met, she was going to ask for a divorce, but then Mr. Maxwell changed, rather suddenly. That surprised Kim. Mr. Maxwell told her he wanted to make amends and rededicate himself to restoring their somewhat broken marriage to the way it had been before the accident."

"Were you angry about that?"

"No, sir."

"Not at all?"

"No, sir. She wanted to try to fix the marriage. I supported that."

"That's very noble of you."

Maggie jumped to her feet. "Objection, Your Honor. Mr. Cahill's opinion is not wanted or relevant."

Judge Brown lowered his castigating eyes on Baxter. "Sustained. Counselor, leave your opinions and sarcasm outside. They have no place in my Court."

"My apologies, Your Honor."

Baxter spent long minutes taking Derek through his duties as Ben's property manager, including his salary and bonus. Derek listed his responsibilities and the properties he oversaw.

Baxter strolled back to his table and stood next to Ben. "Mr. Gray, Ben Maxwell paid you well, didn't he?"

"Yes, sir."

"Ben also gave you a generous bonus, didn't he?"

"Yes, sir."

"Did you continue to have a sexual relationship with Kim Maxwell after Ben wanted to restore his marriage with the defendant?"

Derek hesitated.

"I'm waiting, Mr. Gray. The jury is waiting. The entire Court is waiting."

"Not right away."

Baxter surged back to the witness stand. "Not right away? So you did have sex with the defendant after Ben wanted to restore his marriage? After the defendant agreed not to divorce Ben? Is that correct, Mr. Gray? Yes or no."

Derek's face betrayed nothing. His eyes didn't move. He sat tall and rigid, at attention. "Yes, sir."

The courtroom buzzed with whispery comment. Judge Brown pounded his gavel. "Silence. Silence in the Court."

Baxter whirled to face the jury. "Yes? That was a 'Yes,' Mr. Gray?"

"Yes, sir."

Baxter's voice took on rising strength and satisfaction. He drew the words out to emphasize them. "Yeeessss, surrrr."

Baxter locked his hands behind his back. "Mr. Gray, did the defendant ever express regret or remorse for her actions of this blatant immorality?"

"Yes, sir."

"Oh, so she was well aware of her infidelity and betrayal of her husband, Ben, and yet she continued on, blithely, deliberately, selfishly. You both just continued having sex after Ben had been so open with his feelings and so generous with his money to you and to his wife?"

"There was more to it than that," Derek blurted out.

Maggie shut her eyes. Derek had just played into Baxter's hands.

Baxter glared at him. "Oh, I just bet there was, Mr. Gray. I don't doubt for a minute that there was more to it than that. In fact, I am confident that there was much more to it than that."

Baxter looked at Derek with indignation. "No more questions for this witness. I'm quite finished with this whole round of distasteful and lurid questioning."

Kim slumped, her sad eyes staring, seeing nothing. She felt sick and humiliated. She felt as though she had been punched hard in the stomach. She couldn't bear to look at her mother and brother.

Maggie shot to her feet.

"Mr. Gray, did Kim ever—at any time during your relationship—ever discuss the possibility of poisoning Ben Maxwell?"

"No ma'am. Never."

"On July 29 of last year, the day Ben Maxwell suffered his heart attack, did Kim tell you she was going to ask her husband for a divorce?"

"Yes, ma'am."

"Do you recall what she said to you about ending her marriage with her husband?"

Derek took a little breath. "She said she wanted to face Ben and tell him the truth. She said the marriage was over and she wanted to tell him face-to-face that she wanted a divorce."

"So, on the day of Ben Maxwell's heart attack, Kim was going to tell him she wanted a divorce?"

"Yes, ma'am."

"Did she say anything else?"

"Yes… she said she still cared for him but that he frightened her."

"Why did he frighten her?"

"She said he acted different from when they were first married. She said he'd changed, and that she was scared of him. She said, maybe she'd always been a little scared of him. So we discussed her divorcing him and then both of us leaving town."

Maggie straightened up and turned to Ben. "Mr. Gray, you and Kim were intimate. You confided in each other. As far as you are aware, and to the best of your knowledge, did Kim have any reason, any motive, whatsoever, for wanting to poison her husband, Ben Maxwell?"

"No ma'am. There was no need. She was going to ask for a divorce. She still cared for him, but she did not want to stay married to him."

Maggie continued to stare at Ben. He held her stare, his eyes blazing.

"Thank you, Mr. Gray. No more questions."

For lunch, Kim and Maggie ate Chinese takeout in the courthouse basement room. Kim pushed the chicken fried rice around, still feeling the residual nausea and embarrassment from Derek's testimony.

Maggie ate slowly, engrossed in review and strategy. Snow fell outside the upper window, drizzling the tops of trees. Bursts of wind whistled by, sending snowflakes into a scattering panic, making the world seem blurry and confused.

Kim glanced up to watch the snow as she pushed her paper plate aside. "God, how I miss the summer sun," she said, filling up the long silence. "On days like this, I think summer will never come and I'll never feel the hot sun on my face."

Maggie chewed and nodded.

Kim studied Maggie. Her face revealed nothing. "How do you think it's going, Maggie? Be honest with me."

Maggie picked up her paper cup of coffee and sipped at it, blowing the steam away. "Ben's testimony is this afternoon. After that, I have a few character witnesses and then we do our summations and it goes to the jury."

Kim folded her arms and sighed. "Yes, the jury. I can't tell what they're thinking or who they believe and don't believe."

Maggie's eyes opened on her with compassion. "Don't worry, Kim. Prosecution hasn't proven his case. I'm surprised he hasn't contacted me about a plea bargain."

Kim stared, alarmed. "Would you recommend that?"

"That would depend on the conditions."

"Then you think the jury could go against me?"

"Relax, Kim. Do we know what the jury will do? No. Are most juries mostly perceptive and fair? Yes. Since there has been no discussion of a plea bargain, Baxter must believe he can get a conviction. He certainly wants one to help his political aspirations. We'll see what happens after Ben's testimony. I'll be able to take the temperature of the jury after that."

Kim's shoulders dropped. "I wish I didn't have to sit there and listen to Ben. He's really going to make me look like a whore, isn't he?" Kim shook her head, turning to stare at the white wall. "I guess it's too late for that. Everybody already thinks I'm a whore."

"Some probably think that, others see something else. Everybody brings their own thoughts, opinions and experiences to a trial, Kim. But you'll be okay. Ben's real edgy and volatile. I see it in his eyes. I'm going to go after him. I can't wait to go after him."

Kim nibbled on her lower lip. "How do you think Derek did?"

"He made one slip-up, but I think we recovered."

Both settled back into silence, into their own private thoughts.

CHAPTER 31

Ben Maxwell wheeled himself to the witness stand and was sworn in. He wore a rich chocolate brown suit, powder blue shirt and golden tie. His hair was combed smoothly back from his broad face, revealing cool brown eyes. Baxter approached with a smile.

"Mr. Maxwell, how long have you lived in Scorpio Beach?"

"I've had a house here for nearly 18 years."

"I know you're a modest man, often preferring to stay anonymous, but for the sake of the jury, please tell us how many charitable organizations you support and give money to in this immediate area."

Ben humbly listed them.

"You were also a Scorpio Beach Town Council member, were you not?"

"Yes, for four years."

Baxter encouraged Ben to list additional organizations and friendships with various political and social leaders.

Gradually, he questioned Ben about his activities in Scorpio Beach after his accident. Ben graciously listed local and state dignitaries who were helpful once he'd decided to settle in Scorpio Beach, making the beach house his primary home.

The next part of his testimony included his marriage to Kim and their decision to move to Scorpio Beach.

"Are you happy living in Scorpio Beach, Ben?"

"Yes, very. It's a beautiful town filled with wonderful, caring people. I have a lot of friends here. I feel at home here."

"Did your wife share your view of Scorpio Beach?"

Ben looked suitably downcast. "No, I'm afraid not."

Kim shot a glance at Maggie, who was watching Ben intently.

"Why was that, Ben?" Baxter asked.

"Kim was used to more excitement, I guess. She was a dancer, you know. She had a lot of… well, I guess you'd say off-beat friends. They were artist types. After we moved into the beach house, I sensed she was unhappy. She often told me she wanted more from her life than being stuck in that house, away from all the excitement."

Kim stared at Ben, incredulous. He was lying! She'd never once said anything like that to him. Maggie sat dead still, every sense alert and calculating.

"Ben, was it difficult adjusting to your disability?"

"Oh, yes. Very tough. But I had good friends and good doctors who helped me."

"Did your wife help you?"

Ben's expression was sorrowful. "Oh, I guess she tried. But a lot of time I just didn't see her. She wasn't around."

Kim stiffened in rage. Her face reddened. She wanted to spring up and call him a lying bastard! It took all her strength to stay seated.

"Did you still love your wife, Ben?"

He smiled ruefully. "Of course. Yes. I love Kim."

"Ben… did you suggest to your wife that she divorce

you after your accident?"

Ben's face filled with pain. "Yes. I did."

"What did she say?"

Ben exhaled a heavy sigh. "She mentioned money."

"Money? What did she say about money?"

"She was careful... She said, she'd given up her career for me. She said she didn't intend to walk away without..." Ben stopped to swallow. "She said she wanted to be compensated. She said she deserved to be compensated because we couldn't have... we couldn't have normal relations."

Maggie saw Kim's rage. She cooled her with a calm but firm glance.

"Did you offer to compensate her?"

"Of course. Yes."

"And did she accept?"

Ben took out a handkerchief and mopped his brow. "She said it wasn't enough."

"How much did you offer, Ben?"

"Five million dollars."

The courtroom hummed with comment.

Judge Brown silenced them. He strafed the audience with his eyes. "I will empty this courtroom if there are any more interruptions."

Kim was so astounded, she had trouble breathing. Ben was making it all up. None of it was true. She had *never* asked for any compensation and Ben had never offered.

Baxter stood there, nodding, his hands pushed into both pockets of his pants. "So what happened next, Ben? What did you both decide?"

"Kim said she wasn't going anywhere. She said she knew my lawyers would try to cheat her out of what was rightfully hers. Oh, I tried to reason with her, I even offered more money, but she wouldn't hear of it. She became rather cold."

"Ben... at what point did you suspect your wife was having an affair?"

"Well, like I said, I didn't see much of her. She sort of went off on her own. I suppose I suspected something. I mean, look at me. I guess I didn't blame her at first. Then, little by little, I did get a little upset. Who wouldn't?"

"You hired a private detective, didn't you, Ben?"

"Yes. I wanted confirmation. Well, I got it."

"So then why did you give your wife two million dollars and offer to set her up in business with a yoga studio downtown?"

"Because I was still in love with her. You can't just stop yourself from loving a person, can you? Well, anyway, I can't. I couldn't. I loved Kim. I still do."

"Why did you offer Derek Gray a job as your property manager when you knew he was having sexual relations with your wife?"

Ben wiped his mouth with the handkerchief. "Because..." His voice was choked with emotion. "Because I thought I could stop it. I thought they'd have the decency to take my gifts and stop the relationship. It's the only thing I could think of to do. I didn't want to lose Kim. I loved her."

Ben continued on with his description of Derek—how smart he was and how Ben admired him for his military service. He thought he was a worthy young man, who had fallen under Kim's spell.

Baxter faced the jury. "Ben... did you know you were being poisoned?"

Ben stared hard into the floor. "No. Never. How could I?"

"But you had symptoms. Nausea, dizziness, shortness of breath, for almost a week, didn't you? You made complaints to your nurse, Lois Carson, didn't you?"

"Yes. I thought it was just a virus. Nurse Carson insisted I go see a doctor, but I shrugged it off. I guess I'm stubborn that way. Nurse Carson was very devoted to me and now, in retrospect, I realize I should have listened to her."

"Ben, when the police came to your hospital bed and told you that you had been poisoned, and that they had found a bottle of potassium cyanide in your wife's underwear drawer, what did you think?"

Ben paused, overcome with emotion. His lower lip trembled. He closed his eyes, and then slowly opened them. "I cried. That's all. I just cried."

"Did you believe that your wife had poisoned you?"

He shook his head vigorously. "No. No. It was preposterous. Inconceivable."

Baxter backed away and focused his entire attention on Kim. "Do you believe it now, Ben? Do you believe that your wife, the defendant, did try to poison you?"

Ben wiped a tear. He nodded. It was a slow, painful affirmation.

"I need to hear you say it, Ben," Baxter said softly.

Ben swallowed. "Yes. Yes, I do."

After Baxter sat down, Maggie did not stand. She sat staring at Ben over steepled fingers. The courtroom watched her.

Finally Judge Brown spoke up. "Ms. Stone, your witness."

Maggie pushed up with dramatic effort. She wandered to Ben, staring pointedly at him.

"Mr. Maxwell, when Detectives Saunders and Holder removed Kim's laptop, they went through all her emails.

I have some of them here. Shall I read them?"

He shrugged. "Go ahead."

Maggie went back to the table. She took time leafing through them, deliberately making everyone wait, especially Ben. She turned.

"Here's one. Kim sent this to you on May of last year. 'Ben, darling… please stop talking about divorce. I don't want a divorce and I don't want any of your money. I want you back. I want us back, the way it was. I want the man I married and fell in love with back. I wanted to tell you that in person, but Howard said you didn't want to see me.'"

Maggie lifted her eyes from the page. "Do you remember that email, Mr. Maxwell?"

"No, I don't recall it."

"Okay, I have more."

She shuffled. "Here's another. 'It's dated June 1. My birthday's coming. I'll be thirty. Imagine me being thirty years old. Can we do something special, Ben? Have dinner together? It's been so long. Please say yes.'"

Maggie turned to the jury. "This was your response, Mr. Maxwell. '… No time. Busy with things. Go out with friends or something. I'm not feeling social.'"

Ben smoothed his tie. "I was sick that day. I didn't feel well."

Maggie lifted her eyebrows. "I have more, Mr. Maxwell. Many more. I'll just read little snippets. 'Haven't seen you in days, Ben. Hope you're well. Know that I love you.'" Maggie found another. "'Why do you hate me, Ben? I don't understand. Why do you shut me out? Why do you refuse to see me?'"

Maggie glanced through others. "There are many more like this. Do you recall any of them?"

"You took them out of context," Ben said, flatly.

"Did I? I'm happy to read all of them in their context and in their entirety. I have five months of emails, all very similar in tone, many filled with affection."

Ben stared coldly.

"Mr. Maxwell, isn't it true you blamed your wife for the accident that disabled you?"

"Objection, Your Honor," Baxter called.

"Overruled," Judge Brown said. "Continue, Ms. Stone."

"Answer the question, Mr. Maxwell," Maggie said.

"No."

Maggie found another email. "This email is from you, Mr. Maxwell. I'll read it. 'If I hadn't met you, I wouldn't be a cripple.' End quote, Mr. Maxwell. This is dated June 7 of last year."

"I don't recall it. I may have been angry. It happens. My mind isn't what it used to be since the accident. Things get foggy sometimes."

"I understand. So then perhaps you're a little foggy about other things, say, for instance, when Kim said she'd given up a career for you, or when you stated that she wanted compensation."

"I remember that clearly."

"Do you, Mr. Maxwell? You seem to have a very clever, selective memory."

Baxter shot to his feet. "Objection!"

"Sustained."

Maggie pressed on. "Mr. Maxwell, all these emails show a wife who not only loved you and supported you but also a wife who willingly sacrificed her happiness to try to ensure your health and happiness. Shall I read more of them?"

Ben's voice gathered force. "There's no need to read them. I know what went on. I know my wife better than you, Counselor. I was there."

"Shall I show you receipts of the clothes she bought for you: the 14-karat gold ring she purchased for your last birthday… I'm sure you'll recall the cashmere sweaters, the theater tickets, which you refused to use, the gourmet foods she ordered because you loved them, the silk shirts and the stacks of novels, mostly thrillers, that you love to read. Mr. Maxwell, she paid for these with her own money. If fact, she rarely spent any of your money, did she? Here is an email that states 'You've done so much for me, Ben, but I like having my own money and spending my own money. I've always been independent. I was raised that way by a tough, independent mother. I never want something for nothing.' End quote."

Maggie faced Ben. He was glowing with anger.

"Mr. Maxwell, I counted fifty-seven receipts, just for last year alone, that document many presents your wife bought for you. Do you recall those presents?"

"Some…"

"Some? What does fifty-seven presents purchased for you by your wife suggest to you, Mr. Maxwell?"

His eyes darted about. "I don't know what you mean."

"Mr. Maxwell, does that suggest to you a wife who is cold?"

"Like I said before, I was there. You were not."

Maggie pushed on. "When you heard that you had been poisoned, Mr. Maxwell, why did you believe, with such swiftness, that it was your wife who had poisoned you?"

"Because it was obvious. The bottle was found in her drawer, in her room. It was obvious."

"Obvious? Didn't you once stop and think that maybe it could have been someone else? Did you try to dig a little deeper into other possibilities? You said you loved Kim and still love her. Did you ever—even once—consider defending the wife you love?"

"No! I knew she was sleeping around on me. I knew she was unfaithful. Why would I defend her? She was guilty."

"Guilty of being unfaithful because you'd shut her out of your life, or guilty of trying to poison you? It doesn't matter to you, does it, Mr. Maxwell? It was one and the same, wasn't it? You just want revenge any way you can get it, right, Mr. Maxwell? You just want to punish her."

Ben punched a fist into his chest. "It's a goddamned crime what she did to me, okay? A crime—and by God she's going to pay for it! Nobody does that to me. Nobody makes a fool out of Ben Maxwell and gets away with it. Nobody. And that includes my slut of a wife!"

The courtroom fell into stunned silence.

Baxter wilted a little, his eyes drifting down to the table. His lips tightened. His assistant, Marla Pelts, looked startled, but quickly recovered.

The jury sat motionless, tentative, eyes startled.

Kim was frozen, sweat on her face and neck. Her throat was arid, but she couldn't seem to swallow.

Derek eased back in his seat, a slight grin creasing his lips. He looked at Kim, wishing he could go to her. Touch her. Comfort her.

Ben's posture slackened, and he seemed to wilt by degrees. Some life drained from him and he went pale. He self-consciously touched the knot of his tie, and then he smoothed the tie, and then his eyes shifted about as he slowly realized the sharp impact of his words. He twisted and searched the air in regret, his mind working on recovery words or phrases to change the toxic atmosphere.

Maggie stood like a statue, waiting for him, aware that

whoever spoke next would be the loser.

When Ben spoke, his voice was small and rusty. "Well, that's all I have to say about that. I'm not well, you know. I haven't been well for a long time. Sometimes I say things… I don't mean what I say… that is… sometimes things just come out wrong and…" He left the word hanging in the startled air.

"Thank you, Mr. Maxwell," Maggie said. "I have no further questions, Your Honor."

CHAPTER 32

The following afternoon, Maggie and Kim sat in the crowded courtroom waiting for Baxter Cahill to begin his closing argument. There was an undercurrent of tension hovering in the space, like distant thunder before a storm. There was an unspoken edginess in the faces of the audience. The jury had entered with blank expressions. They reminded Kim of robots, programmed and heartless.

Baxter Cahill approached them with a pensive expression. He looked into each face, smiling.

"Ladies and gentlemen of the jury, good afternoon. The case before you, the case for which you are going to render a guilty verdict is, as I said at the beginning of this trial, a simple case. It is not difficult. It is not confusing. You will not have to deliberate for very long. No. It will be simple.

"You have listened to all the testimony and are now about to weigh all the facts. There should be no struggle with the facts or with the deliberation process, because this is a simple case. You have heard all the witnesses, and you have been presented with all the evidence. You have heard complicated testimony by experts about this and that.

"You have had to determine whether a witness is honest and true or confused or emotional or evasive. You have listened to the defense attorney tell you things that may have touched you in some emotional way because, on the face of it, this case is an emotional one. Why? Because it is a simple case. A very simple case. Why do I say it's simple? Because, ladies and gentlemen, as I said in my opening statement, this case is about one thing only. This case is about passion. Passion which led to greed, which led to lust, which led to attempted murder by poison.

"I hear some of you saying to yourselves, is passion not a complicated thing, a complicated emotion? I say, no. It is simple. Passion means many things, yes: fervor, zeal, enthusiasm, obsession, infatuation and ardor. Ardor? What does ardor mean? It means love, doesn't it? So, what we have here, what we have in this case, is a crime of passion. A crime of love. Ben loved his wife. She fell out of love with him, found another, wanted another and, as a result, she wanted, she desired, she lusted for what she felt was rightfully hers. The defendant wanted her new lover, she wanted Ben Maxwell's money and she wanted Ben out of the way so she could have that money.

"Now, ladies and gentlemen, you have heard a lot of testimony. You have heard of memory lapses and of forgetting and emotional scarring, but I want you to remember something. I want you to remember that Ben's passion was the passion of love for his wife, the defendant, Kim Ryan Maxwell, while her passion was the passion for Derek Gray and a passion for Ben's vast financial fortune.

"It's that simple, ladies and gentlemen, and we have proven this, without a doubt. The evidence bears it out and releases all doubt. How? The bottle of potassium cyanide that poisoned Ben was found in the defendant's bedroom in her underwear drawer. The defendant regularly brewed the green tea for Ben, her husband, and she delivered the tea directly to him. Yes, it is that simple! Very simple.

"Now comes the time when you have to make a simple choice. It is not a difficult choice at all. I am asking you to render a verdict of guilty of attempted murder by poison. I am asking you for that, and I want you to remember the simplicity of this case while considering the facts. As you make your decision, remember, it really is that simple. Hate, selfishness, greed and darkness almost killed Ben Maxwell. His wife, the defendant, Kim Ryan Maxwell, nearly succeeded in killing her husband, Ben, by poisoning him. She planned it and executed it with a greedy, cold heart that is unimaginable to us.

"It was because of her perverted passion. The passion of greed and lust. Shouldn't truth and justice triumph over greed, lust and attempted murder? Well, if it often doesn't triumph over them, ladies and gentlemen, then right now, by God, you have the power to make it so. Yes, you all, every one of you, have the power to right this injustice. You have the ability to reinstate truth, goodness and justice. Yes. Simple, ladies and gentlemen. A simple verdict. Guilty of attempted murder in the first degree. Thank you."

Maggie took her time walking to the jury. She was quiet, nervous and concerned, feeling the supreme pressure of the moment. She didn't show it, of course. It was mastery over emotion and insecurity that she'd learned from her father and by being in the military. She could mask them with a strong, confident lift of her chin and with bold, steady eyes.

Had she said enough during the trial? Had she said

too much? You never knew what was going on in the heads of twelve jurors. What emotions were they feeling? What scars and traumas did they hold secret, viewing the world through those skewed lenses? What formed opinions did they hold? Did they believe Ben? Did they like her? She was not an especially attractive woman. She was overly masculine and often too blunt and abrasive, something she'd inherited from her father, a drinking man, a civil engineer, a distant and practical father, who lacked much capacity for affection.

Maggie was a self-made woman. Her parents were against her joining the military and they were mostly indifferent when she decided to become an attorney. She'd alienated them with her alternative lifestyle. She had a girlfriend. She was an atheist, not a Presbyterian. She would never give them grandchildren in the way they had hoped.

Maggie's father once told her he didn't think she had the aptitude for law, and so she'd busted her ass every day since, trying to prove him wrong. Well, it didn't matter anymore. He'd died of cancer the year before. Only occasionally did she feel the smothering ghost of his presence. Now, unfortunately, at this moment, she felt his disapproval of her.

Maggie curled the fingers of both hands over the railing that separated her from the jury. She looked down at those hands. Her eyes came up slowly as she stifled a throbbing fear.

"Good afternoon, ladies and gentlemen. You have sat here for many days, listening, evaluating, perhaps speculating about this case, and you have been patient, diligent and conscientious. I thank you for that. I thank you for your good, civic service."

Maggie turned to look at Kim.

"Kim Ryan Maxwell is innocent. Kim was a caring, devoted wife to Ben Maxwell before his terrible accident, and she was caring and devoted after his accident. After the accident, Ben Maxwell changed. His passion for his wife changed. He alienated her. He treated her badly. He isolated her and he blamed her for the accident, an accident that hardened him and changed him in dark ways. Now, is that a harsh thing to say, ladies and gentlemen? Is that a harsh thing to say about a man who is wheelchair-bound for the rest of his life? Yes, it is. But it isn't as harsh as Ben Maxwell's accusation that Kim tried to poison him for his money, because she was in love with another man. That, ladies and gentlemen, is harsh. That is harsh, ugly, outrageous, and it happens to be utterly and entirely false. It is untrue. It is, to put it frankly and harshly, a preposterous lie!

"When Ben Maxwell shut Kim out of his life, denying her human understanding, companionship and warmth, did Kim finally turn to another man? Yes, she did. Like all human beings, she needed companionship. She needed warmth. She needed a friend. Did that friendship turn to passion? Yes. Isn't Kim like all of us? Isn't she human? Doesn't she deserve love and understanding? Yes, she does."

Maggie paced back and forth, her voice gathering strength. Maggie drew the silence out.

"Kim is not on trial because she was so cut off from Ben's warmth and love—so blunted and hurt because of his coldness and bitterness—that she found needed human warmth in another man. No. No, she is not on trial for that. She is on trial because it is alleged that she tried to kill her husband by poisoning him with potassium cyanide."

Maggie focused her attention on Baxter Cahill. "Prosecution says the motive was greed and passion. We have shown that Kim had no need for Ben's money. She was a very successful and passionate Broadway performer, who made plenty of her own money and even used that money to buy her husband, who is hugely wealthy, numerous and expensive gifts. Kim was a dedicated dance instructor and a wonderful teacher. Kim chose to give up her successful career to dedicate herself to a husband she loved. Now that is simple, ladies and gentlemen. Simple. Very simple.

Maggie turned back to the jury. "Prosecution has not been able to prove anything alleged in this case. The accusations are entirely unfounded and circumstantial. First, there were many people coming and going in Ben Maxwell's house who could have poisoned Ben Maxwell. We have shown that others made the green tea for him. In his room, others could have added the potassium cyanide after the tea was brewed. Now, as to the detectives finding the bottle of cyanide in Kim's drawer in her own bedroom."

Maggie narrowed her eyes, gazing at each juror. "Ladies and gentlemen, does this make any sense at all? Prosecution could not accurately even prove where the bottle of cyanide came from or who bought it. It is not proven that Kim purchased it or used it. There were no fingerprints on the bottle. None, certainly not Kim's. Additionally, no one ever witnessed Kim put that bottle of cyanide in her drawer or put poison in the green tea that Ben Maxwell drank. As stated earlier, many people were constantly coming and going in that house. It was a busy house. Mr. Maxwell conducted most of his business in that house. Anyone who entered or left the house could have placed that bottle of cyanide in Kim's drawer. Anybody could have accomplished that… simply. Anyone could have put the poison in Ben's green tea, again, simply.

"Again, there is no proof that Kim is guilty in any way. It is purely circumstantial conjecture that it was Kim and only Kim who put the bottle of cyanide in her bedroom drawer. You must consider this when you consider all the facts of this case. You must be sure, without any reasonable doubt, that Kim Maxwell planned, and did intend, to kill her husband by poisoning him.

"Ladies and gentlemen, Prosecution has not proven this. He has not proven his case. There is no proof whatsoever that Kim was involved in this despicable crime in any way."

Maggie folded her hands, lowering her voice to a near whisper. "Yes, this is a simple case. Very simple."

Maggie's voice expanded in volume as she spoke. "Kim Maxwell is innocent. That's simple enough, isn't it? All the evidence is circumstantial, and that is why you must return a verdict of not guilty. Thank you."

The courtroom emptied, and Judge Brown concluded jury instructions. Maggie and Kim were driven to the house where they'd wait out the verdict. Derek stopped at The Dock Café and sat at the mostly empty bar, nursing a bourbon and water. Natalie came over and put an arm on his shoulder.

"You've got friends, Derek. You've got lots of friends."

Derek smiled up at her. "Yeah… thanks, Natalie. Thanks for that."

Ben Maxwell was taken home and, after Nurse Carson left, Rosa meekly knocked on his office door and asked if he was ready for dinner. He declined. Rosa thought he appeared drained and troubled. He told her to go home.

Rosa lingered for a moment in shadow. She wanted to

tell Ben something, but she was frightened. She'd been frightened for a long time. She hadn't slept well for a week.

After Rosa left the house, Ben sat in the darkness, listening to the faraway sound of the sea. It was comforting and peaceful after the stress of the last few days.

His revenge was almost complete. It wouldn't be long now. He smiled darkly.

CHAPTER 33

The following morning at 10:12, Maggie got the call. The jury had reached a verdict. Kim was in the kitchen, standing with her back against the counter, sipping coffee. When Maggie told her, Kim didn't move.

"At least the nightmare of waiting is almost over," she said.

Maggie picked a piece of lint off her dark blue suit. "Kim, if it goes wrong for us, I will appeal. We'll try for another venue."

Kim didn't look at her. "But I'd be in jail… that awful jail, with no sun on my face."

"Let's not go there, Kim. One step at a time, okay? Ready?"

It was a gorgeous, glowing morning. Kim and Maggie rode in the back of the dark sedan in silence, each staring out at the fresh glaze of snow that had fallen the night before. It glistened on the limbs of pine trees that vibrated an electric green against the laundered white snow. They caught a glimpse of the shining sea as they crested a hill and started down the other side toward town.

Kim said, "Maggie, thank you for everything you've done. I was so lucky to have you as my attorney. I will always be grateful."

Maggie looked at her. "What will you do after the trial, when you are acquitted?"

"If I'm freed? Divorce Ben. Marry Derek."

"Will you stay in Scorpio Beach?"

"I don't know. I guess that depends."

"Depends on what?"

"On what Derek wants to do. His business has suffered some, but he still has some loyal customers. One of his employees, Anita, told me they've been doing snow removal and planting trees and shrubs when the ground's not frozen. They've also been hired to put in some artificial ponds and build rock gardens. If things turn out right today, Anita says they'll have a very profitable summer. I hope so."

"Derek was a terrific soldier," Maggie said. "He'll succeed."

Kim turned with interest. "Do you know him well?"

"Not so well, but by reputation. He received his Purple Heart for saving three of his buddies in a firefight. The three he saved have been sitting in that courtroom."

"I didn't know," Kim said. "He didn't tell me."

"He wouldn't. He's a modest guy. Oh, he's a bit wild, but oh so handsome, and oh so reliable, and oh so devoted and dependable once his heart is in it. But then, I suppose you know all that better than I, or anyone else."

Kim thought about that. "I love him very much."

The courtroom atmosphere was tense with anticipation and speculation. Derek's buddies were silent, eyes ahead. Lois Carson and Howard Walker sat in the last row, Lois appearing irritable and impatient, and Howard fidgety.

Ben's friends whispered opinions and annoyance at the unfortunate circumstances. Their faces shined with confidence.

Mrs. Ryan and Scott were struggling with nerves and concern, their eyes busy and somber.

Rosa Sanchez was alone in the third row, sitting in a huddled melancholy. Her silent lips recited prayers. Her right hand was running the rosary through her fingers.

Rachel Cox Kraft and her husband, Dr. Kraft, exchanged occasional comments, mostly about their upcoming vacation to the Amalfi Coast in Italy.

Dr. Kraft said, "From the top of Monte Solaro, you can see the twin bays of Salermo and Naples. It's quite beautiful. You'll love it."

Derek's full attention was on Kim. She looked tired and distracted. Maggie sat still, with her hands folded on the table top. Derek thought he saw hints of weariness and worry on her usually emotionless face.

Baxter Cahill was making notes, but they concerned another trial set for the following week. Marla Pelts squirmed, glancing occasionally at her cell phone and sending texts. Ben Maxwell's confident eyes stole furtive looks at Kim and then at the empty jury box. It wouldn't be long now. He was soon to have his revenge.

Judge Brown entered and the "All rise" brought the courtroom occupants to their feet. After the "Be seated" instruction was uttered, everyone sat—except for Rosa Sanchez.

Those seated next to her glanced up, observing her distressed face. She still held the rosary beads. They still moved through her fingers.

Judge Brown didn't notice her right away. When he heard a low murmuring, he looked up and saw Rosa, standing there, beseeching him with her miserable eyes.

He lifted his head, taking her in.

She raised a meek hand. "Please, sir. I'm sorry, sir."

Ben whipped his head around. Baxter turned sharply.

The entire room turned to view Rosa, standing there, trembling, on the brink of tears.

Judge Brown motioned for the bailiff, who was standing at the far wall near a tall window. His attention became acute as he studied Rosa like a threat.

"Please, sir," Rosa repeated. "I must speak. My dear Jesus wants me to speak."

Maggie's and Kim's eyes were riveted on the woman.

Judge Brown stared skeptically. "Mrs. Sanchez, you had the opportunity to speak when you were on the witness stand."

"I'm sorry, sir… Your Honor. I'm sorry. I didn't speak everything."

The courtroom grew noisy. Judge Brown grabbed the gavel and hammered it down. Silence ensued.

Tears streamed down Rosa's cheeks. "I saw some things, sir. I saw things I didn't say. I'm sorry. I didn't know."

Ben's eyes widened in fear. Lois and Walter stiffened. The room stared at Rosa, rapt.

Baxter sprang to his feet. Maggie leaped to her feet. Both burst out speaking at once, words of protest tumbling out. Judge Brown stopped them, with the flat of his uplifted hand, like a stop sign. Then he brought down the gavel.

"There will be silence in the court. Absolute silence. Now! Is that clear, Counselors? Now, both of you sit down."

Both did, Baxter grudgingly.

Judge Brown turned to the bailiff. "Bailiff, please escort Mrs. Sanchez to the bench."

The tall, solemn bailiff passed through the railing door, met Mrs. Sanchez and accompanied her to the bench.

Judge Brown looked down at her warily. "Mrs.

Sanchez, why have you waited until now to say what it is you're about to say? You had ample opportunity to speak when you were giving testimony."

Rosa looked down at the floor. When she lifted her face, she had a strange, shy smile. "I was afraid."

"Afraid of what, Mrs. Sanchez?"

"I wasn't sure, at first. Then… well, Mr. Maxwell has been so kind to me. I was afraid of losing my job. I was scared if I told what I saw, I would get fired and I wouldn't find another job. I don't want to be on that internet. In the papers. I have to work, Judge. I have a family. My husband is not working. I have a little son. I need my job."

Judge Brown summoned patience. "All right, Mrs. Sanchez. All right. Please take the witness stand."

The Judge motioned to the waiting bailiff. "Bailiff, will you please bring in the jury."

Baxter rose. "Your Honor, I must object to all this. This is some kind of grand theater staged by defense counsel. It's just another one of her stunts."

Judge Brown folded his hands, turning his stern gaze on Baxter. "This trial is still in progress, Counselor. Sit down. I will not tell you again."

Baxter sat down hard, worried. Ben gripped Baxter's arm tightly, fear showing in his eyes. Baxter pulled his arm away. Ms. Pelts' eyes were big and spooked.

Tension was high as the courtroom watched the jurors enter the jury box and sit.

Judge Brown explained the situation to the jury. They looked on, perplexed and surprised.

The Judge looked at Rosa. "Mrs. Sanchez, you are still under oath."

He indicated to the witness stand. "You may sit. You will be questioned by Prosecution and Defense Counsel.

Do you understand?"

She nodded, wiping away tears. After she was seated, Judge Brown told her to begin.

Rosa struggled to find her voice. Her eyes were downcast, her body language closed and timid. She slowly, painfully, turned to look at Kim.

"I'm sorry, Miss Kim, I mean, Mrs. Maxwell. I'm sorry."

Kim struggled to understand, leaning forward.

"Please begin, Mrs. Sanchez," Judge Brown instructed. "Do you need more tissues?"

She shook her head.

"I was cleaning Mrs. Maxwell's room," Rosa began.

"What was the date?" Judge Brown asked.

"Mr. Maxwell was in the hospital. He had his heart attack. I was so sad."

"The date, Mrs. Sanchez?"

"July 30…"

"Last year?"

"Yes… I was cleaning Mrs. Kim's room in the morning. I was in her bathroom. The bathroom door was open a little. I could see through the crack. I heard a sound. I thought it was Mrs. Kim. I was going to tell her it was me, and then I looked. I… I was surprised. It was not Mrs. Kim. It was Lois Carson."

Many eyes swept the room until they found Lois. They saw Lois Carson's face go blank with fear and fill with alarm. Howard stared at her, and his face slipped. He went white.

"Go on, Mrs. Sanchez," Judge Brown said.

"I don't move from the bathroom or make a sound. Lois Carson scared me. She never spoke to me. I don't think she liked me, so I don't move. I watched her. She was nervous, acting nervous. That made me all confused.

She was looking around the room as if she was trying to find something. Then she went to Mrs. Kim's drawer. I'd just washed Mrs. Kim's clothes. I put them in that drawer. The second drawer; Mrs. Kim's underwear drawer."

Ben's face filled first with fright, and then with rosy panic.

"Go on, Mrs. Sanchez."

Rosa wiped her eyes. She grew stronger, more indignant. She sat upright. "I saw Lois Carson open the second drawer and wipe a bottle with something she had in her hand, and then put the bottle inside Mrs. Kim's underwear drawer."

Baxter shot up. "Your Honor, please. This is…"

Judge Brown cut him off. "Sit down, Baxter! Now, or I will hold you in contempt."

Baxter huffed out a frustrated sigh as he sat.

"Continue, Mrs. Sanchez."

"Then Lois Carson, she closed the drawer and left the room. It seemed strange to me that Lois Carson was in Mrs. Kim's room. Why would she be in there? And she looked so nervous. So, I went to the drawer. I opened it and looked inside. At first, I didn't see anything. Then I move some things, and I find the little bottle. I look at it. I don't know what it is. I don't pick that bottle up. I just look at it. I think maybe Mrs. Kim ask Lois Carson for medicine and she had brought it. Then I see the word cyanide. I know what that is. I know it is poison, but I think it must be medicine—some kind of medicine for Mrs. Kim, because she was having trouble sleeping and eating. She was so upset about Mr. Maxwell. She was crying because she think he was going to die."

Lois Carson shot up, her frightened voice ringing out. "I want an attorney. Now. I want an attorney!"

Ben Maxwell erupted. "No, no, no, no, no! This is wrong. This is all wrong. Rosa is lying. She's just a housekeeper. A silly, stupid woman! What does she know? She's lying, Your Honor. This is all wrong."

Judge Brown slammed down his gavel. "Mr. Cahill, control your client!"

Baxter reached for Ben, but he'd already rolled away, making for the witness stand, enraged. "Why are you lying, Rosa? After all I've done for you, why are you lying?"

Judge Brown summoned the bailiff, who hurried over to restrain Ben.

Rosa looked at Ben, choking back tears. "I don't lie, Mr. Maxwell. I don't ever lie."

She held up her rosary beads for all to see. "My hands are on my beads. I don't tell lies. I may be a stupid woman, sir, but God knows I don't lie."

Ben's hopeless, wide and pleading eyes searched Rosa, Judge Brown, the bailiff, Baxter, and then he spun around to look directly at the audience. His hard, resolute stare finished on Kim.

He jabbed an accusing finger at her, pointing it like a gun. "You are guilty. Do you hear me? You are guilty, you slut. You goddamned slut!"

Kim shot to her feet. "No, Ben. *You* are guilty. You killed my love for you. *You* killed us. Both of us. Every day you tried to kill us, and you finally succeeded, didn't you? And then you poisoned yourself and blamed it on me, didn't you? God help you."

Judge Brown had been banging his gavel, but Kim hadn't heard it. She was intoxicated with rage.

Maggie didn't try to stop her.

Ben struggled to roll toward her, but the bailiff grabbed his shoulders, preventing him. Ben's eyes bulged out hatred.

He raised his fist into the air. "I almost did it, Kim. I almost pulled it off. Lois and I almost got you in jail for the rest of your life. May you rot in hell!"

Kim sighed. "Ben, get some help. You are out of your mind. You've been out of your mind for a long time."

Two police officers burst into the courtroom and hurried down the aisle. They escorted Ben out of the room, still cursing and ranting. A female cop came for Lois. She strode away in an arrogant pride, as if she had been offended and tarnished by fools.

In the deep shattered silence that followed, Judge Brown seemed shaken. It took several sips of water for him to gather himself. It was minutes before he spoke to the astonished, now very silent courtroom.

"In light of this new and extraordinary evidence, and admission of guilt, the State dismisses all charges against Kim Maxwell. The defendant is free to go. This Court is adjourned."

Kim was drained. She sagged down into her chair, just as Derek shoved the railing door open and hurried over to her. He took her hand.

"It's over, Kim. It's all over."

Kim looked up at him and smiled. "There you are, my darling. Always there. Always protecting me."

She stood and fell into his arms.

"Always, Kim. Always."

EPILOGUE

Ben Maxwell was out on bail, charged with conspiracy to commit a crime. Lois Carson was charged with criminal complicity.

In May, as spring awakened Scorpio Beach to the first sunbathers, beach lovers and anxious renters, Ben was alone in his office at the beach house. He'd sent everyone home, including his newly hired cook and his manservant. The day was fading, and shadows were gathering across the sea, the cliffs and the beach house.

Ben was at his desk, staring out to sea, watching the disc of orange sun dip into the ocean. Pink and blue wisps of clouds raked the sky, and gulls wheeled and called. He heard a dog barking and saw a kite shaking high in the wind.

He knew Kim and Derek were out there somewhere, probably roaming the beach at sunset. The divorce had gone through. Kim didn't ask for anything, nor did she want anything from him.

"What a silly bitch," he thought. She never did have a head for business or self-preservation. She was just a dancer after all. Just a sluttish, silly Broadway dancer. What had he ever seen in her?

But then he smiled, remembering the warmth of her, her soft skin, her smoky contralto voice that had always moved him to instant desire.

Darkness crept in and chilled him. The house was deathly quiet. Most of his friends had abandoned him. He'd lost business and business partners. He'd lost the respect of the local politicians and even some national politicians he'd snuggled up to over the years.

"What the hell," he thought. He'd had a good run. No complaints. No regrets. Until the auto accident, he'd had it made. He'd accomplished everything he'd wanted to accomplish. His only downfall had been falling in love with Kim. And yes, he'd loved her. He'd loved her so much it had destroyed him. She had destroyed him.

Ben had learned through Baxter Cahill that before Rosa Sanchez's dramatic courtroom declaration, the jury was about to deliver a guilty verdict. They believed the prosecution had proven his case: Kim was involved in an adulterous relationship and wanted Ben out of the way, so she could get most of his money; she made green tea for him nearly every day, and the bottle of potassium cyanide was found in her bedroom drawer. It had seemed simple to them that Kim had, in fact, poisoned Ben. One of the jurors, a local man named Kyle Benton, had led the way. He'd been the deciding factor in swaying the jury in Ben's favor.

In the dim light, Ben tossed back his fourth 25-year-old single malt scotch and toasted Kyle Benton.

"What the hell, Mr. Benton. We nearly pulled it off. Thanks for the help anyway. Enjoy your money. I won't be needing it."

The scotch was smooth and smoky. It felt good, warming his chest. He stared out into the fading light with unfocused eyes, reflecting on his life, as if he were watching an old black and white movie. The alcohol had sagged his face.

He rolled over to the wall mirror to get a good look at himself. He could still see the ghost of himself in there. There was still enough natural light. He stared at his reflection with contempt. He coughed out a low, mirthless laugh.

The semi-automatic silver pistol lay heavily in his lap. He gripped it, hefted it. It felt cool in his right hand. He kept staring at himself, remembering the high points of his life, seeing the movie of that life slowly dwindle away into static.

Ben spoke out loud in slurred disgust. "You're the biggest fool of them all, aren't you? Yes, Ben Maxwell, you are the biggest fool of them all."

He shoved the barrel of the gun into his mouth, paused to laugh once more, and then pulled the trigger.

Ben had been right. Derek and Kim were strolling along Scorpio Beach, holding hands. Colin galloped alongside them, splashing along the edge of the tide, chasing the stick that Kim had tossed into the waves.

Kim and Derek were going to stay in Scorpio Beach. With her own money, Kim had already secured a loan and purchased the yoga studio. She'd also begun classes and hired a masseuse. Local business was picking up, and the promise of crowds during the summer encouraged her to expand.

They lived in Derek's simple beach house and were planning their July wedding. It would be held on the beach, and the reception would be at The Dock Café.

Kim wanted to have a child right away and Derek promised that as soon as she got pregnant, he'd find them a beach house on the cliffs, where they could always look out onto the sea.

They drifted along the tide line, barefoot, occasionally stopping to kiss, to touch and to discuss their future.

When a roaring wave slammed the beach, Derek seized Kim's hand. They sprinted for the sea, kicking, splashing and diving. The May water was shockingly cold, and Kim screamed out. They popped out from under a curling wave and kissed. Another charging wave buried them. They bobbed to the surface, gasping, laughing, wiping water from their eyes. The sunset light bronzed and framed them and blessed the gifted lovers. They floated and touched, and Derek wrapped his arms around Kim's waist and kissed her nose. His eyes gleamed with happiness. Kim kissed him, just as a wave struck and they went under.

Colin barked at them from shore. He had lost the stick.

Thank you for taking the time to read *Daring Summer*. If you enjoyed it, please consider telling your friends or posting a short review. Word of mouth is an author's best friend and it is much appreciated.

Thank you,
Elyse Douglas

Other novels by Elyse Douglas that you might enjoy:

The Christmas Diary
The Summer Diary
The Other Side of Summer
The Christmas Women
The Christmas Eve Letter (A Time Travel Novel) Book 1
The Christmas Eve Daughter (A Time Travel Novel) Book 2
The Lost Mata Hari Ring (A Time Travel Novel)
The Christmas Town (A Time Travel Novel)
Time Sensitive (A Time Travel Novel)
The Summer Letters
The Date Before Christmas
Christmas Ever After
Christmas for Juliet
The Christmas Bridge
Wanting Rita

www.elysedouglas.com

Made in the USA
Columbia, SC
15 September 2019